Tales from a Goth Librarian

17 March 2012 Coast Con

Tales from a Goth Librarian

By Kimberly Richardson

*Janet,
Enjoy my madness!*

Tales from a Goth Librarian by Kimberly Richardson

Copyright © 2008 Kimberly Richardson
Cover photography by Professor Sid Reese
Cover design by Allan Gilbreath

All rights reserved. No part of this book may be reproduced, duplicated, copied, or transmitted in any form or by any means without the express written consent and permission of the author and publisher.

This is a work of fiction. The names, characters, places, and incidents are fictitious or are used fictitiously. Any resemblance to any person or persons living or dead is purely coincidental.

Published by
Kerlak Enterprises, Inc.
Kerlak Publishing
Memphis, TN
www.kerlakpublishing.com

ISBN 13: 978-0-9823745-1-1
Library of Congress Control Number: 2009924168
First Printing: 2009

Special thanks to everyone at Kerlak Publishing for all of the encouragement and assistance.

This book is printed on acid free paper.

Printed in the United States of America

Acknowledgements

To my family, who has always believed in me, even if I am the weird sheep of the family. I love you fiercely.

To my dearest friends, Corrie and Bob Scoby, Karen and Todd, Candis, Neale and April, Kristen, Viking Dan (Valhalla Awaits!), Jeff, David and DJ Mary Jane, Glenn, Kat, Chris White, Brian, and others whose names I can't remember. I love you all.

To the one person who has helped me along the way; my brother Professor Sid Reese. BOOSH!

To my other half - Clayton St. John. The Force will be with you, always.

And finally: To each and every Steampunker, Goth/Rivet Head, and general Freak out there - BE PROUD AND LET YOUR FREAK FLAG FLY!

Absinthe Dreams to you all!

Kimberly
Elder Goth Steampunker who still loves Folk Music

Contents

Prologue 1
Madison de Macabre 3
Non Compos Mentis 5
Silk 7
Dream Guardian 17
Multicoloured Souls 21
Peau 33
Sulfur 59
Purple and Black 95
Cover Her with Violets 139

Goth Poetry:

The Beginning of the End 203
A Night with Edgar (Allan Poe) 204
A Dying Wish 206
Confession of a Corporate Goth Woman 207
A Love Beyond 209
Tighter, My Darling 214
Black and Red 215
Demons and Tea 216
Vampire in Heat 218
Ethereal Girl 220
The Renshaw House 222
Flower of Depression 231
A Beat Tribute to Clive Barker 233
Opheliaholic 235
Lines about Goths 236
Ode to the Topic that is Hot 238

Journal Entry on a Dark and
Stormy Night 239
Werewolves Anonymous 241
A Darke Woman 243
Our Daughter 245
Mayhem, A Wonderful Thing 249
A Last Look 251

Prologue

Twas 'ere the sun did fall into the blackened soil
What we mortal men and women call Earth.
The branches did break, seeping into such mud
That all who witnessed it used their eyes to see.
And the children did play among the vines so thick and coarse
That soon, their sins were forgiven, lost in a fog of forgetfulness.
And I, I who writes it down, a humble author, genuflect if you please,
Will hope that one day my words will be read
As truth shall never be.
I take no claim to the source of my words
But only speak, I was a witness to the play laid out before me.
When nature collided with the force of our limit
Soon, soon, did the play begin, curtains raised and audience
Gasping with last breaths scented with peppermints, old books,
And dreams of a better time.
The curtains lift, the candles lit. . . and now begins.

Madison de Macabre

I am trying to better understand it, but the words escape me. So, maybe I should sing it to you. No? Then, perhaps I should close my eyes and dream it to you. That way, no detail gets left behind.

She danced for him, you know. She danced because she wanted to. Or, she danced because she had to. He would never allow any other action from her. She was too much of a goddess for anything menial.

I watched it all from my little corner of the house where no one would think to look. The family gave up on me many years ago, so I flutter from room to room, not caring what I do. They do not so why should I?

She danced so well last night, so much so that I wanted to reach out to her and tap her on the shoulder, giving her a moment of being spooked before realizing it was I who tapped her.

"Julien," she would say in her usual tone towards me, "how many times have I told you to not scare me like that?" I would smile then flutter off, knowing that she would never trust me again.

But no, this time, she danced well. He stood there, hands tightly wrapped around a silver tipped cane, his black eyes watching her every move, looking for any slip up and finding none. He wanted her to fail simply to show that she was indeed human.

I knew better, however. I knew that she was more than just a dancer. She was his heart and my sister. She was his lover and my tutor. She was everything to him and nothing to me.

So, I watched. She danced. And soon, the house went black.

Non Compos Mentis

They dance for me since I am no longer able to do so.

I watch them, twirling and swaying like grass in a Summer wind, and I am jealous. I want to dance with them, to show them I am still alive, still breathing, and still full of blood. Ah, but that is a dream, is it not? To dance with these gods and goddesses; such a thought makes me smile.

I keep the light burning for them all day and night, should their desire strike them without warning. I want them to know that I do understand. I used to be like them, of course.

They call me by my first name, Drake, giving me a sense of family, but I know it is all lies. They only want me to keep the light burning for them. It does get hard sometimes. The fires that burn come with such a price and yet only I make the payment.

Their clothing changes colour while they move, colours I have never seen before. I wish others could watch this, but I know it is impossible. You see, to watch them dance is to go insane. They feed from that insanity, drinking it down like ambrosia. They are gods, after all.

I keep to a little corner since that is all they offer me and sometimes not even that. I find space where I can and I am lucky if I can before they come. They come at me with sharpness and lust for blood, but it is their dancing that finally kills.

I used to dance. Not anymore. Not since they, in a moment of black humour, tore my legs from my body with their clawed hands. They were bored at the time and have since asked for my forgiveness. I gave it to them, of course, for I know they love me.

It is hard to keep the fires burning for them since I use my own body fat as tallow. A pinch here, a finger there, and they dance the nights and days away while I sit in my spot and cry my tears. I hate them and I love them too much to die. Sometimes, I don't notice the pain. Not at all.

One of them, a woman named Freynai, sits besides me to watch the others. She never says a word to me, but I can feel her two hearts beating for me. She sits next to me because, in some way, she feels sorry for me, but I know better. I know they have the power to make me whole again and she does not do so. All she wants to do is just sit by my deformed side and hum her little songs of mayhem and chaos. She is the one who brings the storms.

I do not know how long I have been like this and quite honestly, I do not remember when they captured me and took me away to their own world. All I know is the here and now. Sometimes, I forget that I no longer have legs. Sometimes, I forget that I am blind.

My beautiful, beautiful creatures of dance and song, frolicking to an endless tune that I am blessed to know.

Sometimes, and this is the strange part, I see glimpses of men in white, stabbing me with long needles, talking to me about my "condition" and how only I have the power to make myself better. Truly they are demons for they want to hurt me. They tell me that I am in a place, a place, a place named Renson. A place for people like me to get better. Lies. I want these visions out of my head, but they keep coming back stronger and stronger.

I am the keeper of the light for the dancers of gods. I am beyond all fear.

I watch.

Silk

I love her.

Such a simple statement, but it means so much more to me. She is the air I breathe, the cool water I drink, the earth under my feet, the sun, stars, moon, everything. She gives me reason to get up every morning and gives me more than pleasant dreams when I fall asleep. She is my own essence carefully wrapped into a perfect being that causes even the gods and goddesses to tremble. Every day, I think of her lips kissing mine, her soft and supple body coming into contact with my own as we make love every day and night. Perhaps other men would pass out due to fatigue or stress, but not I. I would give her every bit, every drop of my self, simply because she is worth that much to me.

I had been working for the company for five years now when she arrived last year. When I first saw her, I could hear buzzing in my ears. She was unpacking her boxes and moving things around in her small, but comfortable office (the last person to occupy it moved to California due to his wife getting a job there) while co-workers stopped by, asking her if she needed any assistance. I walked by her office while carrying some mail and when her eyes met mine, everything around me disappeared. I could no longer hear Kathy type furiously in her cubicle, nor Charles flip through his 540 page report. All I could see, all I could hear was her. She stared at me, I stared back, she waved at me then went back to unpacking while I stood rooted to the spot until Amy, the floor's gossip queen and melodramatic bitch, bumped into me and spilled my mail.

Slightly dazed, I reached down to grab my mail while Amy stood over me and said, "Damn, dude, watch where you're going, 'kay?" She always had this annoying this about her, one that I could never place my finger on, but I knew it was there like a tick burrowing under my skin.

"Sorry about that," I mumbled as I picked up the mail from the floor, "I was preoccupied."

"Yeah, well, whatever." She then walked around the corner and was soon gone, leaving me to still pick up my mail from the floor right in front of the goddess' office. I was embarrassed; I wanted to make a good first impression on her and instead, I looked like a clown. Add to the fact that, because my hands were slick with sweat, the mail kept falling out of my hands, making me look like an even bigger idiot.

"Do you need help?"

That voice.

I could feel my pants tighten in certain areas; that voice. I looked up to the source, but I already knew who it belonged to. She was dressed in a simple yet tasteful black suit with a short black skirt, white blouse, black tights and black clunky shoes. Her hair was pulled back into a ponytail while simple pearl earrings dangled from her ears. Her face was inches from my own and it took all the inner strength I had to hold myself back from ripping her clothes off and ravaging her supple body. Instead, I smiled.

"No, but thank you anyway. My hands are still slick from that . . . (think, damn it!) adhesive I used earlier. Hard stuff to get off my hands (OK, good job! Keep going!) even with soap and water." I kept my smile on my face while she bent down and helped me with my mail. When my hands touched hers, I could feel a slight electric charge, causing me to raise my eyebrows in surprise. When she handed the last of the mail to me, we both stood up at the same time, causing us to laugh.

"Thanks again for helping me," I said in a voice that sounded slightly nervous. "Oh yeah, welcome to the company."

"Thank you. I'm Emily. Emily Shaw." She held out her hand to me, which I took gratefully. I did not wash that hand for a week, even when I went to the bathroom, ate food, picked my nose, or even jerked myself off. Of course, I would use THAT hand for such a moment. She walked back into her office and I walked on towards my own office, drowning slowly in something warm and pleasant, something that only she created. I could barely walk.

The first night after meeting her was a sleepless night. I went to bed at my usual time, but my eyes would not close. I kept thinking of her, her smiling face, her breath that reminded me of warm cookies freshly baked. I wondered what her skin tasted like; would it be light like cotton candy, or spicy like peppers? Would she melt in my mouth as I kissed her lips? Would she melt in mine? I could feel my erection pressing against my boxer shorts, but I resisted; I would not debase her simply for the sake of expending my own bodily fluids, at least not yet. I closed my eyes and saw her floating above me under a clear blue sky, naked, while three red ribbons fell from her sex, thick and slimy from her own wetness.

The ribbons touched my face and I quickly placed them in my mouth, sucking greedily for her juices. She tasted of salty mangoes to me, making me want more. The ribbons kept coming and I kept shoving them in my mouth. She was doing this for me, I thought as I looked up and saw her smiling at me and only me. She wanted me to taste her; such an honour would not be bestowed on just anyone. Soon, my body connected with the land of sleep and soon she flew away, leaving me the red ribbons as a souvenir. If anyone had seen me in my dreams, they would have seen a human bloated like a dead whale, lying in a green valley, slick and wet and smelling of overripe fruit.

During the next couple of weeks, I did everything I could to be around her or her office; stopping by with a cup of coffee in my hand to say hello, or helping her with a file that was stuck in one of the cabinets. She filled my mind constantly and I only wanted more. Her skin glowed whenever I saw her and for a brief moment, I wondered what it would look like spread over my own pale body. She was African American, but race was never a concern. She was a woman - a goddess that only I could see. Trouble was, did anyone else see her true self as well? Was I the only one special enough to see her true self? Did she live alone?

While my workweek was heaven, my weekends were hell for it meant that I could not see or be around her. Two miserable days; why did people look forward to the weekend? I lived alone, no pets, no roommates, just me and my house with many books, some furniture, few art pieces, and one set of dishes since no one ever came by to spend time with me. My parents are dead (the police to this day still watch my every move), killed when I was a child by a freak accident while we were driving to our lake house for two glorious weeks of fun. I was the only survivor, but a certain detective thought otherwise.

I am sorry; I did not mean to digress. THAT story shall be saved until another time, yes? Now, where was I? Oh, yes.

I lived alone and was lonely for I never went out for fun, nor did I invite anyone to my place. I read books in my free time and that was all. I don't even go out to bookstores to purchase my books; I order them online. I had created a shell for myself and so far, it had not let me down. Now that she, Emily, remember she has a name, Emily, Emily, eMILY, EmIlY has invaded my life, I can feel cracks in my shell. I can hear the shell cracking when it gets too quiet; I don't like quiet, no quiet, quietness, slipping downward towards my soon to be Emily.

One Friday, while everyone else did everything else, but work, I walked up to Emily's closed door and knocked on it gently. In the past two months, we had gone from not saying anything to saying hello or making small talk whenever we saw each other. I had also discovered that, through our gossip grapevine, she thought I was a, and I quote, "cute skinny white boy". I had never paid attention to my looks so her words stunned me. She, my goddess, deemed me to be "cute". After hearing that compliment, my esteem went through the roof.

So, it did not bother me to knock on her door for we had become work associates. She felt comfortable around me and that was what I wanted. After several seconds, I heard her say, "Come in," and so I did. She was hunched over some documents while holding a highlighter in her hand. Her hair was pulled into a messy ponytail while two pens stuck out from it; it was her habit to have her pens stuck in her head, for if she ever needed one, all she had to do was pull one from her hair. When she looked up and saw that it was me, she smiled and let the highlighter slip from her fingers.

"Norman," she said with an obvious sense of happiness in her voice, "good to see you." I sat down in one of the chairs opposite hers and said, "Just wanted to see how you're doing, that's all." She relaxed back in her chair and sighed, allowing the chair to touch the window that revealed downtown in all of its dirty yet historic glory.

"It's been a day for me; I'm still working on that Miller case."

"The one regarding our biggest client?"

"That's the one. Anyway, I needed to take a break and thank goodness you dropped by." She scratched her head and I wondered what lay under her fingernails. Gold dust, perhaps? "So, what have you been up to?"

"Working on the same stuff; you know how it goes. Hopefully, I'll have it all done by the end of today, but I doubt it since everyone else is thinking of what they're going to do this weekend." She yawned and stretched and I could hear her joints popping. I shuddered slightly

(Calm down, not NOW! Relax yourself. That's it, relax.)

Then said, "So, have any plans for the weekend?"
"Just me, a couple of books, and some comfort food. You?"
"The same."
"Well . . .would you like to have dinner sometime? Maybe tonight?"
"Sure, that sounds great!" (WHAT?! You're not ready for this. It's too soon! No, I need to be ready. For her. Quiet, quiet, listening please, I need to slow down my breathing; it's only dinner)
"How about if we meet up at Café Risotto down the street, say around 5pm?"
"Sounds good to me." With that, I got up to leave while she picked up her highlighter and resumed scanning her documents. When I closed the door behind me, I wanted to vomit.

For the next two hours, I sat at my desk in my office and stared at the computer screen.
When 5pm arrived, I was already at the restaurant, staring at my watch, when she walked up to me. She smiled and we went in. I will not bore you with the details of that night, sorry to say. The rest of my tale is so much more interesting, as you shall soon see.
We walked back to our cars (we had parked next to each other and did not realize it) in silence; she because she was full and happy and I because I wanted to vomit. I could feel the red ribbons she had given me weeks ago stirring around in my stomach and I almost asked her why she did not take them back since they were making me so ill. Surely, she had to know.
"Norman, thanks again for a great night," she said while leaning against her car.
"T-thank you as well."
"You don't know it, but you've helped me out completely." My smile grew even wider, gleaming like polished bones at night.
"How so?"

"Well . . . my boyfriend and I have had problems in the past and we both decided to take off some time to relax and get to know ourselves better. However, I received a phone call from him today, telling me that he wants to be with me and only me."

I could feel the red ribbons stirring frantically in my stomach, crying to be released.

"Boyfriend?" She looked down in shyness.

"We've been together for three years and this is our first time apart. I needed some time to spend with good friends and family and I have to say thank you for what you've done for me." She embraced me and the ribbons fell silent. "Thank you, Norman." She released my stiff body, blew me a kiss, then got in her car and drove off while I stood by my own car. I leaned over and threw up on my feet. When I finished several minutes later, I noticed I had thrown up red ribbons covered in chewed pasta and bread.

That Friday stayed with me all weekend and during the next workweek. On Monday, I saw Emily in the kitchen pouring a cup of coffee. When our eyes met, hers happy and shining, mine black and dead, I waved hello like a marionette then walked out.

On Tuesday, I slipped into her office before she arrived and set a package on her desk. The package contained the red ribbons I threw up on Friday, still covered in pasta and bread, smelling like a sewer. I found out later that when she opened her package, her screams could be heard on the whole floor. I was locked in my own office with headphones on, listening to static.

On Wednesday, I purchased a knife before work and played with it all day, bouncing it from finger to finger, ignoring the blood that spilled on my desk.

On Thursday, I took the knife home with me.

Friday, I did not go to work.

Monday, I still did not go, but had a package delivered to my work, Attention: Emily Shaw. My name was not on it. It hurt too much for me to write my name.

Sometimes, pain can be a friend to you. You learn to let it linger and love it with experience and patience. Such was the case with me; I learned how to live with my pain for I knew that I had to bear it. It was the only way for me to live otherwise. Emily did not understand; well, how could she? She was beyond my grasp and now . . well, now, she was even more so, for they took me away several days later, claiming I was suffering from stress caused by work. Of course, they knew the truth. So did I. Only Emily remained in the dark, living out her (as I now see it) shell of a life when she was born to be a goddess.

I touch my body every so often, reminding me of what I went through. For her. For us, if that was a possible (yes, it WAS! Don't deny what you know to be true! Sliver of glass, peeling away, sliver of glass dancing on a pin's head like an angel, cover my eyes!) chance that we could be together, then I would have done it anyway.

I get asked now if I would have died for her. I tell them yes.
Would you? Yes?
Did you love her? Yes.
Would you do anything for her? Yes.
Even give the skin off your back?
That's when answering gets hard. It is hard because I did. I don't want to remember it, but I have to.
The package arrived on Monday just before she arrived. I was told that when the delivery guy showed up with the package, he was glad to get rid of it due to the smell. I

imagined then that she shook the box, wondering what was inside, barely noticing the smell or the small leak that had appeared in one of the corners of the rectangular box. She probably said thanks to the guy then closed the door to have some privacy. She did not see a return address, but opened it anyway.

I was so proud of what I had done. It took me only three hours to set up the canvas, but an hour to paint. I did it all for her.

Skin, when stretched and cared for, is like silk in one's hands. I never knew that until I, using my knife, cut off the skin from my back for her gift. Every time I wanted to scream in pain, I instead whispered my love for Emily. Every time I hit a bone or snagged a piece of skin, I said she was a goddess. Every time I wanted to pass out from blood loss, I though of her lips. The paint was my blood and semen; I still shudder thinking that she might have stuck a finger in the mixture and licked it, sighing with delight in receiving such a personal gift. I painted a picture of red ribbons on my own skin. For her. Her ribbons were her love to me and I wanted to show my appreciation for them. Each ribbon was a life when we met had before. That was why I was drawn to her in the first place; we had met before. I know this to be true. I still carry scars.

I was told I was wrong for doing such a thing. They, the same people, tell me that I am in here for a reason, that my mind is addled and has been that way ever since I was a child. They tell me that I am dangerous not only to others, but to myself. They tell me that my back will probably not heal. I will be scarred for life. I understand what they tell me every day, but at the same time, I do not. They tell me I will never leave here; of course, that is fine with me. I have no plans.

Emily does not visit me. After the screams, she refused to see me. I was told that she moved to another city for safety reasons, meaning me of course. I wonder what she does now. Did she keep the painting? Does she think of me? Am I her special friend still? Was she lying when she told me about her boyfriend; did he even exist? I would never harm her. I love her. After all, I did give her the skin off my back to her.

    Isn't that what love is all about?

(red)

Dream Guardian

I woke up and found myself walking down a path shaded by tall oak trees, guardians of old and subjects of legends. I walked because I knew that, if for no other reason, I had to walk. As I walked along the path, I took in the sight of the azure sky through the thick branches of the trees. A very strong breeze scented with jasmine wafted through my hair, mangling it beyond recognition. I was barefoot; I could not remember if I ever had shoes. Soon, I approached a lake filled with water the color of a robin's egg, so clear that I could see the fish swimming along. On one side of the lake was a tree that was full and lush with bright green leaves.

A man dressed in nondescript black clothing sat at the base of the tree, holding a simple fishing rod with a limp line dangling in the water. I decided to walk up to him and as I did, he turned to me and smiled, saying, "Greetings! About time you showed up." He then turned his attention back to his line lazily dangling in the water. Not truly sure how to take his strange greeting, I sat next to him with my gaze now towards the lake. Several minutes in silence passed and then I asked him what he was fishing for. Cod, haddock, shrimp perhaps?

"No," he said in an even tone, "I am fishing for dreams discarded." His eyes never left the lake and it was then that I noticed he was of an ageless sort; at times he looked older than a wise man of a tribe, then younger than a child at others. I knew myself to be within a place that was not a place and so I stayed with the man.

"Dreams discarded?" I asked him, unsure of my own voice and the question that appeared at my lips. His bright, multicoloured eyes now focused on me as he nodded yes.

"I search for those dreams that have yet to be used. I search for those dreams that people forget when they are too lost."

"And what do you do with these dreams?"

"I give them to those who need them more than those who dream them." I turned my thoughts back to the lake, watching the slow ripples echo across the surface. Suddenly, a multicoloured bubble the size of an orange broke the surface and floated over to the man, who had his hand stretched out to catch it. It floated to his hand and stayed there without popping out of existence. He turned to wink at me then threw the bubble up in the air, where it continued to float high in the sky. Soon, I could no longer see it.

"It has gone," the man said, "to one who deserved it more."

"What was the dream of?"

He smiled and said nothing, but focused on the water, leaving me to ponder my own conclusions. Did the person dream of a better job, to be a writer, to no longer be alone? So many choices and so many endings to possibly come from it.

Just then, I heard footsteps behind me. I turned and saw a light blue skinned man dressed in a long red tunic walking up to us. His eyes, blacker than night, stared at me with no emotion. I wanted to look away, but found I could not, so I watched this new person come up to us and take a seat on the other side of the man who still fished for dreams.

"Man," said the blue man with a deep and commanding voice, "tell me of my dreams. Tell me why I can no longer dream of that which I desire."

"You have lost your dreams because you seek that which can not be obtained," said the Dream Guardian (I began to call him that in my mind).

"I am a king in my world, a man who wields power and influence! Surely, man, I deserve my dreams."

"It is because of your status that you can not obtain your dreams." I sat back, fascinated by the conversation. The king was becoming more and more frustrated while the Dream Guardian remained calm.

"At night, when the winds blow scents of wildflowers through my many windows of my home, when I am asleep with my wife, I see nothing. I see black . . . no, something deeper than black. Something darker than black. Man, let me find my dreams." The king stood up, making himself an imposing figure, but the Dream Guardian was silent for several minutes. Then, in a voice a little more than a whisper, he said, "You are a dream discarded yourself. You do not exist." At that moment, the face of the king turned to shock as he disappeared. The man turned his multicoloured eyes to me and said, "I know of dreams and I know of reality. He was a lost dream, one that had not been claimed yet by someone who truly deserved it."

"Could you not help him?" I asked.

"He will be claimed soon. Then and only then will he be able to dream himself, a dream within a dream." I nodded, knowing what he meant.

Time passed as I watched him send off more and more dreams; some were as large as house and yet some were tinier than a grain of sand, but each important and worth a great deal. Finally, the sun began to set and soon the Dream Guardian took up his line and stick and packed it all away. I stood up from my spot and stretched.

"Of course the path does not end here," he said. "The path continues for you. Keep going to the right and walk still." He then turned and walked in the opposite direction, my eyes following him until he walked over a hill and could no longer be seen. Night was now upon me, the moon full and swollen, and I turned to the right to continue on the path. As I walked, I found myself missing the Dream Guardian, wondering how long he would have to walk before he could rest once more.

Suddenly, the night gave way to daylight and soon I was dreaming of a blue skinned man who was a king in his world. Flower-scented breezes blew through his many open windows of his palace while he slept with his wife. A smile played on his lips as his dreams came to him in vivid colours and sounds. I fell asleep.

Multicoloured Souls

When I first saw her, it was raining outside. The fat drops made slow trails down the windows of the bookstore while we were inside, warm and safe, away from the rain that threatened to occupy the entire Saturday. She sat in an oversized chair, reading a book by some author I did not recognize. She wore black-rimmed glasses that accentuated her oval face, making her already intelligent eyes even more so as they ran down the length of each page of her book. Her long brown hair was pulled back in a sloppy ponytail, giving her the look of a university student. She wore dark green baggy pants rolled up to her ankles and a white short-sleeved shirt with sandals sitting next to her chair which I thought was funny; who would wear sandals during a rainy day? Wouldn't they be worried that their feet would get wet? I tried not to laugh, but a snicker came out, causing her to look up in my general direction. Thankfully, I was standing in one of the aisles holding the spine of a book, so I pulled it out from the shelf, trying to read the back of it, hoping like hell she would look away.

When I glanced over to her several seconds later, she was back to her book, immediately engrossed in the written words on the pages. I placed my book back on the shelf and walked along, thinking of her deep purple lips that mouthed the words she read. I walked up and down the aisles, trying to work up the courage to talk to her and not come out wrong in the wash. By the time I reached the cookbooks section I was ready. Smoothing out my hair (short and black – easier to manage), I checked my clothing (jeans, hiking boots, brown t-shirt) then walked straight to her chair. I stood right in front of her, watching her read without even noticing my presence.

"Excuse me."

She looked up slowly with a look on her face that said who in the hell would divert my attention like this, quickly changing it to a lopsided smile when she saw my own smile. "Yes?"

"I just wanted to say that-

Say what? That I wanted to marry her? Get a grip. I felt myself beginning to tremble, but I held steadfast.

"Yes?" She lowered her glasses to get a better look at my face.

"I just wanted to say that I think you are an attractive woman." I said it in a slow, but friendly tone, hoping to not screw up such a simple sentence. Okay, I thought, now it's out. Next move?

She smiled wider now. "Thank you." She held out her hand to me. "My name is Vivian."

"Julian." I took her hand and noticed that it was cool and soft and yet had a powerful grip. "Do you mind if I join you?"

"Not at all." I sat in the chair next to her, watching her change positions in hers as she now faced me and placed her book on the small table in front of her. "So, what do you do, Julian?"

"I'm a writer." As soon as I said this, her eyes widened in appreciation.

"Really? What do you write?"

"Poetry, mainly, but I am working on a novel now."

"What's the novel about or is that bad luck to ask?"

"Not at all. It's going to be about a woman who realizes that the man she loves has been living a lie. So far, I have written a complete description of his background." Vivian hung on my every word as if they held some sort of power.

"Sounds good so far. Is this based on someone you know?"

"Yes, but I'll change the names to protect the innocent." I ended my sentence with a small laugh, letting her know I was kidding.

"So, has your poetry been published?"

"Actually, I have five books published now. The last one was Rusty Typewriter."

The light of recognition beamed in her eyes.

"Wait, you're THAT Julian Hardel? I read all of your work when I was in grad school for my MFA. Your work is amazing!" Her voice became breathless, her dream of finally meeting a famous poet coming to fruition.

"Thank you. Are you still in school?"

"No. Graduated last month, actually. Taking a break from school right now."

"Any plans of going back?"

"Maybe." She shifted again in her chair, leaning closer to me. I could smell her perfume; lavender, I thought. "I'd like to teach literature on a college level, but I don't think I've got the patience to work with college students. I had thought about becoming an academic librarian-

"Just as long as you get to work with books?" She smiled.

"You guessed right: I'm a bibliophile. I love books and would much rather work among them than people." She shifted in her chair and took off her sandals.

"Too many people, I think, have jobs that they don't like because they were told to go into that particular profession, or because they wanted to feel financially secure." I looked over at the book on the table, the one she had been reading before I walked up to her. "What's that about?"

"Oh that? It's the newest Ian McEwan, the British author." I confessed that I did not know him. "Well, he's one of my favorite authors; anything he writes I read and I have yet to be disappointed." I picked up the trade paperback and carefully read the synopsis on the back. It did sound like a good book and I made a mental note to check it out at the library. I placed the book back on the side table, noticing that her eyes followed my every move. I returned her gaze and smiled.

"So, do you have any plans when you leave here?" I asked.

She began to blush. "No, no plans."

"Well, would you do me the honor of having dinner with me? Perhaps Café Moriarty, the new place down the street?" She nodded her head yes.

Within minutes, she put her sandals back on and packed up her belongings in her rather large purple backpack and we soon left. Thankfully the rain had stopped, giving off a faint scent of ozone in the air. We walked down the busy street, coming into contact with others who also decided to enjoy this now cool evening. This was an area full of life, creating a bond among people that could not be matched anywhere else in the city. We walked along the main street as my eyes glanced to her face every few minutes, noticing that she looked down at her feet while walking.

"Do you live in this neighborhood?" My question seemed to break her mental fog as she now blinked her eyes and looked at me with a questioning look.

"Yes," she said, talking to me as if she awakened from a dream, "right down the street in the warehouse. I occupy one of the floors. Rent's just $400 a month, but for all of that space, I consider it to be a bargain." I grunted something to her, allowing my hand to brush against her own. I felt her hand jerk in surprise then relax.

We soon reached the restaurant, walking in together like a couple. The place was small and intimate with small white candles lit on every table. There were two people sitting at one of the tables, deep in a conversation. We took a table by the window and sat down just as a young man handed us menus. When he left, I said, "Would you like some wine? Perhaps a Merlot?"

"Okay."

I had no knowledge of wine, sad as that sounds. I drink what I like and that is that.

Our wine was requested, our orders taken, and soon we sat across from each other, each holding a glass of something that sounded good and was not expensive. I sat back and took the occasional sip from my glass.

"So, what do you do, Vivian?"

"I'm the day manager at Minerva's Bookstore down the street. I've been there for over a year now and I really like it. Ever been in there?"

I confessed that I had not.

"Well, not only do we have a full selection of books written by and for women in all genres and subjects, but we also have a full music selection plus spaces in the back for groups to meet and hang out. Our full service coffee bar never takes a break; anyone who comes in the store can bring their mug for coffee while they look around or they can use one of our own if they forgot theirs."

"Sounds like you're already doing something you really want to do. Working at a bookstore like that sounds good to me."

"It has its good moments, but I still think about doing other things, just to keep myself busy." She scratched her left wrist then took a deep sip of her wine. "If I am not busy doing something, I become bored and, well, my mind starts to wander."

"There's nothing wrong with that," I said in defense; most of my own poetry resulted from my mind wandering when I had nothing to do for several hours.

"I know, I know, but-"

She stopped short of what she was going to say, scratching her wrist again, and then said, "Do you ever wonder why we are here?"

"Pardon?"

"For a while now, my mind has been wondering as to why we are here on this planet, living out our lives like actors performing for an invisible patron. I think about stuff like this in the middle of the night. Usually, my thoughts wake me up and I have to make several cups of chamomile tea before I can go back to sleep." Her eyes now focused on me. "So, what do you think?" I cleared my throat slightly.

"Well . . . I guess we are here on this planet to assist in the ongoing process of Life, whatever that is exactly." Where did that come from? "Without life, there can be no death, nor any re-birth." Sometimes I amaze myself.

She shifted in her seat then took a long sip of wine from her glass. "My friends think I think too much, that I need to just let go and relax and let God handle the rest. But, I don't even know if God is handling the rest. Does he even exist? I used to be a Methodist, but all of that changed several years ago when I- She scratched her wrist again, harder now. "I . . . had questions about God that no one could answer or else they would skirt the issue." She stared at me with eyes that I had seen before; the eyes of a person who was on the verge of doubting everything. I knew those eyes because my own used to be like that.

"Yes," I said with a small voice, "God does exist. He, she, whatever, exists all around us. I used to be like you; I used to question everything and wonder why I was even here on this planet if there was no all knowing, all powerful deity looking out for me." I took a sip of wine to wet my mouth. "I was raised under my parents' hope that I would become a model Catholic. Of course," I chuckled, "things never turn out the way that parents plan. I began to question, to wonder just why I had to do certain things and pray a certain way. I began to look into other religions, wondering about their origins and why Christians thought them to be evil. When I was 21, I traveled, much to the disgust of my parents who lost all hope in me by that point. I was a wanderer, someone who refused to be tied down to a job or some form of a conditioned life. I tried everything and I came up feeling dried out and used up. I was a bleeding heart liberal who could not make up my mind in anything. So, I came home. I felt defeated; I spent so much time abroad trying to learn and expand my own horizons, but all I had to show for it were pictures, souvenirs, and books written by crackpots who used religion as a way to gain some sort of half-assed fame before people forgot them completely."

"So, I guess you felt like I feel now," she said as the food arrived. She took a bite of her meal, set her fork down and said in a small voice, "I feel lost, out to sea without any means of support. Working at the bookstore is great, but, I don't know, I feel empty inside. Call me crazy, but I need some form of reassurance, something to hold on to spiritually. So, what about you? What changed your outlook on God?" She scratched her wrist again, harder this time.

"One Sunday, several years ago, I had stayed in my apartment the Saturday before, doing anything to keep myself occupied, but I felt restless, not really caring what I did. I drank a cup of earl grey tea then went to bed. Another day notched in my belt of Life. On Sunday, I woke up, ate some toast, looked outside and suddenly felt the need to walk. It was a beautiful day with a blue sky over me, birds singing all around me, people spending time with their loved ones or by themselves with a book under a tree, and here I was, moping around and feeling sorry for myself. That's when it hit me; suddenly, I felt a sensation of someone placing their arms around me, comforting me and letting me know that I was loved. Without any word, I fell to my knees with tears running down my face. Everything I had questions or concerns about cleared themselves in my head within minutes."

"What was it?"

"To this day, I don't know. All I can say is that, from that moment on, I knew that I was loved by something that was beyond description."

"So, are you a Christian again?"

"No. I refuse to be labeled. I am spiritual and that is that. I made that decision when I had my moment all those years ago."

"So, what happened to you once you had your moment of clarity?"

"When I stood back up, I raced back home and began clearing out my apartment of bad memories and junk, a task that took several hours, but I felt that I had to do it. When everything was back to order, I turned on my computer and began opening old files of work I had not touched in years, now ready to be cleaned up and sent out to be published. I drank many cups of tea and worked until the clock rang 3AM. I settled in for the night and slept peacefully the first time in three years. When I awoke the next day, I still felt the same so I knew I did not dream it. I took my walk again, noticing everything around me and putting it all into detail with regard for my own life. For the first time I felt alive, a true human. I wanted to tell others of my discovery, letting them know that it was going to be OK, even when Life threw curve balls our way."

"Did you?"

I chuckled in a bitter sort of way. "Can you imagine what people would have thought of me? Some guy running up to you saying, Hey, I don't know you, but don't worry; there is a force out there that protects us no matter what! I would have sounded like a crazy person on the street. I wrote instead, poetry and stories, using my experiences as the basis for them all. I submitted my work to anyone and everyone, hoping like hell someone would publish them. After months of rejection letters, I received my first acceptance letter from a small publishing company in Vermont. I have not looked back because of what I know and what I have felt." I began to eat my own dinner that was now slightly warm while I waited for her to respond. She sat there, still eating in a mechanical sort of way, as her brain processed what I just told her. She took a sip of her wine, drained her glass actually, and then spoke.

"When I read your last book, I felt something inside of me flutter. Actually, I felt that flutter every time I read your books, but I could never figure out what it was. Now that I know, I feel somewhat better about the whole matter. Do I believe now? Well, I feel much better after talking to you about my thoughts. I just want to make sure that it is OK to breathe. It is OK to breathe now, at least for a little while. Thank you, Julian." She scratched her left wrist faintly and smiled.

The rest of the dinner was spent talking about other matters, simple and grandiose, until the wine was gone and the dessert eaten with relish. I was tired, but I still wanted to talk to her. She intrigued me, even after my long (and probably boring) speech about religion.

"So," I said while stifling a yawn, "would you like to go somewhere for coffee, or do you have plans?"

"Well, I was rather hoping we could continue this conversation at my place. I have an espresso machine." I was taken aback at her asking me to come back to her place.

"Are you sure?" No point in trying to sound or look too eager.

"Of course. Besides, is there any way you can autograph my books?"

We walked along the still crowded street, the air slightly cooler from the rain, holding hands. It surprised me that she wanted me to hold her hand after one dinner, but I did not complain or question. I was happy just to do it for she seemed like she needed the closeness.

"I didn't have too much time cleaning up my place this morning," she said with a sheepish grin, "but I still want you to see it." I assured her that I would not think such a thing; I just wanted to be around her.

The warehouse stood at the end of the area, a large building that I thought would be dark and foreboding. However, it was brightly lit with flowers planted all around the bottom while people sat outside in the table and chairs the circled the complex. Conversations were being held with much laughter and noise and I felt more at ease because of it. We went through a side door and down a brightly lit hallway that ended with a freight elevator. She got in first and I followed. She closed the heavy iron door behind us. The elevator lurched with a groan and soon we were going up several flights. I could barely make out the other floors and how their occupants had decorated their living spaces. Finally, on the fifth floor, the elevator stopped and we got out.

My first impression of her floor was of amazement: the entire floor looked to be one large art gallery; pictures of every colour and size hung on the walls or propped up on the floors. Her bed stood in the middle of the floor with surrounding gauze while her clothing hung on racks in different areas. One corner held several plants and flowers. There was even a small tree with large and long green leaves so perfect that it looked fake. To the left was her kitchen while to the right near one of the larger windows was her TV, multi CD player, and couch. My eyes wandered around the floor with awe as I walked around, leaving her without a second thought. She smiled, then sat down on the couch and flipped off her shoes.

"I've never seen so many colours in one place before," I murmured. "Why did you think I would think it messy?"

"Probably because I have so much stuff lying around." I continued to walk around, admiring her paintings, sculptures, and her five bookshelves filled with books on a plethora of subjects. I glanced back in her direction and noticed that she sat on her couch reading a book. I was not surprised.

"Did you do all of the art?," I asked as I held up a canvas painting of a woman with long black hair dressed in a long purple robe. The detail was extraordinary.

"Yes. I went through a creative splurge several years ago and wanted to test my hand at everything, just to see if I could do it. I even took some art classes before I began my MFA." I placed the painting back on the floor then walked over to her and sat down on the couch. She placed her book on the floor and took my hands in hers. I glanced down and noticed scratch marks on her wrists.

When I awoke, it was almost 7:30 in the morning. I blinked several times then sat straight up in bed, not remembering where I was for a brief moment. I then looked around and noticed the paintings and sculptures then looked down at my naked body; a dreamy smile crept across my lips as last night came back into focus; our lovemaking spanned several hours, dwindling down to mere kisses mingled with words that we had to say due to being in the moment. I grabbed my boxer shorts and threw them on followed by the rest of my tangled mess of clothing then walked through the entire apartment in a desperate and futile search for Vivian.

Two minutes later, I found the note in the kitchen by her purple coffee maker.

Dear Julian,
I had a wonderful time with you last night. It was a joy to finally meet one of my favorite poets. Our conversation in the restaurant was stimulating and I must admit, opened my eyes to a possibility of a force and power higher than our own that loves and cares for us. I hope you did not feel like I picked your brain with my endless religious questions, but I appreciated your words. Sorry for the disappearing act this morning, but I have several errands that I need to take care of. Make yourself at home at my place and don't worry about locking the door behind you when you leave!
Vivian

I skipped (literally) all the way home in delight of what happened yesterday. Once I got home, I showered, put on fresh clothes, and greeted the day with a smile that I truly felt inside.

Three days had come and gone and I still had not heard from her since the letter. During that time, I went back to her warehouse place and found that I could not get in, walked back to the bookstore where we met to possibly catch a glance of her, tried to go to her bookstore and found it to be closed for renovations, and just walked the streets of the area with hopeful eyes. She disappeared into thin air, it seemed. I had just about given up all hope when I decided to go back to the bookstore on the third day to get a cup of coffee and relax. I ordered my drink and picked it up at the end of the bar, then found a quiet place to read my newspaper.

WOMAN FOUND DEAD IN HOTEL ROOM

Police authorities answered a 911 from Hotel Aberdeen after one of the maids discovered the body of a young woman in one of the rooms. Her wrists were slashed with a razor and the blood-splattered body was discovered lying on the bed. Police identified the young woman as one 33-year-old Vivian Greenlaw, a resident of the Shady Elm area. Authorities are beginning research of Ms. Greenlaw's psychiatric background since the death was ruled as a suicide.

I stared at the article, my eyes unfocused and brimming with tears. I could no longer breathe. How could something so beautiful be so damned at the same time? I felt faint and nauseous, wanting to run home to scream and yell out my anger.

Suddenly, the strong scent of lavender filled my nose, causing me to turn around in frustration, wondering who had decided to bathe in their perfume then my face lost its tightness as I closed my eyes, picturing her as I last saw her; a multicoloured soul. My hands were wet from my tears.

Peau

Hello there, glad you could come, considering the weather and all. Shall I take your coat? Please, make yourself at home; sit here with me in the living room. I must apologize for the candles being the only source of light in this room, but it makes the atmosphere seem cozier and less of shadows created by the storm outside. I know your sight is not too well in here, but the lights will be turned on soon enough.

Are you comfortable? Would you like a drink, something to sooth your parched throat perhaps? Nothing? Then do I mind if I ask you a question? What is a book?

You seem surprised. Why? Such a simple question and yet you look at me with eyes that are quite wide. However, I must ask you once more: what is a book?

What, no answer? Surely someone as intelligent as you would be able to answer my little question, yes? Someone of your . . . reputation should be able to answer such a simple question, yes? And yet, you sit here, eyes as wide as pools, staring at me as if I have suddenly lost all faculties of my mind. Perhaps you do need a drink. I wanted you to come tonight because I missed you, my friend. The years have been too long and I have terribly missed you since our time at university. I wanted to enjoy my night with you as two learned individuals talking and sharing the night away, and yet all I have received thus far is silence.

Very well, I shall answer my own question then to begin our talk.

Tales from a Goth Librarian

    A book, according to Webster's Dictionary, is a set of written sheets of skin, paper, or tablets of wood or ivory; a set of written printed, or blank sheets bound together into a volume; a long written or printed literary composition; a major division of a treatise or literary work, and so on and so on. Quite a lengthy description, I think, but tell me; is that what you think as well? Do you agree with what the great Webster's has to say about a book? Will you answer me please?

    I see. Well, I guess I must speak once more in answering my question. Your eyes betray you; I thought you to be better than that.

    I see matters quite differently. To me, a book is a journey yet to be taken, but once taken can be repeated over and over at the discretion of the reader. A book is a breath of life, a cool drink of water to a parched throat, a red apple eaten to nourish the soul, a kiss tenderly received from a shy lover. A book is all of that and still much more. When I read a book, I like to sniff the pages carefully, allowing my senses to enjoy the musk and dust of the knowledge contained within. I treat my books like absinthe; languishing in my hazy yet sensual mental fog gives me pleasure beyond all measure and yet I still ache for more. In order for you to understand better, let me grab one from the shelf here.

    Ah, so you can speak! No, no, I can see quite well with the light from the candles.

    Where is it . . . Yes, right here. Please take it and let me get back to my chair.

    No, you did not see anything.

    Now, shall we continue with this?

    See the title you have in your hands? **Indigo** by Graham Joyce; do you remember why I have that title? Remember what happened when we were both sophomores? By that playful look in your eye, I would venture to say yes. I have not forgotten as well, although I still have the clothing I wore on that night; the stains will never come out. Oh well; we were both students in all aspects. I still remember Xavier's face when we told him what we did.

So, take the book in your hand and hold it. Yes, just hold it. How does it feel to you? Rough, perhaps? Smooth like a blushing virgin's cheek? Neither? No, keep your eyes open please. I want you to focus on the book itself and every aspect of it.

OK, give me the book back. Now, I want you to hold it as if it was your lover. Do not be shy; we are the only people in the room. Caress the cover tenderly. Stroke it, softly now, softly. Very good. It seems as though you have done this sort of thing before. I'll give you a few more minutes to let yourself go with it, but remember what I said. Treat it as a lover.

Open your eyes. Now, how did it feel to you? Different? Something . . . alive? Do not lie to me because I can see your true thoughts in your eyes. Do not hide from me what you are thinking. You know I am right.

So, why the experiment? It is because of this experiment that I asked you to come here tonight, leaving your warm and safe surroundings to brave such a horrible storm. I wanted you here tonight because it has been a long time since we last spoke. I still have your letters and I am sure you want to know why I never responded to them. I want to tell you what happened to me after we graduated. Are you sure you do not want something to drink? Tea, perhaps? No? Well, before I begin I must ask you to not ask me any questions until I am completely finished with my tale. No, I will not increase the light. I need the light just the way it is, you see. So, do you swear to remain quiet while I tell my tale? Good.

I had always known our group to be beyond that of anyone else who studied at the university, you know. Our small, but powerful group held the reins for the rest of the lot, paving the way for a higher sense of education. All five of us – Viktor, Emma, Xavier, you and I, we were all giants in our own way. To me, we were the family I wished I had rather than the one I was born to. Our many nights of staying up discussing many subjects still burn in my mind and sometimes, I long for those simpler days. I remember the books we used to read and the subjects that thrilled us so, while we drank cup after cup of that awful black coffee and smoked cigarettes.

Well, when we graduated and went our separate ways, I felt lost and disconnected for a time. I felt as though I could not trust anyone with my life and secrets and so I kept to myself for a period of time. I moved back home, but after six months of ennui decided to travel and see the world, as clichéd as that sounds. I first went to France and studied art history under a Monsieur Yves De Michel. For three months, I was his only pupil, helping him with his own paintings and sculptures while learning my own technique in the world of art. We used to stay up late into the night working in silence with breaks every now and then to smoke his special cigarettes that made my head feel like it was stuffed with cotton. I was glad to be studying with him for he opened my eyes to a world I never knew existed.

He also helped me with my own . . . awakening. Do not scorn me with your eyes. I knew what I was getting myself into and I welcomed it gladly. To me, Yves was a godsend, assisting me in my own path. His styles of lovemaking still haunt me to this day and quite honestly, I wondered how I even survived some of it. He did not beat me or abuse me; his actions were slow and careful, teasing in some ways when I wanted more. When he made his first move on me, I felt my soul for the first time. Do you realize that, for many years, I did not think I had one? I had thought that I was a hollow being that only felt truly alive when I read books and absorbed the knowledge contained in them. No, Yves was beyond all human understanding and I welcomed it.

It all fell to pieces when I walked in on him and a young man engaging in a quite difficult position while their bodies were covered in paint. When I asked him why he wanted this young man aside from me, he simply stated that my training was complete. I felt crushed, my friend, and so I left France and moved onward through the rest of Europe. Back home, my family was under the delusion that everything was OK for I did not want them to know what I was going through, but I was going through bloody hell.

I stopped keeping myself clean, hoping that my slovenly appearance would somehow turn me into a martyr who wanted to show the world the pain I had experienced. I wore the same clothing day in day out and I even refused to feed myself for days at a time. Of course, I had Mummy and Daddy's money, but I did not want to fall back on such a cushion. I wanted to feel the pain. I was so foolish in my thought process, but at the time, I saw it to be my only choice. I made mistakes, my friend, mistakes that young women in my position should not make. I tried it all and did it all; no matter what anyone tells you, chasing the dragon is not what poets make it out to be.

After another two months, my family wanted me to come home and settle down. They felt that I should begin searching for a husband so I could settle down and produce offspring for them, continuing some damn family line. The letters were all the same: please come home Violet, have you begun thinking of more serious matters, Violet? At first, I used to burn the letters after reading them, but then soon stopped. I had grown tired of the life I was living at the time and thought that perhaps coming back home was a good choice to make.

No, no, I am all right. I am not used to speaking so much. Please, let me continue. Do not interrupt me again.

When I arrived home five months later, my family did not recognize me. I had lost weight and my once long black hair was now barely touching the tips of my ears. I still remember when I stepped off the train, boldly facing my stunned family as I gathered my meager belongings and let them lead the way to the car. The drive home was quiet for no one knew just what to ask me. They had the questions, all right, but they refused to speak to me for fear that it would soon turn into a feeding frenzy with me as the sacrifice. When we arrived home, they beckoned a servant to gather my belongings and burn them in one of the kitchen ovens while another took me to my old room, stripping me down to my bare skin and forcing me to bathe. I protested during the entire ordeal, but deep down inside, I was happy. Happy to be home, happy to still be alive, happy to be home. Yes, I did miss them. I closed my eyes and let the servant girl scrub away the dirty past from my body.

For the next several weeks, tension was high at our manor. My family, although they loved me, tread carefully around me when I was out. They were glad to have me home, but at the same time were a little frightened of me. I would wander from room to room while holding a book in my hand while my eyes would focus on nothing in front of me. I was trying to come back to the world of the living, but found it to be difficult. My long nightdress made a whispering noise on the carpet when I walked, giving me the title of family ghost who would be spoken to, but who would not sometimes speak back.

My mother, however, wanted me to drop the "act" and come to my senses so she began throwing parties, inviting young men for me to meet with the hope of possibly marrying one of them. The men were all poufs, toying with their clothing in trying to impress me, but I saw through their false acts. I would dress in my best dresses and allow the servants to "pretty me up" for the guests below. When I walked down the stairs, you could hear the sighs and hints of surprises at watching me glide down the spirals stairs in my aristocratic form. I held the room in awe and my family was pleased.

The men would then run up to me like dogs after a piece of beef, their tongues wagging out of their mouths as they each eyed me as their potential bride and wife and yet I laughed at them all underneath my calm and composed demeanor. I did not refuse them outright, but I did play with them, toying with their minds with my games full of wit and innuendos. They were no match for me and I cherished the defeated looks in their eyes as they slunk off to some corner to nurse their wounds once I finished with them. My family saw the way I treated every potential suitor, giving them reason to be concerned with not only the situation, but with me as well. I was like a stranger to them who only looked like their beloved daughter.

I spent most of my time reading in either my room or the library while the rest of the family went their own way as well. We spoke when necessary and even laughed on some occasions, but most of our time was spent quite gingerly; they were still unsure as to who I really was. That was fine by me; less questions and more time to read. I even began ordering more and more books, filling up every little space that I had in my room in a desperate attempt to shut out everything else that no longer mattered to me. My mother continued on her "Let's get Violet married" quest and every time, I shot down the potential suitor with a gleam in my eye and a smirk that reeked of evil.

One night, as I was preparing myself to go to bed, my mother entered my room without a knock or even asking for my permission. She gripped her candleholder tightly and I could see it shaking slightly and, judging by the look in her eye, I knew that the upcoming conversation was not going to be a good one. I sat on the side of the bed while she stood by the door, our eyes locked and neither one refusing to look away. After several seconds of silence, I figured I would begin this little charade.

"Mother."

"Violet, what has happened to you?"

"Whatever do you mean?"

"I mean, child-"

"I am no longer a child!" For a moment, I did not recognize the voice that came out of me. My mother was stunned as well because it stunned her to silence. Her eyes grew wide at my insolence then narrowed again when she regained her composure. She set the candleholder on one of my dressers then continued to speak in a tone that she only used for a servant who had been caught stealing.

"Violet Winterstone! You will not speak to me in that tone, not now nor ever. You may have graduated from university, but you will always be a child, our daughter, in this manor." I could feel the coldness seeping up my spine, but continued to stare at her straight in the face. I would not break down, no matter the cost. "We, your *family*, have given you everything that a woman of your caliber should accept in life. You wanted university and so we made it possible. We knew that your studies would lead you to a better understanding of the world around you." She walked closer to me, but still kept her distance. "However, when you arrived home from your holiday, we no longer recognized you, Violet. You are now a stranger to us all. Why do you not choose to marry? Do you have someone else in mind? Is that it? Who is he and we'll make sure we invite him to the manor, darling." Her face softened a little; surely that had to be the reason why their golden child of a daughter was acting so strangely lately. Surely. "What is his name? Where does he live? Is he from a good family? Is he-"

"There is no one. I just refuse to marry." You would think I had told her that I wanted to become a man by the look she gave me. She clutched her heart (so melodramatic!) and took a step away from me while I simply sat on the edge of my bed, waiting for her to leave so I could read before retiring for the night. Her eyes were wide like a deer momentarily blinded by a hunter's light; she bumped against the door, but her eyes were still fixed on me.

"Refuse to marry?" she whispered. I nodded yes. "B-but why? You can't possibly expect to become an old maid, do you? Why would you want to live your life like that?"

"But mother, there are many women who decide not to get married. They still lead happy and very fulfilling lives and I plan to do so as well."

"But an old maid? Violet, you're too beautiful to accept such a life for yourself."

"I see. Beauty; is that all you think I have going for me?"

"Violet, please. I am trying to understand, that's all." She sat down on the bed next to me and began to play with my hair. "Help me understand."

We talked long into the night about my plans in life and why I was the way I was. I did not reveal any skeletons in the closet, so to speak, but just enough. When she left my room at 3 in the morning, she actually smiled at me. That night was probably the best sleep I ever had in a long time.

The next couple of months were good for the family, even I. We got along rather well and the whispering behind my back was no more. Violet was her old self, as some of the servants said. I still spent my days reading in the library, pouring over old manuscripts and documents handed down through the generations, and no one bothered me or thought it to be weird. It seemed like, for a time, they accepted my self-proclaimed lot in life. I was in heaven; I no longer had to worry about suitors coming to our home trying to win me over as the future Mrs. Whatever.

However, as I found out later, all was not well. My family, although trying to accept me and the life I had chosen for myself, still whispered about me behind my back. My mother, the one who shared such an intimate conversation with me that one night, still held questions in her mind about me, reservations about my true motives for refusing men. Slowly, but surely, they turned into actors in a play, smiling and talking to me in a good-natured sense in a rehearsed tone. They were nothing more than bloody actors.

Over a period of months, I increased my personal library, ordering books dealing with a wide variety of subjects and some I had just began to study. I wanted to know more the world and why it was the way it was. There were some subjects that a university would never touch and I wanted to be an apt pupil for this new avenue I had discovered. My tastes ran to matters of forgotten corners of history, people and places that were now occupying museums and dusty shelves. I wanted to give these subjects life once more with a hope of sharing that life with others who were searching as much as I, thereby keeping the knowledge alive.

You look tired, my friend. Would you like me to stop for a moment? No, I will not turn on any lights. I will do so when the time is right. Everything occurring tonight is planned right from the moment you answered my invitation to come here. My only concern is that you hear me out completely and not judge me during that time.

Yes, I have changed; such a far cry from the woman you knew so long ago. And yet; perhaps I have been like this during that time as well; only you refused to truly see me. No matter.

There have been studies that claim that we humans only use 10% of our brains. Imagine, for a moment, what would occur if we had the ability to use 100% of it. Think of the things we could accomplish! Would diseases be forever removed from our lives? Would we no longer use currency as a means of buying and selling goods? Would wars be only a smudge in the pages of history? Am I confusing you? You do look rather perplexed right now; perhaps you are thinking that I have gone mad. My family thought so and look what happened to them; oh yes, I have not reached that part of the story yet. Forgive me for trying to jump in time with my tale.

I began to stop eating; only taking in tea and other liquids. My only nourishment was knowledge and I had to have it, no matter the cost. Books had become my only source for anything; knowledge could not desert you, nor reprimand you for something that was insignificant. I used my inheritance to buy books and soon, my life was completely surrounded and inundated with them. For the first time in a long time I was happy. Then came the fire.

I remembered going to sleep after a rousing reading of Darwin's **Origin of the Species**, keeping myself locked in my room. I fell asleep in bed, clutching the book like a child holds onto its blanket when it thinks that the boogeyman is in their closet. Suddenly, I heard or thought I heard someone yelling downstairs, so I grabbed my robe with my book still in my hand and slipped out of my room to the balcony while trying to shake off my sleepiness. I leaned over the balcony, noticing that the lights were on downstairs in the front foyer, but no movement. I turned to go back to bed, thinking that I had a dream, when I heard the noise again. It was my father, Jacob Winterstone, and by the tone in his voice, was not in a good mood. I walked back to the balcony and cocked my ear out as far as possible, trying to hear as much as possible. It sounded as though he was speaking to a servant, but I later realized that he was speaking to my mother.

"This can not go on any longer!," he said in the voice he used when he was trying cases in court. "I can not, no, will not allow her to slowly destroy herself! Not in my home!"

"But dear..."

"Not another word! She will be forced to make a decision; either Violet lives in this house like a true member of the Winterstone family to later be married, or she will leave!"

"She will not make such a choice, you know."

"Then I will make it for her," he said in an eerily calm tone, but I could feel the steel underneath the words. "I will break her, one way or the other." I clutched my book to my breast in shock; my father wanted me gone from my home? I had done nothing wrong as far as I was concerned. All I did was read books; what was wrong with that? I wanted to run downstairs and demand the meaning of his anger towards me, then realized that it would do me no good. Once his mind was set on something, he made diamonds look as though they were made of butter. I wanted to cry, but no tears came. I wanted to scream, but only a soft wheezing noise came from my throat. And yet - and yet deep down inside of me, I wanted him to suffer. I wanted him to truly understand that I had no intention of doing what he demanded simply because I was his daughter. I wanted my mother to suffer as well, for she refused to change his mind and instead let him have his way. It was always his way; he made the rules and we, even my mother, were expected to follow them without question. Oh, how I hated him.

I slipped back into my room and locked the door. My mind was not functioning properly so I sat down at my desk and stared at the book I still held in my hand. Such a simple object and yet it caused my family to hate me with a poison I never knew could exist. I could feel a slow coldness running down my spine; numbness had now taken over me and I was no longer possessed of emotion.

"Violet! Violet!" yelled my father at my door. "Come out this instant!" I turned my eyes to the locked door, listening to my father yell for me on the other side, but I paid it no attention. For a moment, I did not even know who he was. All I could think of was my library; my personal library, my only form of sanity. My father began to knock loudly on the door while trying to turn the knob; I knew that the lock could not keep him out forever. My throat began to close up and I found myself gasping for air, but I refused to run to the door or let go of my book. I wanted to breathe and the air would not come. I could now feel the tears I had expected earlier falling down my face, but still I could not breathe. I realize now that it was all psychological, but at the time, I thought I felt my own father's hands around my throat, choking the life out of me. I dropped my book to place my own hands around my throat and soon, I felt the air coming back to me. I swallowed great gulps of it, savoring the sweet taste, forgetting that my father still banged on my door.

Funny, that; once I acknowledged his fury at my door, I could no longer hear it. I slowly walked to the door and placed an ear to it, searching for any signs and sounds of the Enemy. Yes, at this point, my father had turned into the Enemy with no relation to me whatsoever.

Suddenly, the door shook violently with a loud thud, knocking me off my feet and landing on my back. I groaned with pain then it came again. Scrambling to my feet, I raced back to my bed in fear, knowing that whatever was making that sound could not be good at all. I lay down in my soft warm bed and pulled the covers over my head, trying to drown out the ever-growing noises at my door.

Of course, you do realize that my father was trying to break down the door by using the muscles of several of the servants. After few moments of grunts and hard labor, they finally broke down the door, knocking it off its hinges, to reveal me hiding in my bed like a child. My father pushed the servants away from the door and stormed into my room while I cowered even deeper in my bed. When he reached the bed, he yanked the sheets from me and pulled me up by my arm. There was obviously no love in his action, nor was there any in the eyes that stared at me. His eyes were full of hatred and anger and it was I alone who received such harsh emotions. He shook me by my arm then slapped me across the face with his free hand.

"You little spoiled brat!" he yelled at me and I could smell his dinner on his breath; mutton with onions. "You think that because you live here, you can do whatever you want! Not anymore. Either you learn to live by my rules or you will leave this place and never come back!" He shook my arm once more for emphasis then threw me back down on the bed. I glanced at my arm and saw the very red marks his hand left. I looked behind him and saw my mother silently weeping as she crossed her arms over her heaving chest. Her eyes silently begged me to change my ways, but I knew better. To live in my father's house meant complete submission and I would have been a fool to do such a thing. My eyes then focused on my father's red face and I slowly got up from the bed and walked to my writing desk. I could feel my father's glare on my back as I calmly took one of my lit lamps on the desk in my hand then turned to face him once more. With a smile I dropped the lamp on the floor, instantly causing a small fire on the floor. One of the servants rushed up to stamp it out, but my father held him back, all the while his eyes were locked on mine.

"You have become mad," he whispered while I said nothing in return. I could feel the fire warming my legs, but I did nothing to prevent it from coming closer to me. My father backed away from me, as did everyone else, leaving me standing alone, knowing that the fire would consume the room, the house, and me. I no longer cared; all I wanted to do was sleep. In five minutes, the fire had consumed a little more than half of my room with long tendrils of it sneaking its way out and down the hall. I remained rooted to the spot, watching the flames deliver smoky kisses to everything that it touched. No longer did I notice that the flames had now begun to kiss my nightgown and my legs. The pain felt a little more than a bee sting as I closed my eyes and welcomed its embrace.

Yes, my friend, I was quite mad. I could tell by the look in your eyes so there is no need for you to make a futile attempt in asking me. My mind, at the time, felt like it was torn in two and yet I thought I was the one in control. I felt as though my family had wronged me and that now it was my turn to seek revenge on their privileged and wasteful lives. I wanted them to know that hurt that they brought upon me. I thought that the fire was my only option. Looking back on it, I realize now that I was wrong.

It should have been done in another way.

The fire consumed the house and me with it while my family escaped to safety. Although I am not certain, I could probably guess that once they were outside in the cool autumn breeze, they stared in shock as they watched their home burn to the ground. I am sure that their faces, dirty and streaked with sweat and soot, still held the looks of shock and disgrace while they watched. I am sure that my father did not shed a tear for his daughter; he probably spat upon the ground in disgust. I am sure that my mother watched it all in horrified silence, but refusing to say or do anything about it; she never did have a spine. She was always my father's puppet. I am sure that the servants whispered among themselves, wondering what on earth could have caused Miss Violet to do such an act, while tears fell down their faces. When I lived at that home, I never spoke rudely to any of them, nor did I use them as scapegoats for any of my problems. I treated them fairly and spent time with them when they retired for the night in their area of the manor. It was during those times that I truly learned what it meant to be human. I learned how to laugh and smile through those people. Now, I do not think I shall ever see them again.

The clock has struck 11pm, my friend. Are you tired? The dim lights have made me more relaxed, but I still have more of my tale to tell you. Do not worry; it will all be over soon.

The house burned to the ground in a matter of hours. My family did not try to stop it from burning, from what I was told. According to neighbours who ran into them later in the week, they claimed that my family watched it burn exactly the way I told you they would then turned and left without another glance. My father dismissed the servants and sent them on their way while he and my mother left for good and traveled to Canada. They told their neighbours that the fire had stared due to a fire in the kitchen. My family had no reason to lie, so of course everyone believed them. How strange it would have been to explain that your house burned down thanks to your insane and only daughter?

Firemen rushed to the scene to try to salvage the manor, but it was too late. They too let it burn down to the ground; it made it easier to clean up and start afresh. So they too watched it burn and then left when it was all over. Had they begun working on the rubble, they would have discovered a very shocking and strange surprise.

Yes, how very astute of you. Of course I did not die or else I would not be here talking to you right now.

I did not die. Thanks to the grace of God (or something far more sinister), I was alive, but barely. When the fire reached my body, I remembered screaming until I could no longer breathe. The fire peeled away my layers inch by painful inch, but somehow, I was able to survive the entire ordeal. I lay on my stomach, praying for it to soon be over. I knew that what I had done was wrong, but I had momentarily lost all functioning of sense. I was *non compos mentis* and looking back, realized that I had brought it all on myself.

Days passed as I lay under the rubble. I could not move my body, but my mind was alive. I wanted to scream again, hoping that someone walking by would hear such pitiful screams and come to my aid. But, how could I explain myself to them? What could I say? Everyone knew my family and me, so how could I ask for anyone's assistance? I wanted to die and yet I could not. For some reason, I was still alive.

I felt something wet land on my burned cheek. With that one sensation, I opened my eyes. My vision was fuzzy, but I was still able to see. It was afternoon and it had begun to rain. The fact that I knew that it was afternoon and it had begun to rain meant that my mind was not as messed up as I had thought. I could still think and move. I wanted to shout with joy, but knew that I still had a long road to walk down. So, I blinked and felt the rain trickle down my cheek and into my eyes, cooling them like a balm from the gods. I could feel the rain landing on my charred skin and that too was relief. Inside, my mind was screaming for joy, but on the outside, I barely moved. After several minutes of me laughing inwardly, I calmed by heartbeat to a leveled rhythm so I could think of a plan. I had to remove myself from the ruins, but how? I closed my eyes as the rain now began to pour from the sky, washing away every trace of my past.

When I opened my eyes again, I was no longer wet. In fact, I was no longer lying among the ruins of my former home. Instead, I was lying in the softest bed I had ever felt, with robin's egg blue sheets and a down comforter of a bright and cheerful blue. My skin felt rough against the sheets, but I paid it no mind; I was grateful to be in a bed. I turned my head slightly and could feel the thick down pillows supporting me. Had I died? I could feel tears running down my face; surely an angel rescued me. I then turned my head ever so slightly so as to view my surroundings: I was in a small bedroom that had one window next to my head that was cracked slightly open, allowing a cool and scented breeze to enter and permeate the room. The walls were painted basic beige and there were paintings of every colour and size hanging on the walls. The colours in each painting were so bright that vivid that I wanted to touch them with my scarred hands. The only door was on the other side of the room. After trying to stare at my surroundings, I focused all of my attention on the door, wondering who had saved me and if this was their house.

Suddenly, the door opened without a sound to reveal a man carrying a tray with a bowl of soup and some fruit. When he saw that I was awake he smiled and walked over to my left side. He sat down next to me and instantly I could smell his lime cologne. His eyes were a deep blue almost black that had flecks of what looked to be gold. His skin was pale and yet healthy while his face gave him an aristocratic look. He was dressed in black pants and a long sleeve white shirt with ebony coloured hair that fell down to his shoulders and was pulled back in a messy ponytail. When he smiled, I could see the crows' feet around his eyes and at once I knew he was much older than he looked.

The tray of food sat in his lap, but his eyes were on me. I wanted to thank him for what he had done, but the only noise I could make was a strangled squeak, causing him to laugh.

"Now, now, my dear," he said in a deep voice that reminded me of velvet, "don't tax yourself. It's too early." He then lifted a spoonful of the warm soup (it was chicken and mushroom), blew on it several times to make sure it was at a temperature I could handle, then fed me. When the soup touched my mouth, I groaned with delight which made him chuckle. "I'm glad you like my concoction," he said with a pleasing tone. "I made it just for you." I nodded slightly, giving him the signal that I wanted more. With every spoonful, I could feel my body becoming warmer and warmer with an equal gaining of strength. I nodded more vigorously with every spoonful and he obeyed. Within minutes, the bowl was empty and I was able to sit up thanks to my newfound strength. I smiled, or at least I thought I did, and lifted a hand towards him. He took my hand in his own and it was then that I looked down at my skin. My entire hand and arm were blacker than coal and when his skin touched mine, flakes of my own fell off. In horror, I pulled my hand away from his and stared at him with wide eyes. He stared at me for a moment then took my hand again in his own.

"I do not know what happened to you," he said calmly, "but I am here to help you. I am a doctor." With those simple words, I fell back against my pillow and slept.

When I awoke, it was nighttime, but the drapes were pulled back, allowing the moon to shine her light into my room. I closed my eyes and prayed to Selene, the goddess of the moon, thanking her for her light. Within minutes, I was asleep again.

I opened my eyes again to the sun. My eyes darted around the room, wondering if anything had changed, but it was still the same. While looking around, I noticed that my head did not hurt nearly as much and that the sheets did not drag as harshly across my skin. I wondered . . . I removed my hand from the sheet and screamed. The black coarse skin I last saw was now a grey and smoother. In haste, not noticing that the movements were not causing me pain, I raised my other arm up and noticed it too looked the same.

Just then, my saviour came running into the room, wearing a white lab coat and strange copper and black goggles perched on his head.

"Are you all right? I heard you scream."

"What in the bloody hell do you think?" I screamed back. "Why is my skin now grey? What did you do to me? What happened . . .?" I stopped speaking with shock; my voice had come back! The doctor leaned against the wall, crossed his arms, and smiled.

"It seems that you're doing better," he said.

His name is Lucien William Davenport, MD. That is the name of my angel, my rescuer when I thought I had none. It was he who found me lying in what used to be my room and pulled me from the wreckage. I owe him my life.

Yes, I do still speak to him. I should after all; he is my husband now. In fact, this is our home. But, don't worry; you shall meet him soon.

So, once I got over my shock of having a voice and my skin was on its way to being healed, Lucien sat down in the chair next to my bed and touched my forehead. I wanted to shrink away from those hands at first, for I was still not sure as to how he was able to save me, but his cool hands won me over.

"Hmm, slight fever, but other than that OK," he murmured to himself. I closed my eyes because I did not want to focus on his; somewhere deep inside of me, I was fearful of him. He looked human, sounded human, but yet . . . there was something more to this man that I cared to admit.

"Why is my skin grey?"

"Part of your treatment. It is only Step One towards your full recovery." He moved his hand down to my cheeks and felt both of them for any fever. "You are in capable hands, my dear." Before I could ask him any other questions, he got up and walked out of the room, closing the door behind him. I lay in bed while staring at the door. I wanted to know just what he had done to me and yet I was afraid of the answer. True, I did feel stronger than before, but it seemed too short of a period of time for me to feel this good. I looked at my arms and hands again. The grey colour looked as though I was born from smog and smoke and when I touched my right arm with my left hand, the grey colour seemed to swirl a bit like smoke. I lay back in the bed and closed my eyes, too exhausted to think anymore about my condition. All I wanted now was sleep.

When I awoke much later, Dr. Davenport was in my room, checking my temperature and feeling my face for any signs of fever. When I opened my eyes, his dark blue ones locked onto mine and I could barely speak. The strength behind those eyes was powerful enough to silence me. He checked my temperature as well as my skin then left without saying a word, leaving me puzzled. He seemed different than the last time he checked me, I thought. Was there something wrong?

Looking back on it all, I know why he acted so strangely, why his mood was different than before; his creation. Yes, you are confused; I can see that. But, don't worry; all will be explained. Just be patient with me, please. Don't speak.

I never knew that one could fall in love with someone so quickly. From the first moment I laid eyes on him, I was in love. He could not return the emotion, I thought at first, and so I buried my love for him deeply inside of me, never giving it light. However, I was only fooling myself; the more I saw him, the more I loved him. He was an angel to me, a saviour that could never be repaid. I wanted him to love me just as much as I loved him.

One brisk afternoon I sat up a little higher than before in my bed and gazed out of the window. The verdant meadows rolled as far as my eyes could see and yet the scene brought me nothing, but sadness. I wanted to be out there among the hills, laughing and running, as a normal human should. My eyes gazed back to my now light dusty grey arms and before I knew it, a sigh had escaped my lips.

"Why so sad?" I looked up in surprise and saw Lucien standing by the doorway with a tray of that delicious soup for me. His face bore the look of sadness that made him even more beautiful than before. I looked away, focusing my eyes on anything, but him. "Come now, is that any way for a patient to act when seeing me?" He walked up to my bed and sat down, preparing the soup for me.

"It's just . . . the hills. I've never seen hills so beautiful before." His gaze wandered to the window and he smiled. "Yes, my lands are quite beautiful, but there are other things even more so." I turned to face him, but his eyes were now focused on the soup while he tried to cool it for me; did he mean me just then?

While he fed me and I ate, my mind had begun to wander. Was there any way that someone like him could ever find something like me desirable? Would my hair ever grow back to its original length? Would I ever be pretty again? It shocked me to think such shallow things, but I wanted it for him. I wanted him to look at me the way I looked at him. He fed me my dinner and I took it with gratitude, never realizing that my strength was coming back faster and faster. My hair had begun to grow and I barely noticed it. My skin, however, stayed the same dusty grey. I was coming back to my old self and yet I never knew it. My thoughts were focused on Lucien.

Days turned into weeks and soon, I was out of bed, walking around with his assistance. He would come by my room every other day and lead me around the room, testing out the strength of my body. We never spoke during those times, but words were never needed. If I had known then what I know now, I would have smiled. You see, he loved me too.

For the longest time, I never saw the rest of his home, for my exercises were confined to my room. Strangely enough, I never worried about such things; he came to see me every other day right on the dot. So it struck me as a surprise when he told me, one day after he arrived at his usual time, that he was going to take me out. At first, I was nervous for I had no idea what he meant. He noted the look on my face and laughed like a deity.

"My dear," he said in his usual deep and smooth voice, "I am merely going to show you the rest of my home. Please," he said as he held out a hand for me, "come to me. Do not be afraid." I was unsure for a moment; of course I had strength when he led me, but for me to get up on my own was unthinkable. . . and a challenge. I removed the sheets from my body and sat up rather quickly, surprising myself with my speed. I then swung my legs over the side and with some slight shaking, roused myself out of bed and slowly walked to his inviting hand. When he took my own in his, I wanted to cry.

My room was at the end of a long hallway that seemed to go on forever, at least to me. The walls were covered in dark wine coloured velvet that only added to the overall feeling of his home: sophistication and upper class. Soon, we arrived at the staircase, which wound all the way down to the main room that looked to have been used for parties and other formal and informal gatherings. However, when we reached the lower level, I was in for a shock.

His home was unlike any place I had ever seen, for most of the walls were covered in bookshelves that were set to bursting with books on every subject. I touched some of the tomes as we walked. He pointed out some of his favourite titles to me, watching my reaction to them. Of course, most of the ones he pointed out to me I had already read, which surprised him.

"I've never known anyone, let alone a woman, who had read the same works as I."

"Perhaps you should travel in better circles."

We spent most of the day walking around while he pointed out things to me. I took it all in with my eyes, for I did not know when I would leave my room again. I gripped his arm tighter and noticed that he winced slightly.

"Lucien," I said in a quiet tone as we walked.

"Yes?"

"One question: you never asked me my name."

"Why should that be a concern? For right now, you are my patient. What I need to know about you does not include a name. All I need to know about you I already know." For the first time ever, I was stunned into silence.

We continued our walk through his home and although I enjoyed it tremendously, I was also beginning to feel slightly tired. Lucien took note of my sudden change of condition then, without a word, led me to my room. Once my head made contact with the pillow, I fell asleep and knew no more.

I can not remember the first time I ever heard the noises, but I do remember hearing them the night after my first outing into the rest of the home. After some time of a peaceful slumber, I awoke to the sound of grinding metal. My eyes flew open and I peered into the darkness of my own room, wondering about the source of the noise. For several minutes I heard only the sounds of outside and my own breathing.

Thinking it to be a dream, I smiled then lay back down within my thick sheets and fell asleep.

"Wake up, please."

I slowly opened my eyes to Lucien's face. He wore his usual black and white outfit with those strange goggles perched on his head. His hair was loose and fell down his shoulders like a velvet river. Not knowing what to do, I smiled. He smiled back as he helped me from the bed.

"What's going on?"

"My dear," he said as we walked out of the room and down the hall, "I think it is time for me to show you my project, one that I think will help you finish your recovery." Not knowing what he meant, but excited anyway, I allowed him to lead me down the winding staircase and through the front hall. We walked through the many rooms as I winced from the sunlight coming through the windows. "In my time here alone," he said in a slow tone, "I have noticed that power comes from many forms. Some achieve it through prayer while others achieve it through knowledge." My ears perked at that word: knowledge.

"During my time at university and beyond, I too have been on a quest to seek knowledge in its many forms." I noticed a look of surprise on his face that changed into a grin.

"Ah, so you do understand, then. That is good to hear." We reached a door that I had never noticed before and he pulled out a large brass key to open it. Once opened, he led me inside a dark room then closed the door behind us.

"Lucien, where are we?"

"Where you should be." Immediately, he turned on several gas lamps that he knew of and soon the room gave way to the light, exposing me to his plans. The room was filled with books and a massive oak table in the middle of the room. To the side, however, was what caught my attention; there was a massive black metal box with tubes and spigots coming out on its sides. Lucien left my side and walked over to the machine, caressing it as if it was a lover. "This is my creation, a chance for humans to evolve beyond their own limited thinking." Still not knowing what he meant, I leaned against one of the chairs by the table and waited for him to continue. He walked over to one of the shelves and pulled a book from it then took it over to the machine. He touched a lever on the right side and the box began to groan loudly.

I was frightened; what was I about to witness? The machine continued to groan and as it did, it slowly began to open, revealing a space the size of a human inside.

"For years, we have read books and accepted their knowledge in our minds," he said in a louder tone over the sound of the machine, "but what would happen if we could go further with that book? What would happen if we not only ingested our minds with such a thing, but our bodies as well?" Suddenly, he began to remove his clothing while I watched in horrid fascination. As he removed each layer of clothing, I saw strange markings on his body like tattoos. Within minutes he was completely naked and I could not help, but stare at every inch of his perfectly sculpted body. He then walked up to me and it was then I knew what he had meant. He waved his hand in the air and the machine turned itself off. How did he-

He took my hands in his and with a sigh said, "For years, I have wanted to transcend humanity, giving a new reason to those who surely deserve it. I have chosen you, Violet, to take that journey as I have done."

"How did you know my name?" I was shocked; how much of me did he truly know?

"I know all about you, Violet. From the moment I rescued you from the wreckage, I knew all about you. I know of your passion for the written word and how it consumed you so. I know of your desire to lead a life beyond that of any normal human. I know that you love me as I have loved you all of this time." He held a marked finger up to my lips before the thought of speaking out even occurred to me. "You see, I know it all. Through my own machine, my Genesis, I am beyond that of any mortal. Will you take that same road that I took, my dear Violet? Will you come with me?"

I said yes.

With a grin, he led me back to the black box then turned it back on. The box groaned as if hungry for me. I removed my clothing to reveal my completely naked grey body to him as an affirmation of my choice. The door opened once more and I stepped inside of it. He then closed the door and I was locked in. Strangely enough, I was not afraid, for in some way, I knew what was going to happen. Lucien opened a side slot and threw the book into it then closed it back. I could feel the cold metal against my body, but I was not afraid.

Then, it began.

Inch by inch, my skin was pulled from my body. To be quite honest, friend, I had never known such pain until that moment. Imagine if someone took a razor to your body and with deliberate and sadistic care, peeled your skin off. I had thought surviving the fire was horrible, but this . . . this was monstrous. I screamed for my life and yet the machine groaned. I clawed at the metal, trying to escape and yet the machine groaned, oblivious to my pain and my screams. I wanted to actually die, but the machine would not allow it. To ask for death was to be weak. I closed my eyes as blood, my blood, slid down my arms and into my eyes. I wanted to sleep.

It seemed to be faint at first, but soon the noise grew louder. I could barely open my eyes, but I knew deep in my mind that the box was being opened. I could see light and a figure opening the door with little ease that, suddenly, I helped open it myself with a strength I never knew I had. Soon, I was facing a still naked Lucien who smiled an impossibly wide smile. He took my hands in his and led me out of the box.

"My darling . . . " was all he could say as a tear fell down his face. In haste I ran to a full-length mirror that hung on the wall by the door and almost fainted. There I stood, naked, but my skin . . . I looked at my hands, my legs, and feet, even touched my hair. It was all real and yet . . . I turned to face him again and soon, I was in his arms. When we made love, could actually feel the ground beneath us shaking due to our combined power. I could see time moving backwards; I could see myself back at home with my family who did not understand me. I could read my father's mind as he wondered which mental institution would be best for me. I could feel my mother's anguish as she desperately wanted to be like me, but never had the courage to do so. I saw the stars, planets, and other worlds that we had yet to discover. I saw myself with Lucien, our bodies welded together as one. I wanted to cry; it was too much, but my body only drank it in like wine, leaving me with a hunger I had never known before. I felt like a god.

     When we were done, he then led me to his room and soon, I was his wife, student, partner, and friend. I have him to thank for my life. This, of course, will never be the same again.

Now, you can speak.

Too stunned? Here, let me turn on the light.

You see what happened to me? Do you truly see? Lucien gave the ultimate gift to me and I willingly took it. Yes, those are words you see on my skin. Yes, it is the book **The Red and the Black** by Stendhal. My old skin was ripped from my body, only to be replaced by the pages from the book. Lucien had done the process on his own body, using a book of poems by Emily Dickinson. My hair has grown back to its normal length and yet if you look carefully enough, you can see that my hairs are actually more words tangled together. Touch it; does it not feel like hair? So now you know what has happened to me; now you see what has become of my formerly wasted life. I wish I could locate my family and show them what has become of their daughter, but that moment and my family are in my past.

My strength, due to the book, is ten times greater than men. I can read people's minds as well. You can not leave here, not yet. You see, I asked you to come here for a reason. Lucien and I need others, intellectuals such as you. Come, there is no need to be frightened.

I will ask you again; what is a book?

Sulfur

A hush falls over the street
And the red ladies are silent.
The need for their green fairy is strong
To dull their pains of constant living.

I

Emily was a spinster. It was not that she was ugly or homely; in fact, she was rather beautiful and intelligent with a sharp wit and a tongue to match. She spent most of her time pouring over books and maps, magazines and journals, seeking knowledge where it could be found. She desired to understand the world around her no matter how long it took. She preferred the company of books to the company of men; to her, men possessed a primal sense of knowing the world even though they ruled it. Men were nothing more than a nuisance, a fly upon one's dinner, and she wanted no part of them and their ways. Her father, Wolfe Eldenshire, a more than middle class businessman who was ruthless when it came to money and taxes, loved his Emily so. Although they lived in Victorian London, where women were considered to be the weaker sex, her father thought quite differently of his children. They never fell victim to the ordinary traps of society, where women could not speak their minds, but looked to their husbands to do it for them.

Emily was the middle child in the family of three children; Lysander, the eldest child, worked with his father and was also the company's accountant. He was a tall and lanky man with thick dark locks that fell to his shoulders just like his father, causing many a young heart to swoon just in catching a glance while he walked the streets, his mind filled with voices who spoke languages only he could understand. His eyes could get the truth from a mute person, it was said. When he walked, one could smell the scent of burning leaves and violets in the air. He, too, spent much of his time reading books and walking through forests trails at night, a habit he began as soon as he could crawl. At first, his family worried that he would be killed or kidnapped, but he always returned unharmed and sometimes laughing with leaves stuck in his hair.

Milenda, the youngest, was anything, but young. Her eyes were violet and they sparkled when she spoke, giving life to anything she talked about. Her hair was as red as a bonfire that seemed to move on its own while she walked or even while she stood still. Some claimed that her father had a tryst with a faerie while out walking in the forests and the result of that union was Milenda. Some even claimed that the Eldenshire family adopted her from the Wilde Fae and that she was not their own in blood. While she too enjoyed reading thick books like her older siblings, she also enjoyed studying different languages. To date, she was fluent in over twenty and still yearned to learn more. She was the tomboy of the family, always preferring to sleep outdoors than inside her warm and safe home.

Emily spent most of her free time walking along the dark streets of London, purposely walking in the not so savoury areas of the city, seeking the dirt, crime, pollution, and decadence that so many of London's upper crust refused to acknowledge or, in some cases, accept even though some of their family members dallied in such sordid interests. It was among the prostitutes, drug dealers, pimps, junkies, homeless, and others that Emily walked at night with no fear for her life in any way. She knew and understood these people, knowing them to be just as strange and unusual as she. During her times out, she would take notes on what she saw and observed, adding every detail no matter how morbid or gory. Emily wanted London to know of the dark underbelly of their fair city, giving accounts of real people who walked the same streets as those of the upper class, but whose lives were horrendously different.

One night, however, while she was out walking among the living shadows, a figure clothed in dirty and oily rags approached her, holding out its sore encrusted hand. Emily felt sorry for the poor creature; not once had anyone ever approached her. The people of the slums knew of her family blood and gave her the proper respect. They knew that she, like the others, were more on their level than they cared to admit and so never harmed any of them that passed through their world in any way. As the figure approached Emily, towering over her rather tall frame, she held her ground. She was born with a steel rod for a backbone and refused to swoon at every little foul thing in the world.

Once the figure touched her shoulder with its diseased hand, Emily covered its hand with her own, causing many an onlooker to gasp with surprise; no one had ever touched an Eldenshire before. The figure's face was hidden underneath its rags, but its frame trembled. Emily could tell that it needed food and rest immediately and so, without another word, led the figure to her waiting carriage and horses, all as black as the night, and soon they were off.

Of roses and violets
Smelling sweetly among the grass
Giving no concern to the rotting corpses
That lay just underneath.
My darling, how I love thee so
To keep me forever locked in your embrace
Through Death, there is none better.

II

Light. That's what it was, thought the figure. Light. It sent a command to its brain: open eyes. For several seconds, nothing happened, but soon, the eyes did follow its orders. The light was soft and not harsh like the lights in the places forbidden, the ones where not even the dead would go. No, this was a soft and inviting light, one that welcomed all and turned none away; it was that kind of light. The figure turned its head to the left and saw a side table with several books lying on it and a framed picture of a young woman dressed in purple and black with long black hair. The figure's eyes stared at this picture, its breath caught in its throat. Whoever she was, she was beautiful. No, beyond that; she was stunning.

"How are you feeling?" asked a soft voice from the other side of the room. The figure quickly turned its head towards the source and almost forgot to breathe. Here was the picture come alive. The figure stared at the woman as it tried to speak to her. Emily could see that he tried to speak (after removing the clothing, she realized that the figure was a man) and so propped his head up with many more pillows. The figure could only stare at her and be amazed by her; he had not experienced such kindness in quite a long time. Once his head was up, Emily took a step back to gaze at him.

His pale skin was made even more so by his shockingly long red hair that spilled around his shoulders. He glanced down at his hands and bare arms and noticed that he was clean. She must have done it, he thought, and a smile appeared on his face, causing her to smile as well. He coughed once then tried to speak again.

"Where am I?" he croaked. "Am I still in London?"

"Yes, you are. You are in the Eldenshire home. You've been out for two days. I cleaned you and applied salve to your sores. It is a family recipe; they will be completely healed by the end of the day." He looked down at his arms again and noticed that the sores were indeed fading. He looked up at her and smiled.

"Truly you are an angel." Emily blushed for a moment then regained herself; she was in no mood for anyone's flattery, no matter if she saved them from dying or not.

"If you require anything further," she said with a soft hint of steel in her voice,"please ring for the maid or me. My room is right down the hall and I will be more than happy to help you." She then turned and left his room with a soft click of the door. He stared at the door for several seconds then sank back into the soft down bed with a sigh. Truly an angel.

Emily raced to her room, her mind occupied with many thoughts. Was it so wrong of her to be even slightly rude to him, she thought. After all, she did help him. Perhaps he was just grateful. Perhaps.

Lysander, coming from his room, noticed how deep in thought Emily was as she walked by him without even a glance. He smirked as he slipped behind her and followed her down to her room. His feet made no sounds as he walked behind her, noticing how tightly her hair was pulled back from her head, how her usual attire of all black clothing looked to be slightly out of date on her and yet it complimented her at the same time.

Emily stopped and turned quickly to face her brother whom she knew was following her down the hall. He stopped in mock surprise as a faint smile appeared on his lips.

"I trust the patient is doing much better?" he asked while running a slender hand through his hair. "He seemed to be when I last looked upon him." Even in the semi dark hall, he could tell she was blushing, causing the smile to increase. "What's this, dear sister? Why are you blushing?" Emily held a hand to her cheek and touched it, feeling the slight heat emanating from it.

"I am not blushing."

"You know you could never lie to me, Em. You always had that trouble even when we were little."

"I know, Lys, I know." He leaned against the wall, his eyes still upon her.

"So, who is he, then? Someone you found from one of your usual nightly dalliances in the murky streets of our fair London? Or, perhaps a lover?" Emily smirked at her brother's futile attempt of trying to get the truth from her. So, she did what she could only do: she told him the truth.

"I found him from the streets, or rather, he found me. He was the only person who has ever walked up to me when I walk at night. I felt sorry for him so I brought him home." She glanced up to see that one of the large white candles that lit the hallways was melting wax on the floor. She reached to cup the falling wax into her hand, but Lysander grabbed it instead. He leaned in close to her, giving off the scents of burning leaves and violets. She still could never figure out just how he acquired that scent, but after all, he was an Eldenshire.

"Em, I worry about you when you go out at night," he said in a soft tone, "but I know you could kill anyone with just a look. Please, be careful with this one. Once he has healed, send him on his way. It would not be good for us as well as the other families to know of this . . . intrusion." He released her hand then sauntered back to his room, closing then door behind him in silence. Emily stared at the door for a moment while she rubbed her hand, her mind racing once more with thoughts.

Here we come, men and women fair
With clothing of black and lilies in our hair.
Our eyes, they do glow under the moon's light
And our smiles are of warmth during the night
We dance under the stars and invite to join us
Here, take my hand, please do not fuss.
Closer and closer, see my love for you true
Remove that frown and feelings of blue.
For we are here to love each and every one
To give to your dreams, everyone under the sun.
Come with me, dearest, through the trees dense and thick
Let me make love to you; let our time not be quick.
Do you feel my hand sliding to there?

Do not be alarmed; do not give it a care.
See how much I love you, feel my tender kisses
All of this can be yours if those are your wishes.
A wet sex, an erect cock, a bare breast
Now my darling, lie back and let me do the rest.

III

"Wolfe, we have heard of your most recent guest. You daughter, Emily, brought him home, is that correct?"

"Yes it is. She told me last night. She told me-"

"We already know. You daughter has a rather large heart."

"So it seems."

"Have you seen him yet?"

"Once, while he slept."

"I see. And do you know who he is?"

"I . . . think I do."

"Of course you do. We all do. My question to you is what will you do with him once he has recovered?"

"What do you mean?"

"I mean, Wolfe, will you kill him just like the rest of his kind?"

"That I do not know yet. Must we even consider such a thought about him? After all, the war ended many years ago. We are now of peace. For gods' sake, this is the 1870s! We are no longer savages; we keep to our own and preserve it the best way possible . . . including the Dinashai. We must consider that."

"Yes we must consider that for the sake of all of the families of Aurwen. We have not gone this far without knowing which possible tumours to remove. His family has been a thorn in all of our sides since the founding of our fair city. We have survived because they have not, once we figured out just who and what they were."

"I see."

"Do you, Wolfe? Do you see at all? Tell your daughter, for the sake of all of us, that she must remove him from your home. Once you have taken him to a place of our choosing, inform us and we will take it from there. Is that understood?"

"Understood."

When she was not reading, Emily spent her time with her patient who was getting stronger every day. His eyes, once cloudy and fading, were now bright and shimmering as they glanced at the door every five minutes, waiting to see her face. She was beautiful, an angel sent to help him. He wanted to talk with her about the books she liked to read so much, but he felt too shy to do so; he could barely speak to her when she was around him. He sighed as he lay back in his pillows. His memories were also coming back to him; when she found him, he was little more than an idiot just trying to survive. Now with her care and healing, he began to remember himself, remember why he was found in that horrible condition. Why his family?

Suddenly, the door opened, and he sat up straighter only to fall back when he noticed that the woman's father appeared behind the door. His eyes stayed on the man's face, wondering why he had appeared in his room. Wolfe caught himself for a moment then walked over to the patient's bed and sat down on the side. For a moment, he did not say anything, but just stared at the patient who was beginning to shiver a bit. Finally, he cleared his throat and said, "My good man, it appears that you are doing rather well under our Emily's care."

"Y-yes, sir, I am. You daughter is gifted in healing."

"I have no doubt of that."

"Is that why you are here, sir? Will she not be here today?"

"No, she will. She is reading right now. No, I wanted to talk to you for a moment." The figure rearranged himself on his pillows and focused all of his attention on him. Wolfe locked his slender hands together then said in a low voice, "I have spoken to certain individuals about you, who you are and where you come from-"

"I wondered when that was going to happen." Wolfe stared at the man for a moment; was it going to be easier than expected, he thought. "My memories have been coming back to me. I remembered what happened." He laid his head back on the pillow, clearly exhausted by their short conversation. He closed his eyes and said no more, leaving Wolfe to leave the room with no more answers than questions.

A short time later, the door opened again and he did not need to open his eyes to know it was her. Emily, carrying one of her books, came in the room without a sound then sat down in the same spot as her father. She placed a cool hand on his forehead and sighed.

"How are you feeling today?" she said softly. He opened his eyes, causing her to gasp; his eyes had changed, or rather, they had gone back to what they used to look like before the sickness. They were completely black.

"I am fine, thank you." She smiled then removed her hand and reached for her book, but his hand grabbed hers swiftly, forcing her to look at his now pleading face. "I thank you for your kindness," he began, "but I must leave here soon. I am . . . no longer welcome here."

"I know." His surprise caused her to smile again. "I've known what you were ever since I removed your filthy rags from your body. I've read about your family, but never met one, considering what happened to them."

"I see. And you are not afraid of me?"

"Why should I be? The Dinashai family, although of demon blood, does not scare me, even when I have helped one regain its strength. Most women in Aurwen would have run screaming from you, but I do not."

"I am glad. But, you do realize that because of your kindness, you have placed your family in danger and that I must leave as soon as possible."

"Not without answering one question for me." He arched an eyebrow in curiosity.

"And that would be?"

"Your name, sir." Now he was shocked.

"M-my name?"

"Yes," she said while laughing, "you do have one, don't you?"

"Of course," he replied laughing as well. "It is Sandon. Sandon Dinashai."

"Emily Eldenshire." She extended her hand for him to shake. He looked at the hand for a moment, then took it and instead of shaking it, brought it to his lips and kissed it tenderly, causing her to blush. His eyes looked up at her and noticed she was blushing.

"Are you scared of me?" he whispered, her hand still close to his lips.

"No." Her voice was firm. Without another word, he pulled her towards him and kissed her on the lips. At first, she wanted to slap him for his rash behaviour, but soon those thoughts dissipated as she welcomed the kiss. Scents of burning wood permeated her senses. She could feel his slender hands reach up to her hair, tugging at the tight bun. A second later and her hair fell about her shoulders and back. He pushed her away to see her with her hair down and sighed again.

"Like a true angel," he murmured while running his hands through her coal black hair. Her eyes tried to look anywhere else, but they soon fell back on Sandon's face. "You are my angel, Emily, do you know that?"

"Am I?" He did not reply, but instead pulled her towards him again to kiss her. As their lips met, he pulled her body closer to his on the bed. She could feel heat emanating from his body as his hands began to tug at her clothing.

"WHAT IN THE GODS NAME IS GOING ON?!" Emily pulled away from Sandon to see her brother Lysander standing in the doorway, furious and enraged. Emily tried to pull her hair back into a semblance of a bun, but it was no use. She clutched her book and held it towards her throat. "I said," he said in a lower, but still angry tone, "what is going on here?"

"Lys we-"

"Em, please. I want to hear it from this-" he waved his hand at Sandon, "creature. Well, half spawn, why were you kissing my sister? Don't you know your kind is not allowed such interactions?"

"I know that," Sandon said calmly, but with a touch of steel, now exposing fanged teeth, "but your sister has shown me nothing, but kindness while I was ill. I think only the highest thoughts of her."

"Highest thoughts of her?" he snorted. "Rubbish! If I hadn't come here, no telling what you would have done to her. That's why your entire family was wiped out, half spawn."

"He has a name, Lys," said Emily, clearly not wanting her brother to speak on her behalf. "It is Sandon Dinashai."

"Em, please, stay out of this. In fact, why don't you go to your room? This is something that does not concern you."

"Yes it does, Lys. Sandon is my patient and I am responsible for him."

"Responsible?! He is a Dinashai, Em! They almost wiped out the entire existence of Aurwen or have you forgotten? You were around when the city was trying to recover from their kind. You were around when some of the Mythica's guardians lay at our feet, dying or already dead. Do you not remember how long it took all of the families to wipe the streets clean of blood? Violet blood spilled for their own selfish reasons." He shook his head like a wolf. "No matter. He is to leave now. We are to take him to the Firling Tree!"

"**NO!**" The force of saying that one word caused Lysander to fall back against the wall while several of the lamps shattered. Even Sandon held his ears against the blast. Several of the servants ran into the room, wondering why Ms. Emily had to use her Voice. They saw the trio, patient, brother, and sister then turned and walked back; this was clearly not a situation for them. Emily stood staring at her brother, her long coal coloured hair creating a dark frame around her face. Both Sandon and Lys' eyes were on her. She held the control now.

"We will not take him to the Firling Tree. He may leave, but we are not to take him there. I know what happens there, Lys. I remember seeing such horrible things there when I was younger." She walked over to Sandon and sat on the side of the bed, taking one of his slender hands in her own. "I will take him away from here where the other families can not get to him."

"Em-"

"No, let me do it. I just can not bear it."

Through vale and rock and soot laden winds
My eyes turn to you, my hope against hopes

IV

Hidden under a black thick cloak, Sandon raced with Emily through the streets of London, trying to get as far away as possible from her home before anyone realized that she was gone. Emily held his hand with a vise-like grip, refusing to lose him in the human traffic. They spoke very little unless necessary, saving their energy for running, as Emily directed them to a place where she knew he would be safe for the time being. Sandon, while being led by her, allowed his thoughts and now strong mind to focus on his current situation.

He was the last of his family and that made him an immediate target for Aurwen's hatred. He remembered, now, how the mob came into his family's home and slaughtered them, one by one during a night that never seemed to end. Even the children, those born of innocence, were slaughtered even more horrendous than the adults for they were seen as the future of his line. Sandon hid himself in one of the crypts underneath the house, hearing his family's screams as they were killed off one by one. Although they were half demon, they could be killed with silver in any shape or form. None of the mob ventured down into the crypts; they possibly did not even know they existed. Sandon hid behind his great-great aunt Viria's tomb and waited until all was quiet and the presence of the mob was gone from his senses. When he felt was safe, he crept out. As he began to walk up the immense and narrow flight of stairs with no light to guide him, the scents of sulfur and copper burned through his nose. It was his family's blood that he smelled.

When he reached above ground, he began to cry. Bodies, both of his family and mob, lay strewn all over mixed with blood. He carefully stepped over the bodies of his sisters and brothers, almost tripping over his mother's severed head. He knelt down on the bloody floor and picked her head up, wanting desperately for her eyes to open. It was said their family could still live for several hours even after their deaths. He placed bloodied fingers over his mother's eyes and closed his own, focusing all of his power to her. For a moment, he felt nothing and almost gave up then soon the eyes under the sockets began to roll around. Sandon opened his eyes and removed his fingers just as his mother opened hers and stared into the face of her son. He smiled as the tears rolled down his face.

"None of that, dear love," she said in a whisper as he placed her head on the floor then sat down next to it. "Please, do not cry, dear love."

"Mother."

"Hush now, Sandon. Save your tears and strength. Save them for a much later time."

"Mother, what happened? Why were we attacked?"

"Because of what we are, dear love. The Council came after us, wanted to make our house an example."

"True, we have never been liked, only tolerated, but why this rash attack now?"

"Whispers have been heard, my love. Whispers from the other cities, whispers of 'cleansing' our world, my love, starting with the demon-folk." She rolled her eyes in their sockets once to moisten them then continued. "They want our world to be free from mistakes like us, my love. They are trying to establish bonds and trust with the humans and for their world to be populated with our kind and others is no longer an option."

"Mother, our family has been one of the building blocks for Aurwen. We have never been mistrustful on any level. "

"And yet, because of our sulfur blood and some of our kind who have sullied our name and race, we were all, but extinguished from this realm." She closed her eyes for a moment, giving Sandon a momentary reason to worry, then opened them once more. "My love, hide in London. The Council must never know that one of us still lives."

"Mother."

"Be silent! Listen to my words and heed them. You must hide, my love. Hide where they can not find you." She closed her eyes and spoke no more, finally giving Sandon a chance to let his tears fall.

He raced to London in the cover of the night sky, constantly on guard for anyone who was still thirsty for his family's blood. Once he stopped crying over his family's loss, he gathered their bodies into a large pile and smoldered them quickly and without smoke; his kind possessed the power of flamespeak, setting anything on fire within seconds then quickly extinguishing, leaving no trace. Once done, he quickly said a small prayer to their deity, a dragon god named Filarn who watched over all who possessed flamespeak, to guide their souls well, and then he wrapped his body in black cloak and set off towards London.

When he reached the city, he casually sniffed the air, making sure that no one was looking for him. When all was clear, he set off. Although he had visited the human city many times, London still amazed him. People of every background existed here and each one was unique in their own way. After feeling somewhat comfortable while walking around, he took off his hood, revealing his half demon trait of flaming red hair that hid his knobs of horns on top of his head. Several women glanced his way, noticing how beautiful he was, but none dared go near. He smiled at one, setting her to a swooning fit, then walked on. He caught the face of an Aurwen being, and some of them caught his scent, but were too afraid to acknowledge him. He allowed himself a hint of a smile; he felt free, caught in the human masses and not hunted for the time being. However, he had to find a place that was warm or else he would slip into a coma. He covered his head once more so as not to draw any attention to himself, hoping that he could pass for a full human. He found several places, but since it was the middle of April, none of them had roaring fires going in their fireplaces. He began to shiver and lose consciousness, but still continued to look. Five hours later, he was without any luck and soon had to find any place to sleep, but now the idea of finding an inn was close to impossible; he had begun to break out in sores, another sign that he needed a fire immediately. He tripped over a hole on a street corner and fell to the ground while people walked over him. He could barely keep his eyes open; he needed sleep.

Suddenly, he smelled something familiar. He opened one eye and saw a young woman walking along the streets. He sniffed the air again and realized she was Aurwen. With what little strength he had left, he rose to his feet, completely covered in his cloak, and walked up to her just as she was walking towards him. She had to help him.

"Stop here," she said, jarring him out of his thoughts. He looked around and noticed that they were no longer in London, but in a forest glade. He looked behind him, seeing the lights of London, then back at Emily. She raised her eyes to the night sky and stared hard, looking for something rather important.

"What are you looking for?" he asked.

"A friend," she replied then fell silent. At first, he could only hear the spring wind rustling through the leaves and branches and saw only what the night sky did not cover. He felt, for the moment, safe, although he had to find a fire soon. He was beginning to tire.

"We have a rather large fire prepared for you, half demon." Sandon looked around in shock, seeing no one, then changed his focus to whole demon. There, sitting on one of the higher branches, was a slender figure dressed in a long dark green dress. She, he could see now, walked along the branch now without any regard for her safety; either she had been born in this glade or she spent most of her life here. The figure jumped down to the ground, a good ten feet, and walked over to Emily, who had seen her even before she spoke. The two embraced like sisters and Sandon felt relief even though he still needed a fire.

"Well met, Em," said the figure with a smile.

"Well met, Milenda." Her younger sister then walked to Sandon and raised a hand in greeting.

"Come, embrace my fire and breathe of Filarn," she said in the formal Dinashai greeting, shocking Sandon to the core since no one, but a member of their family would know of such a greeting. He raised a shaky hand and said, "May Filarn bless you with sulfur," he said in reply, then fainted.

The bonfire woke him up immediately. He opened his eyes and noticed that he lay on several thick pillows in the middle of a grove of immense trees. He looked up and noticed the black velvet sky, sighing with loss. He missed his-

"Family is important, you know," said Milenda who sat above him in one of the trees. He smiled without looking up. A group of almost every creature and race in Aurwen was here, talking and meeting, greeting and playing. He was the only half demon in the grove and suddenly, he felt quite alone.

"I miss my family," he said, knowing that she was still there. "I miss them terribly."

"I know, Sandon, but understand; there are those who know what happened and who want to help you. There was no reason for the Council to do what they did simply for the sake of looking more pleasing to the humans." Sandon saw Emily walking some yards away with a centaur. She was smiling and laughing and looked to be in good spirits. "You love her, don't you?" asked Milenda then disappeared into the tree, giving Sandon no chance to answer, but he did anyway.

"Yes, I do."

Emily talked with her friend Bruc, one of the leaders of the centaurs, catching up on old times and unforgettable moments. She laughed heartily when he spoke of his children and how much they wanted to be like their father. As they walked, she looked over and saw Sandon watching her; she looked away and felt herself blushing. Bruc caught it immediately.

"My dear, why dost thou blush so?" he asked. Centaurs were known in Aurwen to speak in archaic tones, much to the frustration of everyone else. He brushed his immense head against her shoulder in affection. "Speak to me of thine thoughts and I shall help in whatever course deemed necessary."

"The Dinashai I brought here, Bruc-"

"You give him your heart, dear child?" Emily blushed even more so.

"I can not answer that, my dear friend."

"Thou dost not need to. I see it in thine eyes, dear child."

Soon, several minstrels picked up instruments and began to play, giving everyone else a chance to find a place to sit and listen. As they played, a young dryad dressed in leaves and trigs began to sing.

In all of my life
There is no one fairer than she
Who loves me still
Who loves me still
And though she be right next to me

Tales of a Goth Librarian

Does she know that I love her too?

Sandon glanced at Emily who had sat next to him after her conversation with Bruc, and took her hand in his. Emily could feel his warmth radiating through his hand and fingers as she stole a glance at him. His hair was brighter than before and his knobs had grown somewhat. He glanced at her, catching her in her glances and soon the two sets of eyes were locked on each other. Everything else disappeared.

"If you hadn't saved me, I would have been dead," he whispered. She said nothing, fearing what she felt in her heart. Was it possible? He took her silence as possible acceptance and pulled her towards him before she could say anything to stop him. The words were on her lips as his touched hers. When their lips made contact, Emily felt his inner heat rise through him, causing her to sweat. She wanted to pull away, but could not; she loved him no matter his background.

For the first time, a woman outside of his own race was not afraid of him, he thought while kissing Emily. She knows of my kind and what we've done towards and for the other races, but still she treats me with no blemish. He could feel his two hearts beating simultaneously against her single one and wondered for the millionth time today why he had to meet her and why he was now in love with her.

"I was right in my wish for her, Bruc. I knew this was going to happen."
"Was their love for one another obvious?"
"Yes, and yet, I know my sister. Most of the Eldenshire women are like Emily; backbone made of steel, yet will melt when a man looks at them longer than a second."
"Thou dost protest such action to be folly?"
"Not at all, but after all, this is 1874. We have come quite a long way, both human and those of Aurwen. Progress is being made by means of machines and art. The humans could not have done it without us and yet look at how they treat us. We

are still seen, to some degree, as stories to tell their children before going to bed so that they can meet with us in shadowed pubs to strike even shadowier deals." They both looked up towards the night skies, watching the thick black smoke curl and twist through the air from one of the many factories that populated London like a debilitating virus. Horns could be heard all throughout, even in their special and sheltered area of the woods. The horns signaled to one another of their progress, their power of being machines rather than flesh and blood. However, it took flesh and blood to create and keep the machines going – Aurwen flesh and blood.

Although human men, women, and children worked and operated the machines that polluted the city of London, it was Aurwen blood and magick that truly kept the machines from falling apart. Due to a treaty created by individuals hiding in shadowed corners for fear of being seen by innocent eyes, it was agreed that the machines would be fueled by those of Aurwen who were sickly or dying from a long and fulfilling life while the humans worked them, thereby keeping a rather strange peace between the two worlds. Those who saw the smoke filling the sky had no idea that it was the souls and spirits of the "magick folk".

Milenda turned her gaze back to her friend with no more answers than questions.

"It chills me to the bone to see what we have done for the short-lived (a derogatory term for humans) and yet they still mock us. Sometimes I even wonder why we are fighting amongst ourselves when we should be building walls against the humans. They have no idea and yet we still help them." She ran her slender hands through her hair in frustration. "Why did Em have to help him, Bruc?" she asked, trying to change the subject. "I feel sorry for him . . . and for her. We were never really that close since I spent most of my time out there, but I still love her dearly."

"She knows, dear childe."

"And yet, I wanted him to be caught and sent to the Tree."

"Confused, hmm?" said Bruc with a chuckle, causing her to smile.

"It seems I am. What-"

"My dear, " said Bruc in a surprisingly modern tone, the formal archaic gone for the moment, "we do what we must do in order to survive. I do not like it any more than you, but that is how it is for the time being. With regard to your sister . . . just let her enjoy this moment. This half demon does not appear to be like his other family members."

"Most of them were not so bad."

"True, but some of them blackened the family name in such a way that those who were good could never be trusted again. But, in looking back, perhaps the other races helped with those stigmata as well. Maybe we should be pointing the finger at us."

The two watched Emily and Sandon kiss for a moment longer then she pulled away only to be nestled in his arms. His horns, during that kiss, had grown several inches and curved away from his head.

"He is coming back, I think."

"Yes, it would appear so."

"I am still not sure whether I should be alarmed or not."

"Nor I, my dear."

Steam and metal, pride and glory
Makes way for progress, a history footnote
To provide children with tales of better days
Rather than the sordid truth when Magick was real.
Truth denied to make way for a better lie.

V

He could feel the heat against his face, but did not open his eyes for he knew what he would see. He was not ready, at least not yet. Before he closed his eyes to the songs of the minstrels, he had Emily snuggled deep in his arms. Her hair felt like satin against his own and he laid a hand on her head just to keep close contact with it. He felt his horns coming back, producing a slight itchy feeling; he was coming back into his own. Emily, he knew, must have felt the change as well, but she did not say anything nor did she glance up. All he could feel from her was that she loved him. He wanted to tell her that it was ridiculous for her kind to love a Dinashai and yet the words seemed to be lodged in his throat. He wanted to push her away from his rapidly heating body, screaming at her to run far away while he disappeared, but he did not. All he wanted to do now was stroke her hair and whisper that he loved her too. All he wanted to do was claim Emily as his own. Far away was London, a city full of smoke, begging waifs, crooked humans, and garbage, but here . . . here was comfort, peace, and love.

The heat, however, was still there. Sandon groaned in frustration; he knew he had to open his eyes, even if only lasted for several minutes. It was necessary and yet he loathed such a responsibility. He opened his eyes and almost smiled; home infernal home. He sat on a volcanic rock that could have burned a human body within seconds, yet he felt only a slight twinge. Such was the way of the Dinashai. Demons and dragons needed such heat to survive, even half demons like Sandon.

He sat in an immense valley that would have been pleasant except for the fact that it was entirely covered in flames and lava with rocks scattered here and there. There was no sun, no cool breezes to help a traveler along the way; the skies were a smoky red while dragons flew the skies searching for their next meal. During any other visit, he would have taken to flight, soaring the skies with distant family members or just others who enjoyed the heat as much as he did. Today, however, was different; the familiar sights and sounds did not remove the weight from his heart. Only she could do that.

"She must be quite a woman to put you in such spirits," said a melodious voice behind him, but Sandon was aware of the figure's presence long before. He kept his back to the figure and said, "I have only known her for a short time and yet she has taken hold of my heart."

"Both of them or just the human one?" chuckled the figure.

"Both of them, actually. I thought you would have figured that out by now."

"I was only trying to lighten your spirits, but I see I was wrong in bringing you here. I thought you would have been happy to come here for a while, but I see I was wrong to assume so." Sandon turned around to face the figure and said in a melancholy voice, "I am happy to be here, Father. You know I am always happy to see you whenever I can." Without another word the demon embraced one of his sons fiercely; father and son reunited again. The demon, a good two feet taller than Sandon's own height of six feet, was covered in red skin that felt smooth and hot to the touch by anyone who did not share their infernal blood. His black hair was long, thick, and pulled into a ponytail while spiral white horns signifying his rank sprouted from his head. His ears were pierced with five golden earrings each while his nose held a bone from a past kill. He wore a black coat that fell to his ankles, white shirt, and pants that hid his legs although everyone in the land knew of him and his physical makeup. He just loved wearing clothes of the human world from time to time. He loved the look of the Victorian gentleman and tried to imitate their style of dress and mannerisms as best as possible, no matter how much his fellow demon folk laughed at him in good spirits.

When father and son pulled away from their embrace, Sandon said, "Father, why did you bring me here this time? Is something wrong?"

"No, no," said the demon as he shook his head, clinking his earrings, "but it is not every day that one of your children falls in love with a non-demon. I wanted to talk to you about her and find out more."

"She saved me and got me back on my feet when I had nowhere else to go, plus she is helping me escape from the

Council. They know of my existence and want me dead, but she and I fled before they could do anything to me. They're probably looking for me, but for now, we are safe. We are among her friends and those who want to keep the peace."

"I am happy to hear it, son." The demon grinned briefly, exposing his sharp teeth, then said in a somber tone, "I am sorry about what happened, son, but you know I could not help in any way. "

"I know, Father. The term sentence you received-"

"Is still in effect and will be for another 500 years." He sat down on a nearby rock, suddenly too weary to even lift his head. "I watched my wife die under the hands of those who claimed to be of peace for Aurwen, but instead wanted nothing more than to rid themselves of our kind. I also saw you hiding and hoped for your safety."

"I had to do it, Father."

"No one is blaming you at all; you did what was necessary. Our kind, no matter the place and history, has always been feared and hated. We can not choose who we are and what runs through our veins. We are of Filarn and nothing can change that."

"I know, Father. I know the Histories; I know of our blood. However-"

"However?"

"However, I love Emily. I . . .think she loves me as well."

"She does, my son."

This is a time to wonder, my dear,
To wonder and explore beyond touch and sight.
To understand what it means to fight like a solider
And to fall with blood splattered.

VI

Wolfe paced the hallways of his home, his mind caught up in a frenzy of thoughts and emotions. He feared for his daughter's life, but knew deep down she was right in helping the Dinashai escape before the Council sunk their hooks into him. The time had come for all of Aurwen to lay aside their differences and focus on the future, Dinashai and non-Dinashai. He was tired, very tired; after 700 years of existence on this planet, he had seen various kingdoms rise and fall, power crazed people climb their way to the top only to be knocked down by an unseen or seen force, and so on. His body bore many scars that would forever whisper their tales in his mind; after all, he did experience their tales firsthand. Now, all he wanted to experience was peace.

Lysander watched his father sink into one of his pensive moments; sometimes it took days for him to completely come out of them if he was mentally wrapped in a dire situation, and those occurred few and far between. However, this one matter was different for it involved family. His own sister, Em, decided to be brave and foolish in trying to help the half demon; such an action would not go unnoticed by the Council. He watched his father for a few more minutes then went back into his room and silently closed the door.

He always kept his bedroom windows opened so as to fully enjoy the sounds of London and its inhabitants, trying to acknowledge the mortals in their colourful and grisly glory. How odd it was that mortals regarded life to be worth nothing more than horse dung steaming in the street. Yet, if they only knew what it would be like if they no longer had to worry about sickness, death of a mortal nature, hunger, any of it, their thoughts regarding their own short lives would be oh so much better. They would take the time to enjoy their life no matter how short it was. All they needed to do was spend one day as a member of his family; their tunes would change within the first hour.

His gaze fell outside where a carriage pulled by four black horses came down the street. Their hooves barely made any sound, but he was able to hear them a mile away. The tall and skinny driver was dressed in a black coat with top hat, but

Lysander saw right through the glamour as it pulled up to their home. He raced to his mirror to check his clothing, then went downstairs to receive their guest although he had no idea what or whom to expect.

When he reached the bottom, he could hear several voices in the parlour to the right, his father's being one of the voices. He walked up to the massive oak doors, took a deep breath, and then opened the doors.

His father sat in one of the velvet wine-coloured plush chairs holding a snifter full of siren mead while two other figures sat on opposite sides of him, both seated in velvet chairs. The man on his father's left was dressed in a sparkling blue robe that fell to the ground, covering his feet, while his smooth skin was pale and almost glowing. His head was bald, save for a long black and thick lock of braided hair that started from the center of his head and fell down past his shoulders. He wore a smile that would make anyone mortal immediately trust and like him, no matter what he said. Lysander swallowed hard, trying not to shake too badly; it wasn't every day that one had the privilege of having a Swandi in their home. Swandi were from the island of Klesta, west of Aurwen in the Delphaen Sea. The race was noted for their high levels of intelligence, sharp wit, and good storytelling, which was why whenever a Seandi spoke, you could not help, but listen. Their magick lay in their voice.

The woman on the right caught Lysander's breath, although he had done it too late for any of them not to notice. Surely not here-

The woman looked up at Lysander and beamed a smile, increasing her natural spicy scent towards him, overpowering his senses to the point of wanting to tear his hair out. It was one thing to have a Swandi here, but another to have the Sylph Queen sitting in the parlour of his own house! She was dressed in what looked to be nothing more than flimsy pieces of fabric that shimmered in every possible (and impossible) colour. The clothing left her arms bare, showing off her dusty violet coloured skin. Her body was slender and tall, giving off the air of a regal being and yet her almond shaped eyes sparkled with pure undiluted happiness. Her long white hair was tightly braided into one long braid that fell past her thighs and as she moved in her chair, Lysander had to keep himself from groaning too loudly at her spicy scent; she smelled of cardamom, cinnamon, vanilla, and strangely enough, clouds, with each scent giving off just enough so as to allow each scent to be savoured. He swayed momentarily then quickly regained his senses, not wanting to embarrass his father, but Wolfe was already trying hard not to laugh out loud.

"You must forgive my son," he said with a chuckle. "It's not every day that he gets to see the Sylph Queen and a Swandi both in his home." Lysander blushed with agreement while trying to compose himself in front of the two guests. "Son, they just arrived and they wanted to speak to me regarding the Dinashai." Instantly, Lysander's mood turned grim; it was time for action even if Em was involved.

"Your Highness and fair Swandi," began Lysander in the tone he used only for business transactions, "I am sure you have been updated as to the circumstances of our situation. I hope you will not hold it against the rest of our family."

"Lysander!" He turned to face his father's anger with his own calmness and continued without any regard for his father's outburst. "We can not allow such a . . . disruption to continue in our family and I am sure you feel the same. Even though Emily is my sister and I love her tremendously, she is still seen as a traitor for helping the Dinashai escape." He walked over to one of the bookshelves that held many of the family's tomes and handwritten books of spells and sources of magick, handed down from generation to generation for the last 5000 years. He traced an imaginary line down the spine of one titled The History of The Yelna (a race of women that lived in Old Europe who were born from rivers and streams and held the power of water magick), trying to form his next words carefully. When he pulled his finger away, it was wet and smelled of blue skies and pleasant dreams. He smiled; their power was extremely strong.

"We are facing dire times. The Council, through years of strife and battles fought with certain human groups, is weakening. Their power is not as great as it used to be and this . . . matter is not helping at all. This is a hindrance that needs to be stopped immediately."

"And what do you suggest we do?" asked his father who had taken a seat while his son talked. He still held his glass and took a small sip of the fragrant liquid, savouring it slowly before swallowing it. "Find my daughter, your sister, and take her to the tree? Or should we just hold back such savage means of torture for Sandon?"

"We must kill the demon spawn, of course-"

"We must bring the half demon before the Council," said the Sylph Queen in a voice that sounded like singing, causing both Lysander and Wolfe to hold their heads in a drunken swoon that lasted only minutes. When their heads were cleared, Lysander continued, "We must not show any form of weakness before him, my Lady. We must kill him where he stands. My sister must be brought before the Council." He turned to face his father and, for the first time that night, he wore a look of genuine sadness.

Sandon woke with a small start, slightly forgetting where he was, then looked down and smiled at Emily who was still fast asleep. The rest of the group had turned in for the night with one or two keeping a night post, watching for any signs of commotion coming from London. Crickets and faint laughter from the spirits of the woods could be heard, but of London, there was none. He wanted to relax like Emily, but knew that he could not do so.

If it weren't for her, he would have been dead like ashes in a fireplace. He owed her his life, his soul . . . and his heart. He loved her from the first moment he touched her hand when she saw him in that dark street. She was not afraid of him or his dirt encrusted clothing. She wanted to help him. That was all that mattered to him; an Aurwen helped him. He sighed, blowing a warm stream of air from his lungs. Since she had saved him, he began to recuperate rapidly, recovering all of the "lost" traits of his kind. Although he carried the traits of a demon from his father, he also carried the traits of his mother who was Dragonkin – half dragon and half human. The Dinasai bloodline was full of dragons, demons, and others who lived of the Fire, but the demon blood ran the thickest in his veins. There was, at one point, underground talk that the Serpent in the human Garden of Eden was one of their cousin kind, but no one wanted to make such a claim in public due to the shame and embarrassment after reading the stories in the Bible.

Emily stirred; momentarily breaking his thoughts, then fell deep in her sleep once more, allowing him to pick up the thread of where he left off. He stroked her hair, but the act caused her eyes to flutter. She blinked once then said while her eyes focused on the still burning fire, "Are you all right? Do you need me to move?"

"No, not at all, Emily. I just wanted to stroke your hair."

"Has there been any word from London?"

"Nothing so far, but there are people keeping post in case anything does occur." He lifted her face to meet his and kissed her lips. Emily felt her cheeks grow warm due to his body temperature; it felt like coming into full contact with a bonfire that had been scented with cinnamon, nutmeg, and cedar. She could feel his arms pull her closer to him, enfolding her completely within his world.

Sandon did not want the kiss to end; never before had he met a woman like her and never again would he want anyone else. He released his hold on her body and lips and stared into her eyes. She stared back, noticing the twin flames that danced around his eyes, flames that came from within and not as a reflection from the fire that crackled behind them. She placed a hand on his cheek as a replacement for the words that she could not trust herself to say: I love you no matter what you are.

As if on cue, Sandon scooped her up in his arms and led her to a small grove of trees, not caring if anyone saw them. He carried her as if she weighed no more than a feather from a phoenix, running through the thick grove with effortless grace. When they reached a small clearing, he set her down on the ground. No sound reached their ears and the only light they received was from Laelrna, the Moon Goddess. Emily's face looked up to the Moon with an expression of peace while Sandon remained standing with a blank look on his face.

"Emily," he began in a voice that was lower than his normal tone, "do you trust me?" She looked at him and noticed that he did not face her.

"Of course I do," she said immediately in a strong voice." Sandon still faced away from her and yet the act did not offend her. If there was something he had to say, then he would say it in his own way, she thought.

"Why do you not fear me?"

"Because I love you." At this, he turned and knelt on the ground by her so fast that she jumped when his face was instantly inches from her own. She could see his now red eyes staring back and for a brief moment, she felt fear. Sandon stared at her for a moment longer then pulled back and raised his left hand next to his face. Emily gasped as soon as a thin line of red appeared on his palm. The coppery scent of blood hit her senses and she almost swooned, but she held her ground.

"How did you-"

"It is called claw magick: the ability to cut any surface." The line began to drip red slowly down his wrist and before it fell to the ground, he pulled her towards him and placed her hand over his own. "Now we are joined," he said, "in a bond that no one can break." Emily could feel the blood absorb into her skin and soon her blood stream. Sweat appeared on her forehead, but she did not pay it any attention for her eyes were now locked with his as the bonding took place.

Sandon watched with fascination as her eyes began to change colour and soon, her eyes looked like his; two dancing flames in a sea of white. He could feel her essence take his blood from him, wanting more, but refusing to overindulge. The two were locked together for several minutes in silence as the blood brought them together. She could feel just how important the ceremony was to him; people who were meant to be together shared each other's blood.

"I share my blood to make you mine," said Sandon in his mind.

"I take of your blood and make it mine," Emily replied in kind then soon her world went black.

Strange; the light in your eyes had dimmed somewhat.
Come closer to me and share my own-
I need not as much as I had hoped.
Farewell to those who thought me selfish.

VII

The ground shook. . .

Elves from the Mountains of Weyland stared up into the skies, not knowing and yet dreading the worst.

The ground shook. . .

An adult blue dragon flying over the town of Skili suddenly landed by a cave and crawled in, instantly going into hibernation forever.

The ground shook. . .

A Storyteller in the city of Galdahae picked up a pen and began to write his memoirs, for it was to be the last thing he would ever write.

The ground shook. . .

Two lovers in a grove of trees in a forest nearby London were in the throes of making love; one being an Aurwen woman and the other being a Dinashai male.

The ground shook . . .

Humans all over the world . . . continued to forget and ignore.

The ground shook . . . as the Dancers of Nightwynd, a coven of witches, expressed their emotions in dance for what had already begun. Nothing could stop them from what they had to do; the dance had to be completed or else all would be lost.

Lysander, deep in studies in his room, dropped his work and ran out of his room just as the rest of the Eldenshire family did as well. When each member saw the others, they all wore expressions of fear except Lysander. His mask was of pain and hate. They knew tat they had precious little time, so they grabbed whatever they thought they would need from their rooms. Even the servants joined in with whatever needed to be done. Soon, they were running at a speed too fast for mortal eyes towards the forest with Wolfe in the lead. At the same time that the Eldenshire family became "aware", the heads of the Council were each startled by the "thread" and soon they began preparing in their own way.

Milenda was soon running through the branches of the trees, trying to locate the two while the other folk began to prepare themselves for a possible battle. When she heard a roar of a dragon coming from a grove of trees, she knew she was too late. She had to save them. She dropped down into the grove and landed soundlessly several feet away from the new couple.

"You sound like a charging rhino," said Emily in a clear enough voice without even looking up from her naked embrace with Sandon. "What?"

"You both need to get dressed," she said in an eerily calm tone. "It has begun." With that, she jumped up into the trees, disappearing immediately. The two began to dress, picking up on the life threads of those now entering the edge of the forest. When they were both dressed, they ran back to the clearing where the others had assembled. When they reached the clearing, they were immediately swept up in the frenzy of everyone trying to assemble as best as possible. Weapons were being stored in hiding spots while the elderly and sick were led off to deeper parts of the woods. Bruc and several young centaurs directed archers to their hiding spots, giving Emily a brief nod of encouragement and slight hope. Even Sandon left her to help others with flame spells, leaving Emily by herself. She wanted to help, but was not schooled in any spells of defense. She had spells of healing, however, which were going to come in handy once the war had begun.

Suddenly, everyone stopped what they were doing as all eyes looked up into the night sky to see a phoenix the size of a lion fly directly over their heads. Its flame coloured plumage lit the night skies while its voice, sounding of angels, rang through everyone's ears, causing many to fall to their knees in praise of this sacred creature. It flew directly over the entire forest then disappeared, leaving many to wonder why they had just witnessed such an event, but others knew better. Throughout the history of Aurwen and other places in their realm, the sight of a Phoenix before a battle meant that those who were on the side of good and right were now protected. The sighting of a Phoenix by humans, however, caused many to go blind or instantly insane, for no one with mortal blood could withstand such a sight. When the phoenix disappeared, everyone went back to whatever they were working on, but with a stronger vigor than before; now they had hope on their side.

All of a sudden, the ground shook with such a force that many were knocked off balance, landing on the ground momentarily dazed. Emily looked up as an ice-cold shiver went down her back; they were here.

"By order of the Council, we insist you release the half demon into our care. Deny this request and we will attack immediately," said a neutral voice that seemed to surround them. "We do not wish to fight, but we will if you do not hand him over to us now." The ground shook once more then all went quiet; the Council awaited their decision.

Wolfe felt like a tightly wound spring; he wanted to run to his daughter and hold her close, protecting her from all of this, but he knew that Milenda was keeping her safe. He walked up to Lady Charlotte Asworth, one of the members of the Council as well as a member of the Windlearners, elemental beings, and stood by her side silently while watching the soldiers prepared themselves for possible battle. Lady Asworth came to Earth from the Planes 1000 years ago, as did other Elementals in seeking a new life in the parallel world. Many found Earth to be a harsh place and left as soon as they arrived. However, some did stay, finding the blue planet to be quite mysterious and adventurous in its own way, appealing to those who wanted more out of their immortal life than just beauty and perfection. Charlotte was one of those beings.

Wolfe found Charlotte's wispy hand and held it with his own in tight anticipation. Nothing needed to be said between; both thought the same thoughts- fear, anxiety concerning the soon to be battle, and sadness. For a brief moment, Charlotte's body became fleshier as she too gripped Wolfe's hand with the same urgency as he.

Of skies in black and salted clouds
Did still the winds that blow in disease.
Prayers, once thought of as saving grace,
Now lay at the feet of sinners and saints.
Blood flows freely through the forest of green
Attempting to wash away the past of glories.
Soon, we must all heed and listen to the winds
For They alone tell of our falling.

1900

Has it come to this? What were we thinking back then? Of course, I remember; we thought of cleansing the world, as it were; to purify and protect what we could see and not see. Such was the way of our folk. And yet, I wonder . . . were we right? Did we have the right do kill innocent lives for the sake of one? Even now as I write this down in my notes, I still ask myself if he truly was as black hearted as the Council made him out to be.

I no longer have the strength to leave my home; going outside during the daylight is unthinkable now. Others, however, are braver than I, but I hear the whispers of their later charred and blackened souls. Fools . . and yet I envy them. All I have are my windows, which give me a view of the new world, this turn of the century. Our kind are no longer needed for the humans to live and survive. We are now left to become subjects of faery tales and stories to frighten young children when they are behaving badly. No one wants to believe in us anymore and if they do, their minds are filled with hatred, distrust, suspicion, and anger.

The world looks the same and yet it is not, thanks to us. We were here, have always been here, and yet, we were the ones who destroyed it all, leaving the humans to do what they had to do. I do not blame them, not at all for if I were in their shoes, I would have sworn revenge as well. I do not blame their hatred for all magick now. I do not blame them for their vile words and slurs against my kind. Once we were thought of as pure forms of beauty; now we are called Viril or Forsaken. Somehow, that name fits us.

I still remember the night when the Council declared war against a young man who had the bad luck of being half demon as well. They came in from all sides and, with their war magick, destroyed the forest where he and his friends and protectors were hiding. Most were killed; even the Council lost quite a number for the magick was strong and not used regularly. London was not so fortunate; most of the city burned to the ground thanks to the Council's magick. The humans came after us with blood vengeance on their minds and yes, we did pay the price. Our treaty that had been set in stone for centuries was now on the brink of being dissolved. Thankfully, we were able to make amends and reforge what was almost lost to us, for without the peace contract, we would simply fail to exist.

Even with the war magick the main target, the half demon, and his lover survived. Their ongoing lives are a constant reminder of what we did and I for one welcome my ongoing penance with humility. Where they are, I know not, but I have heard rumours from the sea elves of Kithing of a strange couple with a demon child living in Ravenscliff, one of the larger cities in the Otherworld. I hope they are happy there if the rumours are true.

The sun has set and soon Night will come. Night is now our time; from dusk to dawn we are allowed out into London, to explore what we used to love during the time of Sun and to spend time with friends and loved ones. The humans have given us that much; I no longer pray for anything more.

Tales of a Goth Librarian

May the Forest Still Grant Us Sanctuary,

Illian Wynderham

Elder of the Quandril Elves, Former High Chair of the Aurwen Council

May 14, 1900

Purple & Black

Working on a manuscript is a bitch.

This was the first thought that entered into Symon's mind as she faced her computer's screen, the cursor blinking in a steady movement, waiting for her rush of words. She stared at it for several minutes while forcing sentences into her brain that would somehow trigger another and another until she was too busy typing to notice anything else. She wanted a word, even a letter, something that would get her going in the right direction. The cursor continued to blink at her in that same monotonous way on the white screen, begging to be moved across due to her insight and literary brilliance. Symon's eyes began to wander all over the monitor while her brain began to consider going online once more to check out her E-BAY items for sale, wondering if anyone was going to place a bid on her three books. She scratched her head and then pulled out a single strand quickly to avoid any pain. She looked at it in awe; it took one follicle of hair to determine the identity of a person with today's technology, a feat that still amazed her. She glanced over to the blinking cursor then back at her strand of hair with the thought of checking out her books on E-BAY, then shook her head and tossed the strand over her shoulder to focus fully on her white screen.

Five minutes later, she walked into the kitchen to make a cup of jasmine tea, her concentration now completely gone. As the kettle began to boil the water, Symon leaned against her sink, trying hard not to fall into a defeatist attitude. She wanted to spend a good portion of her day working on her writing, trying to perfect herself and push herself to write more than just short stories that were sometimes published by magazines. She wanted to be a literary sensation and yet the words felt stuck somewhere deep inside of her, waiting for the right break to bring about the flow. She knew she had it in her, but just did not know what to do in order to get to it.

Soon, her kettle began to whistle, startling her out of her stream of dead end thoughts and to get her cup ready. After she prepared her tea, she walked back into the living room where the cursor still blinked at her, refusing to give up on her. She took a small sip of the fragrant liquid then stared at the monitor.

Ten minutes later, she was walking down the street towards Meridian Books, one of the local bookstores in her area of the city. She lived in the bohemian and artistic area of the city where several of the main streets were filled with coffee houses, bookstores and gift shops, thrift like clothing stores, restaurants of every ethnic background, and a park that everyone loved to walk to, giving them a chance to enjoy nature whenever they wanted it. The day was a typical Autumn day, complete with cool breezes that travelled through the area, giving off scents of cinnamon, burning leaves, and thoughts of warm cider while buried underneath a warm blanket at home. The trees on the sidewalks carried leaves of gold, red, and brown, turning the ordinary area into a place possible of magic and new discoveries.

Symon loved where she lived; it was in this area that one could find painters on the street corners with canvas and many tubes of paint around them, painting scenes that only they could see with their multicoloured eyes, or corner poets reciting their latest opus while standing on top of boxes with a hat on the ground for donations for the "poetic cause" as some would put it. Symon, normally an observer of the flurry of activity on these streets, ignored it all as she walked down to the bookstore. She wanted to get as far away from her own apartment as fast as possible due to the complete lack of spark for her manuscript.

When she entered the bookstore, she sighed with happiness. The bookstore was decorated with a Gothic Victorian flair that would make the most uber-Goth drool with delight. Deep velvet curtains hung at every window while the walls were painted black with silver sparkles, giving off a magical effect. The store catered to the freaky book lover: Horror, Goth subculture, Steampunk, Science Fiction/Fantasy, Poetry, Shakespeare, and anything in between plus magazines, journals of every colour and size, gifts for the darkly/eccentric inclined, plus seating areas for people to read, write, or gaze fondly upon the object of their latest obsession. People who lived their life outside of the norm treated this bookstore as if it were a second home, which in most cases it was. The staff, a mishmash of backgrounds, races, and lives, got along with each other due to their main similar interest: they were all voracious readers.

Symon walked through the aisles of the store, looking at titles, but not really taking any interest in them. She wanted to give her mind a rest from the blinking cursor before feelings of early defeat began to settle in, deterring her from writing for a long period of time.

After several minutes of wandering around, she chose a random fiction book, found one of the comfortable chairs, and began to read. The heaters were on, creating a cozy atmosphere for the customers, while soft classical music floated all throughout the store. Symon's head drooped several times while her eyelids felt like sandbags. She once joked that the chairs were infused with Nyquil because customers were always drifting off to sleep with smiles on their faces. She struggled to wake up, but the chair, the heat, and the music, were too much for her. She closed her eyes.

"Oh my god, can someone PLEASE help me find a book?!"

Symon's eyes opened with a start as her book slipped off her lap. She looked around as if in a daze while trying to find the source of the very loud and very obnoxious voice while she picked up her book from the floor. Other customers looked around as well, trying to discover the source of the interruption of their quiet. Soon, all eyes turned to a woman who stood on top of one of the step stools in the Fiction section. She waved her hands around frantically, desperately trying to get the attention of someone willing to help her, but for some reason could not get anyone's attention. She waved her hands again then sighed as she stepped down the stool and began walking around the store. Many people quickly looked away, as if in fear of what they would see in her eyes. When the woman walked up to Symon, she refused to look away and instead took her in with one long glance.

The annoyance was dressed in a short black skirt with black and purple striped tights, Doc Marten shoes, and a black pullover sweater with a white Oxford shirt and purple tie underneath, making her pale skin even more so. Her brown hair was pulled back into a messy ponytail; showing off her tripled pierced ears. Her eyes, however, seemed to be full of storm clouds, tornadoes, and other catastrophes. The woman stared hard at Symon and Symon stared back.

"Can you help me?" she asked in a rough tone while the corners of her mouth curved downward. "At least you've got the balls to look at me in the eyes. No one else around here seems to be able to look at me. So, can you help me look for a book?"

"I don't work here," Symon calmly replied. "I'm sure-"

"I KNOW you don't fucking work here!" She screamed, causing a neat pile of books on a nearby table to fall on the floor. "I just want someone to help me!" Symon, now at the end of her rope with this arrogant person, closed her book and got up from her place of comfort, her eyes never leaving the woman's face.

"Tell me, are you always a cunt or is this just for our benefit?" Her eyes betrayed no emotion, but her tone of voice was enough. The woman's eyes grew wide with surprise and fury while her whole body began to shake. Several of the customers who were witnessing this event slowly backed away from the two, knowing full well that a fight was about to happen, with many of them mentally placing bets on Symon.

"What did you say?" The woman's eyes were now down to slits as she took a step forward.

"I asked if you-"

The woman suddenly slapped Symon on the face, causing everyone to gasp. Symon stared at her in surprise as she placed a hand to her reddening cheek. The woman now smirked, satisfied that she handled-

Symon's hand moved too fast for anyone to see; she slapped the woman so hard that her eyes rolled around in their sockets. Several customers were grinning; good for her, they thought. The woman's face was a deep red as she stared back at Symon. Then, without any warning, she turned and walked out of the store, much to the delight of the customers, of whom some applauded Symon's "response". She, however, was in no good mood; she quickly took her book, placed it back on the shelf, and then walked out the store in embarrassment. The day was still a beautiful day as she walked down the street, wanting to get away from the bookstore, but she took no notice of it. People walked by her, not noticing her scowl or the way she stomped rather than walked. Then, to the point of near mental exhaustion, she sat down in one of the chairs located outside of Indigo Java, a coffeehouse that had the best blueberry scones in the city. A young male waiter immediately walked up to take her order then dashed off with her order of a large vanilla latte and two blueberry scones. She pulled out a book from her messenger bag and began to read.

"So, you followed me to slap me again?" Symon gripped the edges of her book tightly, not wanting to see who had just spoken to her even though she recognized the voice. With a weary sigh, she pulled the book down and her eyes met eyes full of storm clouds. The woman stood there, arms crossed as if daring her to slap her again. Symon placed her book on the table just as the waiter brought her order to her.

"Look, leave me alone, OK? I don't follow people. I'm just trying to relax a bit." The woman glared at her for several seconds then sat in the chair across from her, causing Symon to give her an incredulous look. "Uh, can I help you?"

"No," she said as she pulled the waiter towards her and ordered a four shot vanilla latte with an oatmeal raisin cookie then pushed him off to do his job. "Like you, I just want to relax."

"So relax and leave me the hell alone." Symon picked up her book and continued reading, not caring if the woman sat and stared at her or not. She pinched off a piece of her scone and nibbled it, quickly forgetting the rude guest who now shared her table.

"So why are you so defensive?" Symon put down her book again.

"Excuse me?"

"I said, why are you so damn defensive?" The waiter appeared with her order and she grabbed it from his tray without even looking at him.

"I'm not-"

"Oh yes you are, ever since I first laid eyes on you."

"Well, could it be that perhaps you were such a bitch to me?" Both took sips from their coffee drinks.

"I wasn't a bitch to you; I just wanted someone to help me."

"Well, did it ever occur to you not to cuss out people who are trying to help you?"

"Is that blueberry scone any good?" She made a motion as if to reach over, but pulled her hand back when Symon slapped it away from her bakery item.

"Look, what's your problem?! Can you please get the hell away from me?" Symon continued reading her book, not caring if she left or not. The woman sighed several times in an exaggerated tone then pulled out a magazine from her bag and began to thumb through it with the occasional sip from her latte.

For half an hour, the two women read without any further interaction. While she read, Symon's thoughts trailed back to her annoying table partner. Who was she anyway? Why did she choose to bother her?

"I'm sorry." Symon laid her book on the table, clearly not expecting such words to come from the woman's mouth. The woman's stormy eyes now looked to be an ordinary slate blue. "I said, I'm sorry," she repeated.

"No need to apologize."

"I feel like I must though." She grabbed Symon's hand in a vice-like grip, causing her to wince in pain. The woman's eyes seemed to be on the verge of crying as she appeared to struggle in trying to find the right words for this moment. "I'm ... not good at talking to people. I tend to be gruff when I speak to others. Please forgive me." Symon wanted to shake this woman's cool and dry hand off her own, but refrained from doing so. "I don't have too many friends."

"Hmmm, wonder why?" The woman tightened her grip on Symon's hand as the storms from before threatened to come back into her eyes.

"Look, I told you I'm not good at apologizing. So, are you going to take my fucking apology or just act like everyone else?" Symon stared into those eyes and actually shivered. "Will you?"

"Yes, I will." Like clouds breaking to reveal a sunny day, the woman actually smiled a bright smile and released Symon's now bruised hand. She rubbed it with her other hand, trying to get the circulation back while the woman finished off her cookie and latte, her eyes still focused on Symon.

"So, what's your name?"

"Symon." The woman sputtered a mouthful of lukewarm latte on the ground.

"You're kidding, right? Simon?"

"My parents thought I was a boy so they named me Simon in advance. When I came out, however, they changed the spelling of it to make it seem cooler. S-Y-M-O-N. My parents are intellectuals, too hip to be hip people."

"Well, it suits you, I think."

"Thanks." Symon finished off her now very cold coffee, wanting to leave this crazy woman here and go back to her apartment to face the blinking cursor. She also wanted to stay and talk to her, mainly because she was a masochist at heart. The woman stared at her in an unnerving way, seeming to look right into her soul and pick it apart for her own choosing. Symon wanted to slap her again, just to make sure she was real.

"So, what are you?"

"Excuse me?"

"What are you? What is your life? Do you have any plans?"

"Oh. Well, I am in graduate school for my Masters in Library and Information Science. Yes, I want to be a librarian when I grow up." She chuckled at that last statement then fell quiet when she noticed that the woman did not share her mirth.

"Why is that funny? Why do you think you have to grow up?" she asked with a serious look on her face, as if she had just asked about the meaning of life. Symon's glance fell to her empty plate, feeling foolish for trying to make a joke with this . . . person.

"I was kidding," she mumbled, trying hard to save face before the woman, as if her opinion mattered.

"Well, to be what you want to become is not a matter of becoming an adult as well. Being an adult is only a state of mind, just like being a child. It all depends on how you view your life against the world and how you choose to live that very life."

"Of course, I only meant-

The woman raised up a hand to stop her. The storm clouds were gone from her eyes.

"I know what you meant. All I'm trying to say is that we should live out our lives the best way we can. If it means that we carry the heart of a child within us, then there is nothing wrong with that, I think."

"I see, and who made you God?" Symon instantly regretted the words coming out of her mouth; the storm clouds were back. The woman sat in silence, her body giving off little shakes, as the storm clouds rolled into view. Her mouth was a tight line that threatened to crack at any second.

"No one made me God," she whispered furiously, causing Symon to feel lower than a worm buried in dirt. "I look to my own self for that." With that, she got up and stormed away from the table, giving Symon reason to breathe a sigh of relief. What a nut job.

The cursor blinked.

The writer sat, wondering when the words were going to come out of her and onto the screen.

The cursor blinked.

The writer got up and made a bowl of Ramen noodles, one of the few comfort foods she allowed herself when she turned vegetarian five years ago. She slurped down noodles with worn, but sturdy chopsticks while walking back to her computer. She slurped down another small bunch of noodles then placed her bowl to the side.

The cursor blinked.

"Urgh," she said under her breath while running her hands through her hair. Nothing? No rush of words to send the computer off to a good start? This was ridiculous. She wanted to go back outside to enjoy the day, but wondered, for a brief moment, if she would run into that crazy woman again. She sighed then laughed; she was crazy. How in the world can someone like that function?

Fifteen minutes later, Symon was back outside, walking down another one of the main streets while glancing everywhere around her to make sure that the crazy woman was not following her. She felt repelled by her and yet intrigued at the same time. She wanted to get to know her and yet run screaming if she did indeed walk up to her, smile and say-

"Looking for me again?" Symon halted her steps at a thrift store and stood there, not wanting to turn around, but knowing that she should. It was better to face one's fear than run away. She turned around and saw the woman once more, except she wore a slightly feral grin on her face. "I said, were you looking for me again?"

"On the contrary," said Symon in a surprisingly calm voice, "I wanted to go back out again. I can't seem to get my thoughts in order."

"Order for what?"

"For a novel I am working on." Suddenly, the smile spread even wider like a child about to get into mischief. She giggled and took Symon by the arm and led her down the street.

"Why didn't you tell me that you were a writer as well?" she cooed in her ear, giving off the scent of violets. "I love writers, just love them! They have the power to kill AND create, you know, but of course you would know that!" Symon nodded dumbly as they walked down the street like sisters, thinking of the many ways in trying get rid of her. When they reached Toothy's, a pastry shop, the woman pulled Symon inside and sat her down at one of the tables then walked up to the counter to order for them. Symon, meanwhile, kept looking at the door, wondering if she could escape without her knowing. The door was only two feet away, the ability to escape within a hand's reach.

"I figured you were a blueberry person, so I got this for you," said the woman as she placed a rather large blueberry muffin before her then sat down with several pieces of baklava. She peeled off a layer and nibbled on it as if it were made of gold while watching Symon nibble on her muffin, then cleared her throat and said, "Lyssa". Symon's eyes darted to her face as she struggled with what she had just said.

"I'm sorry, what?"

"Why are you ALWAYS apologizing?" she screamed, causing everyone in the shop to stop whatever they were doing to turn and stare at the two women, some in disgust, others in awe of the woman who had just screamed. The woman looked around, now feeling everyone's eyes on them, caught the eyes of those looking at her, and allowed the storms to come back. Within seconds, everyone was back to whatever they were doing before with little or no regard for the two women.

"Anyway," said the woman as she took another honeyed piece of baklava and ate it, "my name is Lyssa." She held out a sticky hand for Symon to shake, which she did for a brief second before taking her hand back before Lyssa decided to hold on to it with her vice-like grip. "I figured, Symon, that if I already know your name, Symon, then at least you must know mine, Symon."

"Ok, so now I know your name and you know mine. Now what?"

"Well, now we eat." Lyssa turned her full attention to her baklava and devoured all pieces within several minutes.

"So, what do you do, Lyssa?" Lyssa looked up from her plate with a look that, at first glance, was not sure who was talking to her. She swallowed the piece that was in her throat and said, "I travel," then looked away from Symon's curious glance.

"Well. . . that sounds nice."

"It has its moments." Lyssa continued to look around the place, clearly not wanting to rest her eyes on Symon. "Look, can we leave? I no longer want to be here and honestly, I like your company, but I think you might want to leave me here. After all, I am sure you don't like me." Lyssa's eyes finally rested on Symon. "Be honest; you've wanted to leave my company since I dragged you here, right?"

"Yes, I have." No point in lying about it. "I don't like you, but I'm trying to understand you."

Lyssa snorted. "I'll give you the honesty points for that statement. Can we leave here, please?"

"YOU can do whatever you want to do. I AM going to do whatever I want to do without you." Symon got up and walked out the store, leaving Lyssa without a second glance.

Symon, rather than go home and face the blinking cursor a third time, walked the streets instead. The day was still full of light and cool autumn breezes that it seemed blasphemous to do anything, but enjoy the day. People were out with friends or loved ones, taking advantage of the day as well. She allowed herself to smile and her walking slowed down. She wanted to admire the world around her and power walking was not the way to do it.

"So, can I walk with you in quiet?" asked Lyssa, who seemed to appear out of nowhere. Symon audibly groaned and stopped to face the woman head on. The gloves were coming off with what she had to say.

"Look, I don't want you walking with me, I don't want to buying me any damn muffins, I don't want you sneaking up behind me asking me if you can walk with me, I don't want you around me at all, understand? You're a freak in the really bad way and I want you to leave me alone, understand?" Symon was breathing hard by the time she finished her speech, leaving Lyssa looking more than hurt. Lyssa grabbed her messenger bag tighter as her eyes fell to focus on her shoes.

"Sorry, Symon." Symon could barely hear her apology and at once regretted speaking to her so angrily. "I. . .like you, that's all."

"Yes, well there's like and then there is fucking head-case following me wherever I go." Symon walked off, leaving Lyssa alone yet again, but this time she had her tears. By the time Symon turned the corner, the front of Lyssa's shirt was soaking wet.

Symon, once she could no longer see the source of her recent discomfort, slowed her pace down again and tried to smile. She was finally free of that pesky woman Lyssa or whatever her name was. She stopped in front of a shoe store to admire their Fall line, wondering if she needed a new pair of boots . . . and if Lyssa was going to be OK. She shook her head; that crazy woman could take care of herself.

The sound of someone crying entered her mind, startling her from her thoughts of the boots. She looked up and saw no one, not even Lyssa following her. She returned her thoughts to boots and seconds later the crying returned. Symon looked up again, a tad more frustrated, and saw no one. Rolling her eyes in disgust, she walked back to where she left Lyssa. Maybe God had a sick sense of humour.

When she reached the corner, her heart felt heavy with disgust. Lyssa still stood, her face fixated to the ground, as tears still fell from her eyes. Symon, not really knowing what to do, walked up to her and touched her shoulder, causing Lyssa to embrace her, Lyssa's tears now staining both shirts.

"I knew you'd come back," she whispered in her ear, her breath still giving off the scent of violets.

"So, living room, which is a mess, computer area, bedroom is down the hall, and bathroom is to the right." Symon quickly gave Lyssa the tour of her apartment then walked in her kitchen to prepare some tea. She asked Lyssa if she wanted any, to which she replied no. Lyssa walked in as well and leaned against the refrigerator.

"I like your place," she said in a small voice. "So clean and orderly."

"Um, did you not just see the mess in my living room? I'd hardly call it orderly."

"Oh, no, I meant the order in your overall state."

"Uh, right." The teakettle began to whistle.

"Why do you want to be a writer, Symon?"

"Because I have always loved reading and I have too many stories in my head to just keep up there. I want to share them with the world."

"Sometimes the stories we have in our minds are not necessarily the ones we need to share with others, Symon."

"Of course, but I want to do it anyway."

"Suit yourself."

"Listen, I have to ask: did you choose me as the person to stick to?"

"What do you mean?"

"I mean, did you choose me on purpose? I feel like you did, like you could see something in me that you couldn't see in others at the bookstore."

"Well, now that you mention it, yes I did. You looked at me in the eyes. No one else did that. Everyone kept looking away and it angered me with every aversion. You, however, did not. You had a backbone."

"But, you sounded like a raving lunatic." Lyssa glanced away for a brief moment, and then focused her eyes on Symon's.

"So, how much have you written?" Symon waved a hand towards the computer screen, blank with the blinking cursor still going strong. Lyssa got up from sitting on the floor and walked over to it. She stared intently at the cursor as if she was willing it to produce words then turned to stare at Symon. The storms were back.

"Come here." Symon walked over to Lyssa who immediately grabbed her and slammed her into the computer chair with enough force to knock the wind out of her lungs. "Do you see?" she hissed in her ear, giving off the scent of violets. "Do you see what needs to be done?"

"W-what? What are you talking about?"

"You have no words inside of you, admit it! You've wasted so much time thinking you have the words when actually you do not, do you, Symon? Do you?!" Symon wanted to cry; she was right. She had no words inside of her, for if she did, she would have spent all of this time typing rather than sitting in front of the screen, staring at the blinking cursor. She closed her eyes and allowed the tears to come. Lyssa, noticing that she was crying, softened slightly and patted her back. "You are much more," she whispered, "and yet you waste it in trying to force words that do not exist to come out. Let me help you, Symon, let me help you." Lyssa placed a hand on either side of Symon's head and closed her eyes. Symon felt the slight pressure of her hands, but did not think anything about it.

Suddenly, she felt it. Words, deep and dark, thoughtful and intellectual, suddenly coming up from another source, a place she never knew existed. Her eyes were still closed with tears, but her fingers were now on her keyboard, quickly typing away. Symon opened her eyes and, seeing her hands now typing out words, phrases, sentences, everything, she began to laugh. Lyssa's hands were still on her head and remained there for the next two hours. Symon was so engrossed in her writing that she did not even realize Lyssa was still there.

Around one in the morning, five hours of straight typing later, Symon stopped to stare at her screen for the first time; she had written 40 pages of a story. She blew out a breath and leaned back in her chair then shrieked when she realized that Lyssa was still there, still holding on to the sides of head. She jumped out of her seat and stared at the strange woman. Why was she still there? Was she quiet that entire time? Did she say anything during those hours? She stared at her hands then up at Lyssa, who was staring at her with a calm demeanour and a slight smile on her face.

"What happened?"

"You typed. I helped. Enough said."

"But, how-

Suddenly, Lyssa's lips were on Symon's, her arms wrapped around Symon's body. Symon, almost gagging, tried to pull the woman off her, but soon felt her own arms wrap around the woman's body, pulling her closer as the scent of violets cloyed her senses, making her want to vomit, but still she held on to Lyssa's lips. Lyssa, with surprising strength, pulled Symon up from her chair, breaking their kiss, and led her to Symon's bedroom, where she ripped Symon's clothes from her body with no trouble then removed her own as well, revealing a slender pale body with muscular arms and legs. Symon, never having been with a woman, did not know what to do. She could only stare at this woman, this creature, with eyes of uncertainty, but soon Lyssa snatched her in her arms and resumed their kiss. Her long and slender tongue snaked its way into Symon's mouth and twisted itself with Symon's thick and dry one. Lyssa's hands wandered all over Symon's body as the two stood there in the darkness of her room; she could feel Symon's body warming up to her touches and kiss while still holding onto a sense of reservation.

"Don't fight me," Lyssa whispered in Symon's ear while licking the outside of it. Her left hand wandered down to Symon's sex and rested on top of her pubic hairs, gently brushing the coarse hairs. Symon, in a moment of clarity, grabbed Lyssa's hand and pushed it away then pushed her own body away from hers. She gasped for breath then sat down on the corner of the bed with her face turned away from Lyssa. Lyssa remained standing, her face a mask of anger.

"Why did you push me away?"

"Because I don't know you. Besides, I have never been with another woman before."

"And why should that stop you? Flesh is flesh, Symon. What we do in the dark has nothing to do with reservations. I want to make love to you because I know what you are." Lyssa then walked over to Symon and knelt down then forced her legs apart. Symon tried to push her away, but Lyssa was too strong; her head slipped between her legs and soon she kissed Symon's now extremely wet sex. Symon gasped at Lyssa's slightly cold lips touching her body, causing her whole body to shudder. Lyssa grabbed her legs to keep her from running away and buried her head deeper, enjoying her warmth with her tongue. Symon lay back on the bed and grabbed the back of Lyssa's head, pushing her further and further in. Lyssa moaned with every flick of her long tongue, causing Symon's body to shake and quiver. Never before had she felt something this intense. After several minutes had passed, Lyssa released Symon's legs then crawled up to the bed and lay next to her. Symon tried to slow down her breathing, but found that she could not. She felt like all of her senses had been used to the extreme.

Lyssa turned on the side, facing Symon, and began to stroke her cheek. Symon could smell violets as well as her strong musk odour coming from Lyssa's sweaty body.

"Do you see now what you are to me?" she said as she cupped Symon's chin and turned her face so that she was looking into her eyes. Symon wanted to look away, but found that she could not.

"Please, don't do this to me."

"Why? I have so much to give you; why do you refuse it?" Lyssa then slid closer to her and began to gently pull on her nipples, causing Symon to moan. Lyssa tugged on her right nipple then took her left one in her mouth and began to nibble on it. Symon moaned even louder and soon her own fingers wandered down to her still wet sex, her fingers sliding in and out with practiced ease. Lyssa bit down her nipple then pulled away, watching a thin trickle of blood flow down Symon's chest. Symon looked down at the blood then up at Lyssa again in a daze as her fingers continued sliding in and out of her.

Then, without any warning, Lyssa took her left hand and slid it neatly into Symon's chest. Symon's fingers stopped moving as she registered what was happening to her. She began to scream, but Lyssa covered her mouth with her other hand as her left hand slid deeper within her chest. Although she felt no pain, Symon still could not believe it. Lyssa's hand felt like ice as it plunged deeper. Lyssa's eyes locked on to Symon's and the storms came back, full and furious, closer and closer.

Symon woke up to the sun beaming down on her face and a cool breeze coming through her open windows. She blinked sleepily for a moment then, as last night's activities came back into her mind, her eyes snapped wide open. She sat up in bed, her naked body revealed, clean and cold from the open windows. She ran a hand down her chest, right over the area where. . . did it really happen? It seemed so real and yet. . . Symon grabbed a shirt from the floor and put it on while walking to her living room. The screen saver was on so she touched the mouse to get the last screen up.

The words were still there, words that told a story, a story that was not her own. Symon touched the screen, still wondering if it was all a dream. But the words were there, the blinking cursor satisfied. She printed off a copy of the document and stuffed it in her messenger bag. Perhaps if she had time later in the day, she would go over it again and edit it.

After grabbing a quick breakfast, Symon walked down the main street to her job, the main branch library, where she worked as the administrative assistant for the library director. Thanking the gods that she worked in an environment that was free from stress and backstabbing as her previous job in a securities firm, Symon tightened her grip on her black messenger bag and hurried along. If she made it in enough time, she would be able to get a cup of Jasmine's gourmet coffee that she always made for everyone in Administration. Jasmine was one of the coolest librarians around; a Goth woman just like Symon who loved to read all sorts of books except romance. The two became fast friends on Symon's first day of work; as soon as Jasmine noticed Symon's Steampunk attire, she squealed with delight and scooped her up within seconds.

When she walked into the Administration office, the smell of cinnamon coffee greeted her. She smiled as she let her nose lead her; surely there was some coffee left in the kitchen. She laid her bag down next to her desk in her small, but nice office then briskly walked to the kitchen with fingers crossed, hoping that someone was gracious enough to leave a drop of Jasmine's coffee.

Her crossed fingers proved to be good; there, on the burner, were two full pots of Jasmine's coffee scented with vanilla and cinnamon. Symon smiled as she grabbed her personal mug that said I LOVE BOOKS in dark purple. She filled her mug half way then added her usual creamer and sugar then took a deep sip. The smooth flavours, blending into one luxurious moment, caused her to sigh while her eyes were closed. She took another sip; thank you Jasmine, she thought.

"Well, you finally got some, huh?" Symon opened her eyes to find her friend leaning against the doorframe with a wicked smile on her face. She, too, held a cup of coffee in her hand, taking short sips every few seconds. "So, what did you do on your day off?"

Symon took a long sip, not wanting to answer that question because she was still unsure if it really happened; did Lyssa really exist? Did they really make love last night? Did her hand actually slide inside of her chest?

"Nothing really, just worked on my story."

"How far along are you?"

"Actually, can you come with me to my office?" Jasmine moved to the side to let Symon walk through the door. Jasmine walked behind her, taking now noisy sips from her mug. When they reached the office, Symon closed the door behind them then reached into her bag to produce the manuscript. Jasmine sat down in the chair on the other side of Symon's desk, anxiously waiting for what Symon had to tell her.

"I wrote this yesterday," she said as she handed it to Jasmine, "so don't make any criticisms yet; I haven't edited it." Jasmine grabbed it and soon began to read it while Symon sat in her own chair and turned on her computer.

Suddenly, Jasmine started to moan deeply. She reached for her cup of coffee and nearly missed it as she continued reading Symon's work. Symon, not knowing how to take such a noise, started working on her latest assignment given to her by the director. Soon, Jasmine moaned again, causing Symon to peer around the side of her monitor at her friend who was engrossed in the story, her eyes scanning every word, every phrase. Symon went back to work, trying her best to ignore her friend.

Thirty minutes later, Jasmine slapped the pages down on Symon's desk, breaking Symon's concentration on her work. She peered around the monitor again and this time caught her friend's heavily kohl-rimmed eyes staring back at her.

"Well, what did you think?" Jasmine said nothing for several seconds, just staring straight at her friend who was anxiously awaiting any kind of response. Suddenly, she whooped and threw her arms in the air.

"Oh my god, Sy, I knew you were a good writer, but damn!" Symon double blinked; it was THAT good? "I've never read such a piece of work! You don't need to change a thing, not one word, understand?" Jasmine grabbed her mug of now cold coffee, yipped again, then let herself out of the office, leaving a purely stunned Symon still seated at her desk. That good? She picked up the manuscript and read it again, making sure she did read it and not just skim through it.

It told the story of a young woman who lost everything in her life for the sake of being something greater to the world. The woman wanted to give the world herself as the ultimate gift, but she paid a dear price for it. She, too, fell under the spell of the words, ignoring the e-mails that popped on her screen, the phone calls that seemed so distant, everything. All she wanted to do was read her words. They were her words and yet they were not, for she did have assistance, Lyssa. Her mind wandered back to an image of her face, frowning deeply while her eyes held storms at bay. She was cruel and yet she did help her with this piece of work. But, how could she get in contact with her? She did not leave a phone number or an e-mail address so it was futile to try to look for her. However, deep in Symon's mind, was the thought that she would see the strange woman again at a time when she did not want her around.

I helped her. That is what I do. She came to me and I helped her.

It tasted good; I had not tasted that in such a long time. I want more, but I know.

She was scared of me.

She tasted of fear and sanity. Vanilla and apricots, sunshine and tears.

I want to taste her again. I feel cold.

Soon, very soon. I am tired. I am tired. I am tired. I am tired.

My eyes feel heavy. I am awake now.

I do not remember what year, where am I, who are these people? Did I die?

I am tired.

Symon. Symon with a Y rather than an I. Symon, a woman. Flesh, skin, taut, tight, tingle me, tingle me, relax, please, let me love you.

I am tired. I feel slightly sane. I hate that. Blueberries. Skin tight and taut. I am tired. Lean on me, dear friend. I shall give you words, words, words. Sing. The letters came in droves. Acceptance letters from publishers wanting her little manuscript, offers of thousands of dollars, contracts for years, all wanting her; "Symon, darling, we never knew you could write like this." When the first acceptance letter arrived in the mail, Symon celebrated by having Jasmine over for dinner and then going out to Goth Night at Club Masquerade, the only club in the city that fully catered to the Goth scene. However, as more and more letters arrived from other publishers offering her longer and longer contracts with more money, Symon's pride began to dwindle a bit. She should have been happy, ecstatic even, but something lurked in the back of her mind, something that told her that all was not well with this situation.

Plus, strange thoughts, thoughts she would normally not have, began entering in her mind, followed by a soft whispering voice. This voice spoke in fragmented sentences, telling her stories and truths, or were they lies? She could not tell the difference. At times, she could barely hear it, but it never stopped speaking to her. It always spoke to her, but barely over a whisper. The thoughts would slip in and out of her mind like a silk scarf that was caught in a gentle breeze on a Spring day. Sometimes the thoughts were pretty and simple to comprehend. Other thoughts, however, kept her awake at times; fearful of what she would see once she closed her eyes and slept. She began using a journal in order to keep up with these thoughts that seemed to have no direction or reason.

Day One

I don't know where to begin in all of this, but I feel like I must. I don't know. This whisper in my head; a dream? Too much going on in my mind? I wish I could tell someone about the thoughts in my mind, but I know people would think I was nuts.

For example; I have thoughts of wondering what it would be like to watch a reversal birth. I have no idea why I am thinking about that??????

Makes me think of Lyssa. Crazy ass bitch. No, I shouldn't say that about her. She had her moments.

I actually would like to see her again.

She chose a small independent publishing company that offered her a substantial amount as an advance in the hopes that she could write at least one novella a year. She agreed and signed their contract. Symon continued working at the library, but soon fans of her book discovered where she worked and began to follow her around, claiming her to be the new Literary Voice of the Gothic subculture, of which she had no real interest in. True, she lived the life of a Goth, but she was in no way any subculture's literary voice. All she wanted was to be a published author. Her fans thought differently, however. Symon had to politely shoo a devoted fan from her office at least twice a week after she would listen to how much her words meant to them and how it would mean so much to them if she signed their book, of which she would with a shy smile. Her co-workers would snicker under their breath when she would gently, but firmly push them out of the library while their eyes were completely focused on her and nothing else.

"It seems you've become the Goth Messiah," said Jasmine one morning as she poured coffee for the both of them. Symon smirked then took a deep sip of her coffee, not willing to give her an answer. All she wanted to do was write, not become a celebrity.

She ran into Lyssa quite by accident weeks after the huge success of her first novella. The number of fans making their pilgrimages to the library were rising, causing a concern to the general patrons of the library who went there to study in a quiet atmosphere. Symon, although flattered that so many people read and supported her work, wished that it never happened to her. It was only one novella; was it truly that important to so many? Yet, somewhere deep inside of her lay the answer: of course it was important. To her fans, reading her work was like finding a pitcher of cold water after walking in a desert for a day. Her words provided nourishment to their souls and she was glad to do it.

One extremely cool day, Symon decided to go out for lunch. Before she became such a hit, she had to watch her money, making sure that every purchase was accounted for. That worry no longer bothered her; after paying her small, but annoying bills completely out and bulking up her savings account, she found that she had enough money to stretch and enjoy when the time came to be impulsive. Her co-workers wondered why she still worked at the library, but she quickly told them that her job there would always be one of her greatest passions in life, even more so than writing.

So, as she sat outside, eating a veggie pita sandwich and re-reading the latest Clive Barker, she felt the small hairs on the back of her neck rise, causing her skin to break out in goose bumps.

"And how do you like success thus far?" Symon lowered her book to the sound of a flat voice, knowing instantly the source as she groaned and inwardly leapt for joy at the same time. She looked up to Lyssa's face that betrayed no emotion as she stood in a rigid pose, tightly gripping her shoulder bag as if she was afraid it would jump off her shoulder and run away. She wore a long sleeve black dress that reached her ankles, meeting her thick black Victorian boots, along with simple silver hoop earrings and a necklace with a strange circular design at the bottom. Her hair was still in a messy ponytail, a desperate need for a hairbrush. "So," she said again in a slightly higher tone, "do you like it?"

"It has its moments, why?"

"No reason." Lyssa then sat down next to Symon and reached for her sandwich with Symon not stopping her. She took a generous bite, her eyes never leaving Symon's, then placed the sandwich back on the paper in her lap. "Good," she mumbled as she chewed thoughtfully. Symon looked down at her sandwich and instantly lost her appetite.

"So, how have you been?" she asked in a futile attempt to begin some thread of conversation with her. Lyssa chewed for a several seconds in silence then swallowed and actually grinned a grin that lit her entire face.

"Doing well, actually. I wanted to apologize for the last time we saw each other. It was not right to leave you like that with more questions than answers. I am sure you would like to know why I did what I did."

"Actually, more like how. How were you able to-?"

Lyssa quickly clamped a hand down on Symon's mouth just as two young men dressed in business suits walked by talking frantically to each other with no notice of the two black-clad women sitting on the bench. Symon tried to pull her hand off her mouth, but it was held fast by an abnormally strong grip. Lyssa's stormy eyes followed the two men as they walked by, waiting for them to be out of earshot. When they could no longer be seen, she removed her hand from Symon's mouth then said with a calm voice, "Sorry. I demand solitude when we speak of such matters."

"What such matters?" asked Symon as she wiped her mouth furiously with her napkin. "What in the hell are you talking about?"

"I am talking about the connection we shared that night. How I was able to touch you deeper than anyone else before."

Lyssa turned Symon around so that they faced each other as her sandwich fell to the ground with a soft plop. Symon did not want to look into her eyes, but the storms came furious and strong, wreaking havoc in everything and nothing at the same time. She did not want to be a witness to the power the woman held, for she did believe that Lyssa held power. This woman was not normal and she knew it. But what? What was it about her that pulled her deeper into those eyes, the eyes that showed her different worlds, periods of time, a glance of when gods and goddesses walked the earth? Why was she having such thoughts now?

"Do you see?"

"Yes . . ."

Symon wanted to pull away, but soon she no longer felt her body.

"I give you an offer. Will you take it?"

"What is the offer?"

"I want to be your Muse, Symon. Take me into your mind and let me help you find what you have been searching for so long. I can make you a Voice. The one story you have now is only the first step."

"The first step . . . " Symon could no longer feel her skin.

"The first step, Symon. Will you take me as your Muse?"

Day Twelve

Perhaps, I have made a horrible mistake. After all, she is crazy, and yet, I wonder about the offer made to me; the one that I so quickly accepted. To take her on as my Muse sounds exciting, something that will benefit me greatly, I think. And yet, I wonder if I have made the right decision. Did I make the right choice? She's coming over tonight for dinner and to talk about ideas; perhaps I shall have my answer then.

The whispers are still there in my mind, increasing in intensity. Question is: do I want them gone?

Symon spent most of her day off cleaning up the apartment; she wanted it to be perfect for her guest, making sure that all was in order for her and that she would not suddenly decide that her offer was a bad idea. At every hour she would take a break with a piping hot cup of tea and a scone, relishing in her progress thus far. She had three hours to go before Lyssa arrived, but it still felt as though she had all the time in the world. In the background, Voltaire sang with dark mischief about killing all of his ex lover's lovers as she brushed the crumbs from her shirt and continued on. Every book had to be in place, every speck of dust had to be removed, and everything had to be in order for her Muse. She chuckled as she thought of that phrase: her Muse. Someone who would provide her with ideas, inspiration, insight, and perhaps a little of her own thought process. That last thought caused her to stop and stare thoughtfully at a wall. Would she even dare attempt to enter Lyssa's head? If so, what would she find there? Would she even be able to understand such a twisted individual, or would she, quite possibly, like it and never want to leave? Curiouser and curiouser, she thought as she went back to her work. Now I know how Alice felt.

Lyssa arrived right on time, just as Symon finished lighting several candles that instantly gave off the scent of patchouli in the living room. One quick knock and soon Lyssa stood in her living room with no storms and no attitude. She wore a long deep purple dress with long sleeves and her infamous boots and her hair was down for the first time. Her face held a hint of a smile as she walked towards Symon and embraced her like a sister.

"Are you ready, my dear?" she whispered in her ear, her breath scented with violets. Symon, too stunned to believe this display of softness, nodded yes. Lyssa released her and walked around the living room in search of something. Symon's eyes followed her every move, wondering what she was looking for and, for the millionth time, if she indeed made a big mistake in taking her offer.

"What I seek," said Lyssa as if she heard her question, "is a place to sit. I need to find a spot that will give us both a chance to flow with ideas without any hindrance." She then walked to the middle of the large rug on the floor and closed her eyes, breathing deeply in calmness and peace. Symon, still not knowing what to do, walked over to her and closed her eyes as well. Suddenly, Lyssa grabbed her hand . . .

Symon stood on a cliff overlooking a vast area of water. Was it a lake, an ocean, or something greater than that? A wind carried her thoughts out to a place that was too far for her own eyes, a place where she had to be, but did not know how to get there. At once, her eyesight focused and soon, she could see where she needed to go. It was a lonely rock in the middle of the water, a rock that looked to be older than the Earth itself. It gave birth to the planet, she thought as she stared at it. A faint humming could be heard coming from the rock, vibrant and full of life. She blinked and now realized that the rock was an island. The waters lapped the coast, caressing it gently like a lover with his first conquest, as she could now see a white clothed figure walking along the beach. She blinked once more and now she was on the beach, watching the white clothed figure walk up to her. She could smell violets and instantly knew that it had to be Lyssa. When the figure was only a foot away, it raised an arm and pointed one slender finger at her, not in accusation or protest, but merely pointing. The figure's head was covered so she could not see if it truly was Lyssa or not, but deep down she knew it had to be.

"You seek something grand," said the figure as it walked closer to her. Symon felt rooted to the spot, wanting to know just what she was looking for. How did it know?

"You claim to know what you truly want, and yet you take inferior routes in order to get it. You set yourself up for failure time and time again and yet you still do it to yourself. How many times must it take for you to see that the cycle is vicious?" Symon wanted to look away, but found that she could not; the figure was right. The figure had yet to reveal itself to her, but she knew it had to be Lyssa. Who else knew what lay at her innermost core?

"So," she began with false bravado, "what do I do?"

"You ask for it and it shall be given to you."

"Am I speaking to Lyssa?" The figure said nothing, but reached for its hood and pulled it away from its face. Symon gasped.

The figure was Symon. All went black.

At first, it hurt. It wasn't the kind of hurt that can be handled all day, giving it the proper respect when due, but all the while knowing that one could ignore it. No, this pain was something too real to be ignored. It was the kind of pain that could bring a king to his knees, send a strongman to weep in a corner, or give a deity a reason to kill itself. This was the pain that left someone exposed and vulnerable, raw and oozing with truth coming from every dry and bleeding crack. This was the kind of pain that stripped all of the debris away, leaving only a fraction of what was once a human, a being with thought and emotions. Reason into nothing, sanity into raw madness. This was the pain Symon felt when she tried to open her eyes. Lyssa stood above her, waiting for her to get up on her own; she would not help her in this way. Symon was curled into the foetal position on her living room floor, shaking while silent tears fell down her face.

"Open your eyes," said Lyssa in a dry tone. Symon heard her voice and wanted to, but the pain was too much for her to bear. She rocked back and forth, mewling because she could not make any other sound; she did not trust herself to be able to speak. "Open your eyes," said Lyssa again with no emotion. She crouched down so that their faces were inches apart from each other then laid Symon on her back and tried to relax her body. Symon, at first, resisted the change in the body's form, but soon gave in although she still refused to open her eyes and face the woman that was causing the pain. When Symon was laid out like a board, Lyssa began to strip, throwing her clothing all over the living room. There was no seduction involved in her action; she needed to remove her clothing for her next step. When she was completely naked, she straddled Symon's body and placed her face only inches from her own.

"If you can not open your eyes for me, then I shall have to do it myself," she said in the same flat tone as before then placed a slender hand on Symon's chest. Instantly, Symon's eyes flew open, wild and rolling around their sockets, then they finally rested on Lyssa's face. She broke out in a sweat as she tried to speak, her body giving off little shakes in the process.

"W-where-?"

"Relax, you're at home. You never left."

"But, I thought-"

"It was only a dream. Now, relax." At once, Symon's eyes closed and her body stopped shaking. Lyssa placed a hand on either side of her face and leaned in closer. When their lips barely touched, she smiled then kissed Symon. Symon's eyes flew open once more, but only in surprise. She tried to raise her arms up to embrace the other woman, but Lyssa sat on them. She struggled for a moment then relaxed her body, enjoying the sensation of kissing another woman. When they first came together, Symon did not know what to make of it; she was not interested in women. Now, however, her thoughts began to differ. Would she ever entertain the idea of being in a relationship with another woman? Lyssa's tongue, cold and slender, slipped in between Symon's lips, touching Symon's tongue, awakening in it to a new sensation. She moaned a little and arched her back slightly, but still Lyssa held her down with her own body. She fell into the kiss, not wanting it to stop. Lyssa pulled away without any warning, causing Symon to open her eyes once more in confusion.

"Lyssa, why did you stop?"

Lyssa then plunged her hand straight into Symon's chest. Symon's body began to shake as her cold alien hand snaked its way through her chest, searching for something. The woman's eyes were closed in concentration while Symon's were wide open; the other night had not been a dream. She stared with horror at Lyssa's arm moved around; she could feel the hand moving around and once again noticed that it did not hurt. On more than one occasion, she felt her hand graze against her heart, sending little ripples of a weird nauseating sensation through her body that left her within seconds.

"What . . . are you looking for?" she whispered. Lyssa did not answer; she was still lost in her concentration. Lyssa knew what she was looking for, but knew that it travelled when it knew it was trying to be found, something that it did not want to happen. "Lyssa?" she tried again.

"I am searching." The words came out in a calm tone as if the two were discussing a novel they had just read. "Something that does not wish to be found."

"What is it?"

"Something that needs to be removed." Suddenly, Symon felt her hand close around something small and hard like a ball. Lyssa's eye opened in success as she pulled her hand from her chest. Symon expected her whole hand to be covered in blood, but it came out just as clean as when it went in. In her hand was a small black round object that shook violently in her hand. Lyssa removed herself from Symon's body then stood up with no help, her eyes focused on the object in her hand. Symon, after feeling around on her chest for any signs of blood or holes, got up on shaky legs, her eyes focused on the black object as well.

"What is it?"

"Something keeping you from living up to your true potential," was all she offered as a response. She rolled the object around in her slender palm as the object gave off the scent of burnt rubber. Symon walked over to her, still not sure how to take the news that a small, black, foul-smelling object had kept her from writing. She wanted to scream.

"Why was it there?"

"Someone placed it inside of you, keeping you from ever becoming a success in whatever you did."

"But, I just published my first book-"

"You did, but you received the idea from me. I am talking about your own ideas placed on paper. You have yet to do that, correct?" Symon stared at the black object a few more minutes then sat down on her couch as a cold numbness settled into her body. Who was she kidding? Every time she tried to work on a story, or try out a new recipe, or even take up a new hobby, she always began with a burst of speed and gusto only to peter out miserably in the middle then finally giving up nowhere near the end. Although she had a good heart and intelligence to match, she was never asked to do anything serious because she would always quit the job before it was ever completed. Now, as her eyes focused on the small black item in her strange friend's hand, she knew why. She never had a chance.

"Who could have done such a thing to me?"

"Someone who wanted to see you fail, Symon."

"But, I don't know anyone who hates me that much!" she protested.

"Doesn't matter right now. What matters is that it is now out of you and you are no longer in danger." At once, Lyssa's hand tightened its grip on the object, trying to crush it. At first, the object refused to be crushed (Symon could feel the object's "emotions" in her mind), but Lyssa held on firmly, refusing to let go.

"This is for everyone who has ever thought you were a failure," she said in a calm voice although her body was tense and slightly shaking. "This is for anyone who ever wished you to fail miserably. This is especially for your parents."

"My parents?" asked Symon weakly, her eyes still focused on the object.

"Of course; they were the ones who put this object inside of you." Symon closed her eyes, allowing thoughts long buried to come up fresh and unearthed in her mind: the many times her parents made fun of her when she tried to talk to them about her love for all things Sci-Fi and Fantasy, how her mother always berated her when Symon refused to wear makeup and instead focused on her inner beauty; how her parents said in their own way that she would never amount to anything because she was not an attorney, physician, or anything else that required several degrees, how they never supported her when she made the career change from junior attorney of a small, but prosperous firm to an Library Assistant with hope of going to graduate school for her masters in Library Science, how her parents focused more on money and material items rather than the fact that her daughter was finally on the right path and that was successful with every step. Tears fell down Symon's face, her eyes still closed, as she experienced every disappointed thought her parents ever had for her and why they would never accept her no matter how many times they smiled in her face and said that they loved her no matter what.

"All of it a lie," she whispered harshly. "All of it."

"No." Lyssa now sat next to her, the black object gone from her hand. Symon opened her eyes and began looking around the living room for it. "It's no longer here," she said in a calm tone. "It has returned to its creators. "

"So, now what?"

"Well," said Lyssa as she shrugged her shoulders, "we go out and get drunk." She offered her a smile free from the storms in her eyes. Symon smiled back as if for the very first time.

The two worked every afternoon when Symon got home from work. As soon as Symon reached the door, Lyssa would be there, ready to drag her to the computer to type for two hours with no breaks. Symon, at first, was not sure if she could keep up with such a schedule, but after one day found that she could. She no longer had any lingering and detrimental doubts inside of her; she was now clean and free to live out her dreams turned reality with no qualms.

However, her thoughts always turned toward Lyssa when she was at work. Just who or what was she exactly? True, her craziness had abated somewhat, making her more and more likeable as the days wore on, but there was something about her that she could not put her finger on. Of course, she mused sarcastically, it had nothing to do with the fact that twice she was able to put her hand in her chest with no blood. No, of course not. So, what was she?

"What are you?" she asked Lyssa one day after many good days of writing. Lyssa looked up from editing her pages and offered her a weak smile in silence. This was going to be harder than she thought. "What are you? No one who is just anybody can put their hand in another person's chest. What are you?" Lyssa continued to stare at her in silence, the smile now fading from her face, but thankfully the storms did not come to her eyes. She placed the pages on the floor, her eyes watching her moves, then they refocused on her face again. Symon gulped; the storms were building up, but they still had not arrived in full force.

"Why?" asked Lyssa in a calm voice.

"I want to know who or what I am dealing with, that's all. Makes for a better relationship."

"I am your partner and your Muse. That is all you need to know." Lyssa then reached down to grab her papers, but Symon snatched them from her and put them on a side table. This was not over yet.

"Well, I want to know for my own sake. You're not human, obviously, so why don't you come clean and just tell me." Lyssa's eyes were focused on the stack of papers on the side table. Now was not the best time.

"I will answer that question another time, but for now, let me get back to work." Lyssa made another attempt to take her stack of papers, but Symon refused to be moved on this. She took the papers and laid them in her lap with her crossed arms over them.

"No, you will answer the question now!"

The storms came rolling back in full force. Suddenly, the room felt colder although her heater was on at full blast. She shivered a little, but she refused to back down on this request. After all, she had every right to know just who or what she was working with, right? Lyssa stood up in one fluid motion, closed her storm-filled eyes, and began to hum quietly. The song sounded disjointed, but Symon fell into the humming instantly, her body rocking back and forth to the rhythm. She closed her eyes.

At first, there was darkness. Symon could still hear Lyssa humming and she could still feel her body rocking back and forth. Suddenly, she saw a small pinprick of light almost too faint to even notice. She stopped rocking and instead focused on the light. It was small, but she could see it. Soon, the light grew and grew, bouncing in time to Lyssa humming. The light now became the open end of a tunnel where Symon could see several trees and a small hill in the distance. She no longer noticed that she stopped rocking and instead got up and was now walking toward the tunnel opening. Lyssa continued to hum her strange song.

The sky was a clear blue as Symon walked toward the lonely tree on the hill. Several birds flew overhead, their chirping breaking her of her reverie. She stopped walking and stared at the tree, still not realizing that she could still hear Lyssa singing.

The tree was a massive oak; Symon was still several yards from it, but she could tell that it was a majestic being full of life with roots deep. She continued her walk towards the tree, not looking back, not seeing that Lyssa now walked behind her. All Symon knew was that she had to get to the tree. When she reached the hill, she began to climb. She glanced up several times, making sure that the tree was still there and that perhaps this was all a dream. The tree still stood, its branches swaying in the light breeze that carried scents of jasmine, oranges, and dried leaves. Lyssa stood at the bottom of the hill, still singing while watching her patron climb. She would know soon enough, she thought.

Symon found the climb to be easy with little exhaustion and soon she stood at the foot of the tree. She walked up to its trunk and placed a hand on it; warmth flowed through her arm, leaving a tingling sensation that made her laugh.

"Why do you laugh?" asked a small, but strong voice. Symon quickly stopped laughing and tried to remove her hand from the rough bark, but found that her hand was now stuck to the bark. She pulled and pulled, but the hand remained fastened to the tree. She soon gave up and decided to answer the voice.

"I laughed because I am happy," she said in a matter of fact voice. "Is that OK?" The voice did not answer so Symon tried to remove it again from the bark and rather than her hand pulling free, actually sank into the bark up to her wrist. She struggled harder this time, but her hand would not move from its spot. She took a deep breath and knelt before the tree, simply because she had no other option, and laid her head against the cool bark.

"The tree is a part of me," said Lyssa's cool voice behind her. Symon, shocked to hear her voice in this strange place while she was in a compromising position, struggled to stand up, causing Lyssa to laugh. It was one of the few times when she actually sounded sane. "Don't worry about trying to get up," she said then sat down next to her perplexed friend. She laid her head against her shoulders and sighed, the scent of violets filling her senses. "This is a place I come to when I feel the need to escape."

"Are we dreaming?"

"Far from it." The way Lyssa said those words made the hairs on the back of Symon's neck rise up. She shivered then said calmly, "You never answered my question earlier. Who or what are you?" Lyssa stared ahead, her stormy eyes not truly focusing on anything, as the words filtered through her mind. How to truly answer, she thought for a brief moment then said in a (reasonably) calm tone, "I am the Goddess of Madness."

Symon laid her head against the tree's bark and her whole body slipped into the tree. She asked me and I told her.

I am not of pride.
She asked and I told her.
My tree then consumed her.
I am not of pride.
I told her.
Told her.
Told her, told her, told her, told her.
Telling me of what lies, dear one?
Dear heart, who loves me.
I am the Goddess of Knowledge, TRUE Knowledge.
Symon, with a Y and NOT an I, fell.
Down, down the hole.
I am not of lies. I hear her scream. I watch her fall.
She sees for the first time.
I can smell the sweat.
She sees me. Truly. Images. Coming.
Colours blending, her own mind not able to see—
No, she can see. Give her time.
Time for What? She is mine already.
Faster, faster, give me speed! Caressing the inner roots—
NO!
I am not going to lose her.
I will not lose her to my own.
My own.
My own, resting comfortably in her space.
Now she sees, she sees, sees, dancing across a table of blood.
Of course, the plan is different, now. Now, I am—
(screaming)
She wanted this, didn't she? She WANTED me—
To love her, love, yes, bright red in a box, a BOX!
Box with shiny paper, bow, given to a little girl who hates me.
Symon falling.
She falls.
She fell, quickly, down, down, down, down.

And landed in her bed. Symon continued to scream, even though she felt her own unmade bed under her body, even though she knew she was in her room, even when Lyssa herself walked up to her and cupped her face in her cool hands, silencing her at once and forcing her to actually look into the storms, braving the winds and rain, clouds and lightning, to see what she could truly be. Symon shuddered as the knowledge fell into place within her (now realized) locked mind. She opened the door and let Lyssa in. Feeling the walls come a-tumblin' down, Lyssa smiled.

"I am a drink of water," she murmured as their lips met.

Day Twenty

Lyssa. She still scares me terribly. A Goddess, no less. When she told me of her true self, I wanted to run screaming in the other direction, but something kept me from making such a mistake. Every day, I feel it, a little more and more and yet I still think I have a chance of redemption when it is over.

She steals my sanity in order for me to write. Every story, every poem, is wrapped in doors now wide open and revealing. I am no longer hiding from people; every story reveals more of myself than I would like to admit, but it must be done.

Every story brings me praise. Every story opens a new deal with my publishers, more money than I can stand, more attention than I think I deserve. People know my face as I walk along streets just trying to buy a cup of Earl Grey tea.

Lyssa is strange (of course!) because she is of this world and yet is not. When I ask her how long she has been here (which tends to be every day), she shrugs and smiles in that eerie, Stephen King kind of way. One time, however, while we sat during a break, drinking tea, she said , "Before Man was ever born," then resumed drinking her tea. I still don't know what to say to that.

Some modern things are beyond her understanding: she can not work a toaster at all. Every time she tries, I eat black toast. She does know the computer and the Internet, though.

She tells me that the gods and goddesses of old are still around, walking in human disguise so as to blend in with everyone. "So, why don't they come back to be deities?" I ask her.

"They are afraid of the world now. There are so many things out there now that people have become quite attached to, things that have no soul or are even alive. Who wants to believe in Aphrodite anymore? Or, Dionysus, Athena, Zeus, any of them? Why should humans believe in deities when they have their overpriced coffee drinks, obsessions with weight loss and/or gain, video games, fast cars, and dreams at a snap of their fingers?"

"So, why did you choose me? Why not some other writer?"

"Because I saw something in you that was of possible hope. I saw a seed trying to grow. I saw a fish learning to swim in concrete. You are there and not, surviving and living with no sound." I could only stare at her while she said those words to me and I still have no idea what she meant . . . and yet, I do.

I can feel it. Slowly sliding inside of me like molasses, cold and thick, priceless and dirty. It is her madness, what she is and what she is made of. I can feel it taking over, and although I am trying to fight it, I want it. Oh god, how I want it.

Symon wrote. Lyssa reviewed and examined the pages, looking for any imperfections in her words, then mailed the manuscripts off to different competitions, contests, and general publications. Symon wrote. Lyssa slid her essence inside of Symon more and more, giving her the literary nourishment she needed in order to continue while siphoning her sanity, little by little. Symon wrote. Lyssa woke her up at 5 in the morning every day, pulling her arms, slapping her face, pinching her cheeks until she woke up grunting and slightly disoriented. Lyssa never slept, but sat on the floor, watching her pupil, looking into her thoughts and seeing the possible stories underneath the layers of tissue and muscle, blood and bones. Symon wrote.

Acceptance letters came in twice a month. Lyssa poured through each and every one of them, reading them to Symon who just sat back and listened. Her mind was in a constant state of writing with scenes and dialogue revolving around in her mind. There was no room for anything else; she gave her two-week notice at the library, much to the disappointment of her co-workers who understood, but still hated to see her go. She went outside twice a day to walk around among other people while Lyssa edited her work, but soon gave it up. Every time she walked along the busy streets, she found herself wanting to scream; with Lyssa's "intervention" she could read people's darkest thoughts, thoughts that their dear ones never knew or suspected:

The man in the business suit, waiting for a taxi, who wondered what it would be like to sleep with a young boy.

The woman opening her flower business for the day who dreamt of drowning puppies in a well.

A young girl skipping rope who wondered why her father touched her as often as he did.

A couple walking hand in hand: the woman wanting to be with another woman while the man dreamt of strange coloured mushrooms growing in a field far away that only he knew about.

She wanted to scream; she could hear the thoughts of everyone who walked by her, amplified to make her deaf. She covered her ears and walked a little faster, keeping her head down, but still being able to see. She saw faces distorted, monsters pointing their fingers at her accusingly, calling her a liar and a god at the same time. She was brilliant, talented, disturbed. She saw bursts of colour all around her, some not even known to humans. She walked faster, but the words kept coming at her, shouting, loving, playful and truthful.

These were the thoughts that made her stop walking completely.

Lyssa stood in the kitchen, drinking an extremely hot cup of Earl Grey tea, watching her writer pupil type away in the next room. Her eyes glanced to ten different things within a second then focused back on Symon, her back hunched over her desk as the words poured from her, sometimes too fast for her to even write down. Lyssa could see her aura, a deep purple, the colour of madness, slowly taking over her original blue. For a moment, she hesitated; was this right? She placed the cup on the counter and walked into the living room then lightly placed a hand on Symon's shoulder.

"Symon." Symon typed, not hearing her, caught up in her words vomiting from her mind. Lyssa shook her shoulder harder as she called her name again. Symon's fingers stopped typing as she turned around slowly to face the source of her disturbance.

"What?"

"Symon, I . . .we need to talk." Symon stared at her with bright eyes that flashed something Lyssa was not too entirely sure of. "Come. Sit with me on the couch." Reluctantly, she got up from her chair by the computer and sat down next to her, but her eyes glanced longingly at the computer and the flashing cursor, ready to take in more of her words. She could even hear it talking to her, a soft sibilant whisper like a child, begging her to come back. She made as if to get up, but Lyssa placed a steel like grip on her shoulder and forced her to sit down again. She turned Symon's face towards her own and held it there. Symon's eyes were still slightly glassy, but soon she came back fully. Lyssa allowed a smile to appear on her face.

"I think you need to stop for a while. The writing, I mean." Symon's eyes went wide at her request. Wasn't she the one who wanted this for her?

"Why?" she asked while trying to hold herself back from shaking her.

"Because. . .you need a break. That's all."

"But this is what you wanted, isn't it?" Symon's voice had taken a slight condescending tone. "After all, you were the one who told me that I needed this and you, right?" Lyssa felt the sting behind the words and wanted to slap her.

"Yes I did-"

"So why all of a sudden do you want me to take a break? Now that I am finally getting my name out there for the literary world to see. Why now, Lyssa, hmm?" Symon stood up too fast for Lyssa to pull her down. Her eyes were glassy once more as she continued her rant. "Finally, finally, I am where I want to be and NOW you want to take it away from me, Lyssa? Why now? Why? WHY?" Lyssa stared at her creation and wanted to scream, but held her tongue. "I wanted to be a writer and now . . . well now I have no idea what I am now. I can read people's minds, see their darkest thoughts! I can see colours I never knew existed!" She sat down again and gripped Lyssa's shoulders tightly, staring into her eyes that, surprisingly, held no storms. "I think I am going mad," she whispered. Lyssa nodded her head yes, breaking Symon's rant immediately and calming her down. She held her head and squeezed it like a ripe melon while moaning. "I am going mad," she moaned over and over again while Lyssa placed a hand on her shoulder, trying to comfort her, but not too much.

"You wanted this." Tears of every colour fell down Symon's face.

Day

I am still here.
I am still here, waiting.
I gave it away. I want it back.
Lyssa knows.
I can see. I want it now.
I am here.
I am still waiting for her to take it back.
I no longer know of the light.
I am still here.
This is my own.
This
This . . . .

Tales from a Goth Librarian

I can finally see, see what it means.

I found you when you were right on the edge of where you needed to be. I found you when you constantly doubted yourself with everything, even what kind of toilet paper to buy. I saw a light in you that was about to go out, a light that needed to be brighter than ever. I know why you mistrusted yourself, why you thought you could not do anything right, and I removed it from you. Now that you are where you needed to be, now you feel the need to question my doings and the reason behind them. Why? You knew. You knew who I was and am and now you feel the need to question me. Do you think you are the only person I have assisted? Why do you think that those of the creative nature go insane one way or another? They requested my help, to help them see beyond normal, and I give it to them without any sugar coating. And yes, some of them were like you, asking me why they were the way they were. I used to laugh in their faces, but now. . . Madness. Why does the world think of it to be such a curse? Mortals think of madness to be detrimental and crippling, but to me of madness itself, it leads to a path beyond everything anyone could ever dream of. Colours so bright it hurts and yet you still want to see. Ideas and thoughts so powerful that you wonder why no one else ever thought of it. I gave it to them out of love and concern and not out of darkness and curses. So it is with you and yet not. You are my special, the one beyond all others. It is because of this that I will do what I have never done before: I will give you a choice. Stay or leave. If you stay, you will be influential beyond all human understanding and comprehension. If you stay, you will See. If you leave, you will be sane and without me. I give you the choice. Choose.

(decide)

It hurts from time to time, but Lyssa helps her with the pain, letting her know that her doors are opening.

She hears everything around her and laughs at no one.

People follow her around, clutching their copies of her books to their chests as tears stream down their faces. They want to see, but know they can not, but through her books, they know of something else.

The other deities see Lyssa's disciple and wonder.

When she walks outside, she holds her head high and looks at people, right into their eyes. They see her ocular storms and quickly look away, but they feel as though they were just given a glimpse into a world that will never be theirs. They see her and they know. Lyssa walks next to her and smiles.

Somewhere deep inside of her, she is screaming.

Cover Her with Violets

When she was a child, Jane would talk to herself.

She had a handful of friends, kids that occasionally came by her grandparents' home to play with her and her toys or ride their bikes with her down the quiet streets of the neighbourhood. Even though she had fun with them, she did not care to be around them so much simply because she liked her alone time. During her moments of being alone, she would talk to herself, imagining that she spoke with a person from another country or even another world. Her imagination was far better than actual people, she thought. These figments could not disappoint her and she could not disappoint them; a sea elf would talk to her about the mysteries of underwater life, or a deity would stop in for the night to converse with the lonely yet fascinating girl.

She would talk to them about school, recently read books, or her thoughts about the world around her. She, at first, limited her conversations to just her bedroom, but soon felt the need to talk long walks while she talked. She packed a small bag with snacks and a book and would head out after school to a secluded place not too far from her grandparents' home to relax and talk to those who truly understood her.

Aside from talking to herself, she would also spend her free time reading books of every subject. She was a voracious reader, a trait that would follow her into adulthood. Every Friday, her mother would take her to the library to check out five books, only to finish reading them by Wednesday. To her, books were free vacations that could be repeated as many times as the person desired. Books never left her for someone cooler, they never let her down, just like her imaginary friends. As she grew older, however, her barrage of imaginary friends dwindled down to one, a being that had no gender specifics, but listened intently to her and gave her silent advice when she needed it.

Her life while growing up was a normal life; a mother who wanted the best for her even when it meant having to show "tough love", a stepfather who loved her dearly in his own down to earth way, a small circle of friends that she could rely upon when she needed the support, and her imaginary friend that she refused to fade out. The friend stayed with her throughout her grade school life, then high school, to college and beyond without a concern, for it knew that she needed it just as much as it needed her. It was special because it was real to her, even if no one else could see it. She knew it was real because it believed in her and that was all that mattered.

Jane looked up from her paper to face her classmates, ready to gage their reactions to her words. One person was asleep and drooling on their notebook, but the rest stared back with wide eyes of appreciation, letting her know that she had done well with the latest writing assignment. Suddenly, they clapped, congratulating her for a job well done. Jane blushed as she smiled at them while neatly folding her paper, relieved that she completed this assignment on time; tonight called for a celebration of veggie pizza with a good merlot and several movies at home. She walked to her seat with her paper as her classmates continued to congratulate her for a job well done.

One person in the room, however, did not add his own support for he was too busy still savouring her words spoken to them, well, him, actually. He wanted to close his eyes and sigh with delight; everything she wrote was for him, but she did not know that. His heart began to beat rapidly, an aftershock of listening to her read which occurred every time she spoke to him. He loved her, worshipped her, and wanted her all to himself, but knew that she would never consider him. She was a genius, just like him, and yet no one told her of this. Perhaps it should be my job to let her know, he thought, before someone tells her otherwise. Would she believe him? Would she understand just how much she meant to him? He had to act fast and he would not be denied.

"Ms. Collier, would you mind giving me your paper before it turns into an origami nightmare?" Jane, talking to one of her classmates, snapped her head to the source of that slightly cold voice and groaned inwardly. Dr. Jason Phillips stood to the left side of the room, his body relaxed and leaning against one of the oversized windows that revealed yet another beautiful fall morning, ready to be enjoyed by the students in the classroom. He was tall with a healthy pale complexion and on the lean side as a result of being a runner for many years. He always wore the same outfit: black Doc Marten shoes that were slightly scuffed up, black slacks crisply pressed with a long sleeve white oxford shirt with the sleeves rolled up twice, and a colourful tie. His jet-black hair had some grey mixed in and locks of it fell in his eyes, giving him the look of a naughty schoolboy. He wore black-rimmed glasses that framed eyes that were too blue to be real, making him the object of crushes held by some of his students. Whenever he spoke, his thick London accent that he still had even after living in the U.S for several years shone through every word. Everything he said took a higher purpose merely because of his accent, a fact that he used to his own advantage. He used his voice purposely to get his way on matters and people gave it to him without a complaint. The English department thought of him as someone who could do no wrong and he knew it, but he still kept a sense of humility about him; too much cockiness and he would be back in England, teaching for a much lower pay with no hope of ever going tenure. He was adored in the United States.

Jane, however, saw him quite differently. She saw him as a bastard who had nothing better to do than make her life a living nightmare. Ever since she began graduate school to obtain a MA in English Literature, he was the constant thorn in her side. Every class he taught that she took was painful; he singled her out on many occasions to berate her work. He seemed to expect more from her and that she was wasting his time, but she knew she could not avoid him; he taught most of the classes that she needed and going to the board was not an option. He hated her, pure and simple. For two years, she lived with this fact and knew that she was powerless against him.

"Jane, may I please have your work?" he said with a slight frosty tone. "I do need that, if you please." Jane almost stumbled as she got up from her desk and walked over to him to hand in her assignment. The class knew of his treatment towards her and all eyes were glued to the two of them as he snatched her paper from her hands. "You've done your assignment, Ms. Collier, but of course, well. . ." He let the statement finish itself; her work was not good once again. Jane's shoulders slumped in defeat as she walked back to her desk; a couple of her classmates noticed she had tears in her eyes. She was a delight in all of her other classes, Dean's List every semester, and yet he treated her like dirt. Dr. Phillips, now smiling, moved from his spot of leisure and walked to the podium. "Well," he said in a slightly nice tone, "I must say that I am pleased with the majority of your papers for this assignment. It was a pleasure to read most of your work." Jane sank lower in her seat in embarrassment; she knew he was not pleased by her work and actually had the gall to say it. "So, remember: your next assignment is due in three weeks. If you forgot what the topic was, just e-mail me and I will provide the question again." As the end of class finally arrived, the students began to pack up their belongings to head to their next destination while Jane packed up her messenger bag with burning cheeks of shame. How could he be such an asshole to her?

"Ms. Collier, if you please." Jane looked up and saw Dr. Phillips seated at the desk, staring intently at her. She sighed then sat down again, watching her classmates leave the room while a few of them glanced back at her in confusion; whatever was about to happen would be heard about later in the day. When the last student closed the door, Jane gulped nervously, causing Dr. Phillips to actually laugh. "Jane, do you know why I come down on you so harshly? Do you have any idea what I think of you?" he said in a soft tone with a hint of steel underneath.

"I know that you hate me." Jane, not really sure what he wanted from her, decided to give him the truth, no matter what. If it came down to worse case scenario, she would transfer to another school. She had had enough.

"I don't hate you, Jane, but I feel that, well, I have been unfair to you." Jane sat up straighter in her chair; he actually admitted that he was wrong? Now she was very interested in what he had to say. "In my 25 years of teaching, I have come across a couple of students who are bright lights in the world of academia, bright lights that I personally assist in molding and shaping. You are different. You are by far one of the best students I have ever had in my teaching career and yet you give me work that is beneath you. I know you are far beyond what you give to me. I have heard from other professors about you and your work. What you give me, well. . . " Jane could not believe what he said; he actually admired her? She took his abuse with no complaint for years, only now realizing that he appreciated her. She smiled with relief, but it soon turned into a frown. What was the catch?

"Dr. Phillips, you've given me nothing, but hell these past couple of years. I have been afraid of you, thinking that you disliked me intensely. Now, I find out that you appreciate me and my work, right? Did I hear that correctly?" She knew she sounded sarcastic, but she could not help it; this was beyond a simple explanation. "I'm sorry, but I just can't take your oh so simple words to take away what I had to endure under your teaching for the past two years."

"Jane, you have every right to hate me for what I did to you. All I can say is that I am sorry."

Jane wanted to slap him across the face, but knew that it would get her nowhere. This was not the time to lower herself to the level of whiny airhead bitch. She closed her eyes for a moment as her mind relayed to all of the times that he insulted her, demeaned her in front of other students, and the like. She wanted to finally release her body from their poisoned hooks, but found that she could not. It was her pain that motivated her to do her absolute best, regardless if he acknowledged it or not. However, today was different. She had been looking forward to the words he just spoke to her, but somehow, it was not what she had expected. She shook her head in confusion then stared into the slightly amused eyes of Dr. Phillips.

"You know what, Dr. Phillips?," she said, accenting his name with a heavy dose of sarcasm, "for some reason, I just don't believe you. Not at all. You expect me to just forget everything you ever put me through, everything I allowed myself to endure from you? This . . . apology," she said while waving her hands in the air, "is not going to wipe the slate clean." She got up and grabbed her messenger bag, not noticing the absurdly shocked look on his face, as she made for the door.

"You're right, Ms. Collier, I had no right to be so mean to you and I do apologize profusely," he said as he got up from his desk, stopping her from walking out. "But I want to, as you put it, wipe the slate clean." Jane lowered her bag to the floor and stared at him, still not completely trusting him, but curious to know what more he had to say. "I want you to forget what I put you through the past two years. I want you to understand just how much I admire you and your work. You are one hell of a student and perhaps my methods of trying to better yourself were wrong and ill prepared. However, as you know, I am working on the Shakespeare research for the yearly review. I need an assistant and I can think of no one better for the job than you. Consider this as my way of trying desperately to remove the scarlet letter from your chest, Hester."

He knew one of her favourite books was <u>The Scarlet Letter</u> so he felt propelled to make a reference to it, no matter how cheesy it might have sounded coming from him. He looked into her eyes, gauging her reaction to what he had said and instead received a blank slate. He felt as though he needed to open his mouth and put his foot inside. He ran his slender hands through his hair nervously; she was the only person he had considered for the position. If she refused, he had to come up with someone else for the job and that was the last thing he had on his mind.

Jane did not make a move, but inside she was screaming with joy. To be an assistant to a professor on a project was a dream come true. She wanted to laugh while watching him squirm in trying to make amends for how he had treated her and, in some deep dark place inside of her, she felt sorry for him. Sometimes, in holding onto the past, one could be oblivious to what the present and the future had to offer, thereby allowing wonderful moments, learning lessons, and just plain fun slip right by. Today was not going to be one of those days. She allowed a smile, letting Dr. Phillips know she was interested. He smiled back and continued with, "You'll be paid, of course, plus we will go to London, my home, for several weeks for more research. Can you come by tonight to my home so we can work out the details?" Jane said nothing, but nodded her head; she was simply too stunned to say anything at this moment. Her world just flipped.

"So, you meant to tell me that after all of those times when he treated you so badly that NOW he wants you to be his assistant?" Paul, one of her best friends and schoolmates, and Jane sat in their favourite seat at Java Bean. She said nothing to his question, but sipped on her vanilla latte; should she have said no to his offer, she wondered. Was it all some horribly crafted joke on her part? Paul stared at her, waiting for an answer, but replied to his own question without even acknowledging her presence. "I don't buy it, not at all. If I were you, I would go to the board and ask if this is the real deal or not, understand?" He snapped his fingers for emphasis, causing Jane to snicker. Paul, on first impression, looked like a linebacker for a professional football team, with chocolate brown skin rippling over many muscles. He, too, was working towards his MA in English Literature, but had hopes of also working towards his PhD to teach on a university level. However, once he opened his mouth, one knew right then and there that he was a raging queen. He squealed when a shoe store had a sale, delighted in wearing tight shirts that showed off his muscles, and was completely in love with Roger, his very opposite, but still loving partner of ten years.

"He told me why he acted so rudely around me-"

"But that should not be the band-aid to cover up how you felt, honey. Do I even need to remind you about the many nights you came over to our home crying and chain smoking, feeling sorry for yourself, about how you hated yourself and how-"

Jane held up a hand to indicate that he should stop before they began to fight. She knew how she felt during that time and now was not the best time to bring up the past; as far as she was concerned, she left the past in the classroom. Paul shrugged his shoulders and took a long sip of his caramel cappuccino.

"I think it meant a lot for him to consider me for the position. I know I do; one hell of a way to begin the weekend, huh?" She looked into the still disbelieving eyes of Paul then said in a soft tone, "I can't keep holding on to my baggage, Paul. You know that. Look, my parents are coming down on me hard this semester. I can't afford to fuck up now. You know that."

"Why? You have a 3.9 average right now. You're the golden child in our class."

"They know all that and they are happy, but they know about Dr. Phillips. You know my parents; they think I am responsible for his attitude towards me."

"Even when you told them your side of the story? Even when you told them of how much of a bastard he was to you?"

"Like I said, they are my parents. Sometimes it can be a blessing or a curse. Sometimes, having them in my life is more than that."

"Well, now you can tell them that he thinks very highly of you. That'll make their day and perhaps get off your ass in trying to make you reach sainthood," he said sarcastically that Jane quickly picked up, causing her to smile. She smacked her lips once, tasting the chemicals in the deep purple lipstick on her lips, then sipped from her latte, now suddenly deep in thought.

"What do you think? Should I tell Dr. Phillips no?"

"Hell no, are you crazy?"

'Wait, I thought you were against me taking the position?"

"That was a different me five minutes ago. Now I'm telling you to take the job and do what you need to do, understand?" He snapped his fingers to emphasize his point, making Jane cough while laughing.

My beautiful goddess, he thinks while sitting on his couch. All of the lights are off, creating such a perfect blend of darkness, giving him time to think about her and only her. The darkness allows him to think clearly with no room for any digression. I wanted to talk to you, really talk to you today. I wanted to tell you that I am here for you, that I love you. He frowned; will she accept my love for her when I tell her? I have to tell her, but how? Should I take her out on a date? Maybe symbols are better; roses delivered to her apartment? Me dressed in a black suit, ready to take you out, or a vanilla latte? She seems to like those all of the time. He has watched her before, spying on her activities any chance he can get. Why does she sometimes sit in shadowed corners, crying and smoking cigarette after cigarette? His hands itch; he wants to touch her skin, softly, lovingly, making her know that she is loved by someone. When?

Jane walked through the quiet neighbourhood, searching for Dr. Phillips' address. The sun was beginning to set, colouring the sky with purples and blues, as a slightly chilly breeze caressed her cheeks. She giggled at the touch, smiling like a child as she walked along. Then, without any thought, she stopped on the sidewalk, and not caring if anyone saw her, raised her arms to the sky and closed her eyes, allowing herself to be in the moment. It was this moment, right now, that meant everything. She felt connected to a thought of consciousness streaming through her like a live wire. No matter what, she thought as she lowered her arms and continued walking, this is my time.

Soon, she reached his bungalow home and walked up the driveway, careful not to touch his BMW mini that was parked outside. She rang the doorbell and he opened the door, grinning from ear to ear as he let her in and closed the door behind them. Once inside, he gave her a tour of his home with pride. He lived modestly in colour and design with bookshelves packed with books, papers, and knickknacks. There was no sign of a significant other, cementing the fact that Dr. Phillips lived the life of a lonely, but clean bachelor. He wore relaxed jeans with a white oxford shirt and no shoes, giving him the look of a hipster man who had just returned from a poetry reading.

"I have some documents that I think you might want to read now," he said as he led her to the living room. Papers and books covered the coffee table while some books lay on the floor around the couch. Jane laid her bag on the floor and made herself comfortable on the floor while picking up a group of papers to read. Jason walked into the kitchen to get something to drink for them and when he returned, he sat down behind her on the couch.

"What I hope to do," he said as he tried to organize some of the papers in his lap, "is to prove that Shakespeare was indeed the true author of the plays and sonnets. So many people have claimed that Shakespeare did not exist, or if he did, was in fact someone else. As you can see here-"

He stopped when he noticed Jane trying to rub her shoulder while grimacing. He set the papers down and said in a softer tone, "Are you OK?"

"I have tight shoulders," she said, still trying to massage herself, "and I get knots in them all the time. I'm always tense."

"Come up here and let me see what I can do." Jane moved herself to the couch and allowed Dr. Phillips to massage her, ignoring how this situation might have looked to an outsider. She was in pain and he was offering a release from that pain. Instantly, the relief came, as his hands worked out every kink and knot in her shoulders. "I'm a licensed massage therapist." He located a rather large knot and began to work harder, causing Jane to groan loudly then giggle.

"Sorry."

"No problem. Like I said, I am used to tight people like you." He worked her shoulders harder, grunting with the effort. "My god, are you ever relaxed? It's like trying to massage concrete."

"I'm relaxed only when I'm drunk," she joked, making him laugh as well, a sound she had never heard from him towards her. She sighed deeply, releasing a breath that felt old and musty inside of her while Dr. Phillips continued working on her shoulders and neck. His hands felt like cool putty, she thought, and then closed her eyes as he moved closer behind her to work out a tough spot in her neck. She could feel his thighs tighten against hers as a result of some emotion she did not know and was not made aware of. All she focused on was his hands.

Suddenly, she felt his lips brush against the back of her neck, causing her eyes to snap open in surprise. He pulled away for a brief moment, feeling her body stiffen, not wanting to scare her away. He coughed, making a noise to break the silence as he placed his hands on his thighs, but made no move to slide away from behind her.

"Are you OK?"

"Fine, but did you just-"

He then leaned forward again and brushed her neck with his lips, allowing the tip of his tongue to taste her skin, as his arms wrapped around her chest and pulled her even closer to him, exposing her neck for his entire mouth to explore. She felt his wet and soft lips slide carefully on her neck, giving it little nips with his teeth every so often. He could taste her perfume on his lips, the one scent she always wore no matter the season; it was a special blend of honeysuckle and jasmine that filled his nostrils every time she walked by him in class. He had to know what it tasted like on her skin. His hands wanted to touch every part of her body, finally fulfilling his aching dream that cost him sleep at nights, but instead stopped and removed himself from her back.

Jane kept her eyes focused on the wall, trying hard not to allow herself to give in to the rush of emotions she felt when his lips first brushed against her skin. Her emotional protective wall was slowly coming down and she had to act fast in trying to get it back up. She stiffened then pulled herself out of his grasp, standing up and walking over to the other side of the room, her eyes never leaving his searching face. She touched the back of her neck as if she was struck and asked in a whisper, "Why did you do that?" as he too got up and walked over to her.

"Was it wrong?"

Jane wanted to leave. He took a step closer to her, his arms out and pleading. "Can I hold you for a moment?" Jane shook her head no and made as if to leave, but he blocked her and wrapped his arms around her. "Don't fight me," he whispered as he pushed her against the wall and lowered his face to hers, their lips meeting for the first time. She could taste his lime lip balm as well as her own perfume as his soft lips covered her own. She did not pull away, but fell into those lips with her own desire. The wall was now down and she hated herself for it while falling into his kiss even more so.

One of his hands slipped under her shirt and began to fondle her breasts as they kissed, the hand tugging on her bra, wanting to release them from the contraption. His lips moved from hers and slid down the side of her neck, giving it little bits and licks along the way then back up to her ear. She could feel his erection bulging through his jeans, pressing insistently against her, wanting to be inside of her. He lifted her skirt and stroked her panties, feeling her warm wetness. He slipped a finger through the side and found her sex wet and extremely warm, ready for his touch. He slid his finger inside of her, causing her to gasp and him to moan softly in her ear. She reached for his jeans and began to pull on the zipper as his finger moved faster and faster. Suddenly, she began to feel sick inside as the wall rose up once more; this was wrong, no matter how good it felt. This was wrong. Her body stiffened and she removed her hands from his jeans, letting them fall loosely down either side of her body.

"Do you want me to stop?" he whispered while sucking on her earlobe. For a moment, she could not answer him. What would he do if she told him, yes, get your filthy hands off me, you sick bastard. Even though she was 33, an adult by society's standards, he was 43 and her professor. And yet. . . Her body turned to stone; the walls were up and nothing could get them back down. He stopped sucking on her earlobe to look at her straight in the eye, trying his best to read her and if what he had done was wrong. He ran a hand through his hair then stroked her lips with his other hand. Even after kissing her, her lips still felt soft and inviting. He wanted those lips again, but this time all over his body. He leaned closer to her so that their lips were barely touching each other. Jane turned her head, giving his lips a taste of her ear once more. He sighed in her ear in slight frustration; this was not what he wanted. For some reason, he thought she was going to fall into arms and love him just as passionately as he loved her. He did not factor into the equation of what she used to think of him and how he treated her.

He stopped and pulled away from her, his hair falling into his sad eyes. He could tell she was scared. "I'm sorry, I thought . . . . Jane. Forgive me." He walked away from her and sat back down on the couch to pick up reading his pile of documents. Jane leaned against the wall, not sure what to do. He would not look up at her for fear of whatever she was feeling; it was a bold attempt after all.

"Dr. Phillips." He looked up with an expectant look. Her eyes wandered for a bit around the room then rested once more on his face. "Why did you do that?"

"Because I like you, Jane."

"Is that why you asked me to come over tonight?"

"No. I do need your help on my project, but. . ." There was silence, but both stared at each other, not really knowing what to do next.

"I don't know if I should go or not."

"Do you want to?" He got up once more, papers spilling all over his bare feet, but he did not make a move towards her. It was too soon to make another move right now.

"I don't know."

"Come back to the couch, then." He held out a hand, olive branch for this moment that she gratefully took because she had nothing else to hold on to during this moment. She walked over and took his hand in hers as she allowed him to embrace her once more. She could feel his body trembling against her and wanted to tell him that it was going to be OK, but knew that it would have been a lie. "You are beautiful," he sighed as he buried his face in her neck, resuming his kisses. He then sat her down on the couch then walked over to his CD player and turned it on. Instantly the sounds of Vivaldi could be heard throughout the entire home. He turned back to face her and began to take off his clothes while Jane watched him. She felt numb; a part of her wanted to run from this place and yet another part wanted him to undress just for her. No one had ever shown her this much attraction, not even the men in her past. Each one of them pursued her for their own selfish reasons, but no one had ever pursued her because they thought her to be beautiful. This was new to her and she was not sure how to take it. Was it a joke? Was it because he was single and desperate? Had he ever done this before? Did it even matter?

When he was down to his boxers, he walked back to the couch and sat down next to her. Dr. Phillips took her hand in his and began to stroke it while his eyes were fixed on it. He could not face those eyes right now, not with what he had to tell her.

"I want to make love to you tonight," he said with a soft voice, eyes still lowered while his hand continued to stroke hers. She could smell her own musk scent emanating from him, causing her to feel slightly giddy.

"Dr. Phillips-"

"Jason, please."

"Jason, you're my professor. I can't do that with you." He stopped stroking her hand and looked into her eyes with defeat and longing.

"Understood." She pulled her hand away from his and got up, leaving him still on the couch, his shoulders slumped and his face worn. Once she had her bag, she walked to the door and grabbed the knob, making as if to open it and walk out for good, but instead stood there, facing the door, still not sure what to do. Jason faced away from her, angry with himself for pushing such an idea on her. How could he have been so stupid? Vivaldi continued to play, but neither one in the room noticed it. Just then, Jason got up and walked over to the CD player to turn it off. She walked up to him and pulled his hand away from the player.

"I like Vivaldi," she said. "It was a nice touch." He refused to look at her and, pulling his hand away from hers, turned the CD off then sat back down on the couch, still not looking at her in the face. Now she felt like an ass, but she was not sure if this was something that she wanted to pursue; once down the rabbit hole, you can't go back.

"Jason." She still stood by the CD player.

"What?"

"Can you at least look at me in the face? Don't treat me like this." Jason turned to face her and she realized he was crying.

"Are you happy now?" he said as two tears slid down his cheek. "I wanted to make this night special for us and instead I've ruined it. I was stupid to assume that you felt anything for me. I should have just kept my feelings to myself." Jane said nothing, but let herself out of the house, feeling too heavy with her own emotions to do or say anything in response to his defeating words. She needed to breathe, but lacked the strength to do so.

As she walked back home, her mind repeated the events, leaving her to wonder if she made the right choice in leaving him there. It was a nice touch to play Vivaldi while they made love. How did he know that she adored Vivaldi? Once again, no one knew that she adored classical music; all people ever saw was a highly intelligent black woman who dressed as though she lived in the 1860s, Steampunk to the extreme. No one ever tried to go beyond her looks and her cerebral humour, wanting to either fuck her and walk away or just walk away. No one had ever tried to get to know her and for him to play Vivaldi for her was something that went beyond all comprehension. She stopped walking and turned to face his home. The lights were still on.

Jason picked up his clothing from the floor and threw it all in the laundry room. All he wanted to do was get in the bed with a several shots of gin and call it a ruined night. He had failed in trying to obtain an assistant as well as a potential lover. Since being in the States for ten years, he refused to date any American women, claiming them to be too wild and loose for his tastes then changing his whole concept of them once he met Jane. She was unlike any woman he had ever met which was why he knew he did not have a chance in hell with her. She was beyond his league and she had no idea.

True, she did dress as though she came from a Dickens novel, but in blacks, reds, whites, and purples, but she was amazing. Sometimes, while the class spent some of their time reading or working on their papers, he would just stare at her, wanting to touch her and hold her because she looked as though she needed it. He never saw her with any male friends except for her rather large and muscular queer friend. She seemed to be in her own little world and was completely content with that draw of a straw. He hung his head low between his shoulders, wanting now more than ever to get drunk and go to sleep in a gin-filled dream.

Just then, someone knocked on the door. He slipped on pajama pants and a shirt and walked over to the door. He knew who it was before he even reached the door, but decided to play along with it anyway. She was scared and had every right to be that way.

"Who is it?"

"It's Jane." Without another word, he opened the door and let her in. She stood in the doorway, clutching her messenger bag strap, with a look of uncertainty.

"Why did you come back?" His chest began to hurt.

"How did you know that I adored Vivaldi?" He chuckled at the question while relieving his inner tension; she came back to ask him that?

"He's one of my favorite composers so I figured it would be nice and fitting to play him tonight. I had no idea you liked him as well."

"You had to have known. No one else does aside from Paul and I know he does not run around and tell people about me. I do enough of that on my own, I guess." She fidgeted with her clothing; the tension was at an unbearable level for both of them. "Look, that's all I wanted to say, um, yeah."

"Would. . .you like to come in again?" Jane walked in with no hesitation and he closed the door behind them, locking it with certainty. Jane sat down on the couch and took the glass of water he had given her before and took a long sip. Her throat was completely parched. Jason leaned against the wall and crossed his arms, wondering about the next chain of events and whether it would be good for both.

"So, why did you really come back?"

"I told you; I wanted to know if you knew I adored Vivaldi."

"Well, we've answered that question. Next?"

"Did I come back at a bad time?"

"Oh, I don't know, perhaps you did. I mean, after all, you did refuse me earlier."

"I did not refuse you!"

"And what happened, Jane, hmmm? I told you what I wanted and you walked away. That sounds a bit like a refusal to me. So, why did you come back? It's couldn't have been for the stimulating conversation." Jane grabbed her bag in fury and stood up.

"You bastard," she whispered as she made to leave yet again, but Jason blocked her and held her tightly, making her drop her bag. He wanted her to face him, wanted her to actually look into something that she was about to throw away all in the name of pride.

"Why did you come back?" he asked in a loud voice. "Why did you?" Jane did not want to look at him, but it was hard not to; she did not want to answer him and she did not want to hear what she wanted to tell him.

"Because-"

"Because why?" Jane leaned forward and kissed him before he could argue any further, releasing his grip and turning it into an embrace. Slow at first, increasing in intensity, the two were soon in his bedroom with the door closing behind them as the crickets chirped outside, welcoming the night once more.

Hours later, the two lay side by side naked on his bed, both fully awake and conscious as to what had happened between them. Jane rolled away from him and closed her eyes for a moment, trying to replay all of their previous actions, wondering for the millionth time if she did the right thing by sleeping with Dr. Phillips. When she opened them again, she saw her imaginary friend sitting on the floor, staring at her with no emotion. It was a translucent being of neither sex with long brown hair, wearing a long purple robe. She wanted to talk to it, but knew that now was not the best time to do so. It knew as well and sat on the floor, watching the play progress between the two.

Jason lay on his back, staring at the ceiling, with a smile on his face. He was happy for the first time in ten years. He rolled over to Jane and draped an arm over her stomach, sighing as he did so. His breath smelled of her sex: overripe salty mangoes.

"Jane?"

"Yes?"

"Do you hate me for-"

"No." He snuggled closer to her, his semi limp penis grazing her back.

"I enjoyed it. Did you?"

"Yes, I did." She could feel warmth deep inside of her wanting to come up again. She arched her back, sliding her, butt against his penis, giving him the signal that all was OK. That stroke caused him to become erect again instantly. He found one of her nipples and began tugging at it. She then rolled over to face him and began to stroke his erect penis, but he removed her hand and slid himself inside of her, continuing with their lovemaking. Her imaginary friend watched with detachment.

She awoke at 5 in the morning thirsty. The two had been asleep for several hours after their last moment. She rolled over and saw that her imaginary friend was gone. She wanted to talk to it, but knew that she would have plenty of time once she returned home, but for now she wanted a glass of water. She got up and crept out of the bedroom, careful not to disturb him, and walked into the semi dark living room to grab her glass of water. The central heater hummed white noise, almost lulling her back into sleep, but she wanted her water first. She sat on the couch and drank greedily from the glass, parched and almost dehydrated.

"Are you OK?" Jane turned around and saw Jason in the doorway, naked, rubbing his eyes like a child. "I reached for you, but you weren't there."

"Just thirsty." She raised her up her glass.

"Is mine still there?" He walked over to the couch and Jane handed his glass to him. He drained it in one sip then burped, causing Jane to laugh.

"Glad to know I can make you laugh," he said as he returned the glass to her. She placed both glasses on the table then walked back into the bedroom with him following.

Jason woke up at 9 and smiled again. The windows were full of Autumn sunlight; hazy, but still beautiful. The windows rattled with a cool breeze that blew through the trees and bushes. He stretched then glanced over at Jane, who was still asleep. He leaned over and kissed her on the cheek, awakening her instantly. She blinked sleepily then smiled when her eyes met his.

"Good morning."

"Good morning."

"Hungry? I make killer blueberry pancakes." He leaned over to kiss her again and she welcomed it in kind. When he pulled away sometime later, he got up and put on his pajama pants and shirt then walked into the kitchen to begin breakfast, leaving Jane to her thoughts. She rolled around on his bed, the scents of their lovemaking sessions permeating her senses, flashes of last night coming back to her. She walked into the living room and put her clothes on then joined Jason in the kitchen.

He was whistling God Save the Queen while flipping pancakes on his electric griddle, his back turned to her. She sat down at the table and waited for him to realize that she had entered the room. When he finally turned around and saw her, he grinned and waved his spatula at her.

"I hope you like them slightly crispy," he said.

The two ate in silence with the occasional grin at one another, neither one really sure of what to say. Was this the infamous day after awkward moment when the people who were so vocal during sex had nothing to say to one another afterwards? He said things to me, she thought while she ate. He thought I was beautiful, telling me that over and over again. Should I be ashamed of myself giving in last night? It had been a long time since . . .

Jason wanted to say something to her, something to let her know that he was glad it happened. He, too, had been without sex and comfort from another human being for such a long time that he clung to whatever she had to offer him at any level. He desperately needed what she had, no matter the shape of it. He set his fork down on his empty plate and reached for her hand. He needed to touch her right now for his own sake. Jane saw his hand reach for hers and she dropped her fork and took his hand, glad that he made the first move rather than leave it up to her.

"I am glad we did what we did," he said, tightening his grip momentarily. "There are so many things I want to tell you, Jane. Do you have anything planned today?"

"No."

"Good. Spend time with me today, if you don't mind." He released her hand then took up their plates to the sink. Jane got up from her chair and walked over to Jason, wrapping her arms around his midsection while she leaned her head against his back. He stopped washing dishes and placed his wet soapy hands on top of hers. It was going to be OK.

For weeks, he had been stalking her, waiting for the right moment to announce his presence to her. However, he did not plan on him making the first move. He saw her go into Dr. Phillips' house the other night then leave then come back. For a moment, he wondered if she was going to come outside again, but then noticed the lights go off in his house. What were they doing now? Why did she leave then come back? What was it? He closed his eyes and let his terrible imagination do its job. He pictured the two of them, talking then undressing, getting into his bed, him kissing her tenderly...he began to hyperventilate. He had to do something. He wanted to know about her as well.

He wanted to cry and smash things in response to what he had witnessed, but knew better; it would only lead to physical pain. He had to remember that feeling of control, although it was getting harder and harder to do so. He could not allow the black to come back, no matter how sweet it tasted and how badly he wanted it. He wanted to tell her that he was not a threat, unlike the professor. Always the bloody professor. For years, he wanted to stay away from him, trying to eke out a living on his own, but found himself drawn to him again. And her. She was not ordinary, that was for sure. He could see why the professor was so enamoured of her. He could see why he had thoughts of fucking her, leading him to crying alone in his bed. He knew because he had felt those thoughts as well. He closed his eyes; his head was starting to hurt again. The black was coming back.

"I had no idea that you were going to come back. I thought I had crossed the line with you when I told you what I wanted."

"It did bother me when you asked me that, Jason, but I had to come back. I wanted to know for myself if you meant it or not."

"I guess you can safely say that I did mean it. For crying out loud, Jane, we had sex three times last night. I think that is a safe assumption, wouldn't you agree? By the way, were you trying to get me going again when you woke up and had your glass of water?"

"No, I was thirsty." Jane laughed as she snuggled closer to him. "You actually thought I was trying to seduce you by getting up and drinking my glass of water?"

"Well, don't make fun, but a man my age takes any kind of symbol to be a sign of sex. Sorry about that." She kissed him on the nose.

"I never knew you had a sense of humour. I just thought you were just some pent up freak."

"Well, now you know." The two said nothing for several minutes, not really thinking of anything to say. The two lay in his bed naked, holding each other tightly after making love. "You've made me quite happy, you know. I can't even remember the last time I was truly happy," he said with a thick voice.

"Are you about to cry?" She asked as she turned around to face him, stroking his face with her hand as he began to laugh.

"Should I? Would you like to bathe in my tears?"

"I thought I was the only Goth in this relationship." Jason pulled away to get a better look at her.

"You're one of those Goth kids I hear about on the tele?", he said with slight disbelief.

"Actually, I claim no label, but I do lean towards Goth and Steampunk."

"What's Steampunk? I know all about the Goth thing, but you've lost me about the Steampunk."

"Well, Steampunk is for those who enjoy the Victorian age, especially the history concerning the steam machinery. Ever seen the movie League of Extraordinary Gentlemen?"

"Yes, I have. That's Steampunk?"

"Well, kind of, but the mood and theme of it is pretty close." She snuggled against him, wanting his body heat to cover her own cold one. "Actually, ever seen The Golden Compass?"

"Yes, I have, actually."

"That's Steampunk."

"Ah yes. So, you're into Victorian literature, I take it?"

"Of course, but not just because I am into Steampunk. I have always loved Charles Dickens, Oscar Wilde-"

"Jane Eyre, hmmm? I remember you carrying around a tattered copy of that book in your hand like it was a sacred text or something. Don't get me wrong; I loved that book, however, I don't think it carried as much weight in my life as it did in yours, right?"

"Of course, Dr. Phillips. So, you had no idea what Steampunk was, huh?"

"No, I had no idea and don't call me Dr. Phillips, at least, not while we're together. I just thought you were a dark and interesting person."

"Well, I guess that would be the best way of describing me. Thank you . . . Jason." He snuggled against her again and sighed in her hair.

"Jane?"

"Yes?"

"Would you…like to spend the night here? It's been so long since someone has stayed with me . . . well, I miss it. You can go home to grab some clothes, if you wish. Tell you what; I'll order delivery for dinner tonight. Sound good?" She did not respond, giving him slight cause to be worried. "Jane, I hope I'm not trying to force myself on you, but I want you to stay. I'll understand if you don't." Jane was still quiet. "Jane, did you hear me?"

"I heard you."

"Well?"

Jane turned to face him again and took his limp penis in her hand. She made her decision.

Images, the sun rising and falling as he slid himself in her over and over, his long hands touching every part of her, her body responding to his caresses, his eyes now wet with tears.

She did stay.

"Have you ever been married?"

"Once, years ago, but she left me for another professor, my best friend in London, actually. Bloody bitch; she had been having an affair with him for months and I never knew about it until it was too late. When I did find out, I was crushed beyond belief. Jeremy and I had known each other since we were children growing up in London and I loved him dearly. It still bothers me to this day what he did to me. I thought I could trust him with everything. Seems I was wrong."

"So when did it start?"

"I think it was when we joined this particular country club for the sake of trying to get back in shape. Jeremy and I had started putting on weight that we had gained while eating blueberry scones for tea every day for a month and so we thought it would be good if we worked it off together. My wife wanted to join as us well and I thought that was a grand idea. Little did I know that they set that up so they could spend more time together. Looking back, I realized that while she was smiling and waving at me while I played cricket, she was probably thinking about how big Jeremy's penis was." He chuckled, causing Jane to vibrate. "My god, I sound like some old stuffy fart, don't I?"

"I don't think so. You sound like a man who felt the bitter stings of adultery."

"My parents would agree with you, but I do sound like some bitter old man who can't get over the fact that my wife preferred to be with someone else rather than I. They think that I should not have married her, that I should have married someone who was interested in the same things as I rather than some trophy wife."

"Well, how did they feel when you got divorced?"

"They were happy, to tell you the truth. They knew I had been through hell with that woman for so long so for me to be free from her was good news to them. After the divorce, I wanted to get away for a while, so I came to the States, as my father puts it. I'm glad I came here." He stopped for a brief moment to kiss the back of her neck. "I told them about you being my exceptional student and how I treated you."

"Uh huh, and what did they think of that?"

"Just like you, they couldn't understand why I was so hard on you. They felt that I should have just told you outright, but I explained to them that I wanted to see your absolute best and that you were not giving it to me."

"How would they feel about me sleeping with you now?"

"Not really sure, dear, but right now I don't want to think about that. I'll handle that later." He sighed. "When we go to London, I want you to meet them, if that is OK with you."

"I have no problem with that."

Silence.

"Have you ever been married?"

"No and I don't want to. I know about people like you; people who spoke before their god stating that you would never leave your partner and yet your partner ends up doing just that. To me, people like your ex-wife make marriage a sham."

"Well, now, I wouldn't say that. That is quite harsh. There are many people who are still married. Take my parents for example, and I am sure yours-"

Jane moved away from him. He tried to reach for her, but she pulled away. "Jane, what's wrong?" he asked with grave concern. "I hope I did not say the wrong thing to you about your parents."

"My mother left my father when I was a year old," she said, talking as though her imaginary friend was in the room. "He was a horrible man and I'm glad he never tried to look us up after we left. Although my mother married a really great guy when I was 13, I still think about the fact that I share genes with such an asshole. I guess that's why I learned how to be fully independent; I vowed I would never go through what my mother went through. I remember when she used to cry in the middle of the night for no reason, but I knew better. I knew she was still in pain over him and how much she still loved him, although in looking back, I wondered why. " Jason tried once more to hold her and this time was successful. She could feel his heart beating against her chest and relished in that comforting sound.

"You have beautiful skin," he murmured, tracing patterns along her arm with his fingers. "How do you make it glow like that?"

"What?"

"Sometimes, when I touch you, I wonder if some of the glow will rub off on my skin so we can glow together. In case you haven't noticed, I am a typical pasty white man from Great Britain. I do not glow; I just burn." Jane was black, but it was obvious that she did have white relatives rather close in the family tree; her skin was like light caramel that paled during the autumn and winter seasons. Most of her sexual experiences were the result of many white men wanting to just touch her skin. . . along with other parts of her body as well. She was exotic to them, like an endangered species, one that they thought they could easily trap in their "cages" with wily words and original seductions.

"Jason, please."

"Please what?"

"There's no need for that. You've gotten me into your bed so-"

"Jane, I did not say those things just to get you in bed. I told you that because. . ." He wasn't sure if he should tell her so early that he was in love with her and had been for the past two years, ever since she walked into his classroom the first day of her graduate program, wearing her scent of jasmine and honeysuckle that he had now tasted and treated like ambrosia.

"Yes?"

"Because I wanted to know, that's all." He released her and faced the window, watching the rain fall where it was once sunny and cold. Jane rolled away from him as well and saw her imaginary friend smile while it sat on the floor. *At least you don't lie to me*, she thought, making it smile even wider.

The two acted like professor and student, neither one betraying the other during class. Jason wanted to touch her skin while he lectured, but refrained from doing so. In the course of one weekend, he went from a bitter and slightly lonely bachelor to a man now very much involved with one of his students on a regular basis; they worked on his project every night, sometimes staying up until one in the morning since their schedules did not begin until 10am. He asked her to bring several items of clothing in case she could not make it back to her apartment, slowly getting her to eventually move in with him. He even began buying little toiletries for her like the special baking soda toothpaste she had been using that she recommended to him, deodorant, even tampons, of which he was proud to purchase. To him, it meant that she trusted him with her hygiene and well being. He knew he was slowly pushing her to become a permanent part of his life, but she was worth it. She was everything he had ever wanted and she still left him wanting more. For the first time in his life, he felt complete. He was, in short, addicted to her.

He was careful whenever they had sex, pulling out at the last minute and sparing her from becoming pregnant, but he wanted to feel himself explode inside of her, releasing himself in such an intimate manner. He would instead ejaculate on her stomach or in her mouth or even in a napkin, although he hated doing that. He and his wife never had children, a choice that he later regretted, but got over with reluctance and time.

Jane was happy; Jason was the first man who truly understood her despite their age difference. Some nights, while they read documents and made notes, neither would make a sound for several hours, but it only added to their relationship. Jason, from time to time, would glance up to see her chewing on a pencil while reading. He wanted to kiss her and tell her how much he was in love with her, but refrained; she, however, already knew how he felt about her. Jane wanted to let her parents know about her relationship with Jason, but knew that they would not understand at all, even though she was completely happy. For the first time, she was with someone who did not try to change her to please their own inner checklist, only to dash her against a rock and laugh while her inner self fell from her like sludge. Her last boyfriend, a man who claimed to know and understand her, was a complete mistake; he claimed to be a literary fanatic like her, but instead had only read two books in his life. He was also very good at laying guilt at her feet, blaming her for his every problem, even the ones he had before the two even met. After praying the entire rosary one rainy Sunday (something she did only when the situation called for it), she removed him from her home and left him at his old house that was falling apart and had no electricity due to him not paying his utility bill. When he called two days later, screaming at her for over an hour about how his life was ruined because of her, she calmly listened to his bullshit then hung up the phone. He never called back.

Two months later, Jane moved out of her apartment and into Jason's home at his request. He had more than enough room in his home for all of her clothing, accessories, and books so it was not putting him out of his own home. To him, she was comfort on a completely different level and he welcomed it gratefully.
"It's nice to come home to someone, even though I just saw you in class," he said over dinner one night. The two decided to actually leave their home for dinner; their meals had been delivery since both were too tired and busy to cook. Jane chose the place for the night as a celebration of their relationship and as roommates. They also decided to go out since it was their two month anniversary of being together and Jason wanted it to be special. Jane smiled and sipped her glass of wine, feeling a sense of calm for the first time in her life. This was what she had wanted for the longest time and never achieved due to her own shortcomings., but now, now it was her time to actually live and laugh.

Two tables down, Paul and Roger sat, enjoying a romantic dinner as well. Paul looked up and saw the two seated at a table. Jason caressed Jane's cheek and leaned over to kiss her, causing Paul to gasp and almost drop his glass.

"Paul, what's wrong?" asked Roger in a concerned tone. Paul said nothing, but his eyes showed it all; Roger followed his partner's eyes and gasped when he saw the two kissing. "Is that Jane? And…is that your professor?" The two quickly looked somewhere else when they saw them get up from their tables to leave. Jason wrapped an arm around Jane's middle and kissed her on the cheek then the two were gone into the night, giving Paul and Roger much to talk about.

"Tell me what you like."
"In regards to?"
"Well . . . in regards to everything. I want to know more about you, every little detail about you."
"I love books-"
"I already know that."
"Who's telling the story? Anyway, I love reading, traveling, which, by the way, I am very excited about going to London with you."
"Well, I want you to enjoy yourself. I want to show you everything and give you a taste of my own life. More wine?" Jason took her glass and got up to refill both in the kitchen while Jane sat on the living room floor. When he returned, she took a sip then said, "I really want to go to the London Review Bookshop; perhaps I'll see Ian McEwan there."
"Ian? Oh good lord, don't tell me you love his work?"
"Of course I do, why?"
"His family and mine are good friends." Jane couldn't believe it.
"You?! You knew Ian McEwan?"
"Well, know, actually. We still keep in contact with each other. In fact-"

He got up from the couch and walked over to one of his overflowing bookshelves, pulling a tattered book out from a tight spot and then handed it to her. She scanned the title and squealed with delight; it was an advanced reader's copy of one of his novels that she cherished. The book was heavily underlined with handwritten notes all over the pages, presumably notes from the great author himself. She looked up at Jason and grinned.

"You shouldn't get rid of this, you know."

"I know, I want you to have it." Jane looked at him incredulously then sat up and kissed him on the lips, grateful at that moment to be in love with a man who knew her so well.

He sits in the dark because he prefers it that way. In the last month, he has gone through anger, sadness, resentment, fury, depression, and love, even love, still at this point. He wants to know why he loves her. The professor. He knows now about the two of them, knows where they go and what they do. He wants to scream and shout, letting the world know of their blasphemous union, but knows such an act would be futile. He has to do something with the professor. Always the professor. She must be a treasure. A treasure that must be loved and cared for. A treasure that would be so easy to break into little bloody pieces. He smiles, thinking.

"What are your passions in life?"

"Don't have any." She lightly punched him in the arm.

"Don't be so daft."

"Ah, picking up on my speech, are we? Soon you'll be saying cheerio, pip pip and all that rut, what?"

"Well, what are your passions in life? Don't change the subject."

"I told you, I don't have any. I read, I enjoy opera, and I love wine. I'm boring."

"You're not boring, Jason." She moved and sat next to him on the couch, holding his hand. "We're two of a kind." He folded his arms around her, drawing her into his body warmth.

"I . . love you, Jane," said Jason hesitantly. He knew she knew of his feelings for her, but this was the first time he had ever said those words to her. Jane sighed, releasing a breath she did not realize she held until she released it. "I love you," he repeated with more conviction.

"I love you too, Jason." Suddenly, she felt his body shaking against her own. She turned her head and noticed that he was crying.

"Tears?" He wiped his face.

"Sorry, luv. Kind of let myself go, huh?"

"Not at all."

"I am glad, you know. Glad you told me that you love me."

"Well, I meant it. What else did you expect me to say?"

"Hello, Mom?"

"Janie, dear, how are you? How's school going?"

"Rather well, Mom."

"How's the research project going?"

"Oh that, well, pretty good I'd say. I can't believe I'm going to London with Jason!"

"Jason? Who's Jason?"

"Sorry, Mom, Dr. Phillips. Anyway-"

"Are you allowed to call him by his first name?"

"Of course, Mom. We have been working together for a while now and he thought it would be better if we went on a first name basis."

"Hmmm, well, I don't think it's right, but if he says it's OK, then it must be OK. You know your father and I are very proud of you. You turned your life around so well after that disastrous relationship with that boy, what was his name?"

"Eric, Mom."

"Well, it's good that you've been doing so well in school and on this project."

"Jason said I was his only choice for the position. I was honoured that he picked me." Jason walked out of the kitchen and wrapped his arms around her, kissing her neck tenderly for a moment, making her giggle.

"You OK?"

"Yeah, sorry." She was trying hard not to laugh in her mother's ear; she waved a hand at Jason to knock it off, but he was in a silly mood. He grabbed her again, trying to tickle her and this time she did laugh.

"Jane!" Jane pushed him away, still snorting with laughter.

"Sorry, Mom, you were saying?"

"I wasn't saying anything."

"Well, I need to go. Jason and I need to get back-"

'Wait, where are you calling me from? Are you at his place?"

"Uh, yes. That's where we work." Jason mouthed the question what's wrong? after seeing her face change in emotion. She looked at him and waved him back.

"Jane Amanda Collier, why are you at that man's house? What will his wife say about that?"

"He's not married, Mom."

"Not married!" she yelled. Even Jason heard her voice and knew something was wrong. "Give him the phone, please." Jane handed the phone to him, knowing that whatever she was about to say to him was not going to be pleasant.

"This is Dr. Jason Andrew Phillips," he said while using the voice he used to use when he used to treat Jane like dirt in class.

"Dr. Phillips, this is Jane's mother. I know my daughter is an adult, but I want to know why she is at your home. Isn't that inappropriate? She is your student, after all."

"Yes, she is my student, but I asked her here. There is nothing with what I have done, Mrs. Collier."

"But, you're not married!"

"And?"

"And, it is not appropriate for a man of your profession to have one of your students with you in your home!"

"I see. And what if I was to tell you that not only is she invited to my home whenever she wants, but that we are actually living together? That she is not just my student, but my girlfriend as well?" Jane almost fainted from shock; why in the world did he just do that? She could see her whole world falling down all around her. She wanted to vomit.

There was silence on the other end for several seconds then a very dry, "I see."

"Yes. Well, I wanted to let you know. I felt it right to do so, although Jane might not agree with me on that point." Jane looked as though she wanted to kill him right then and there. Jason said a few more words then hung up the phone, not caring if Jane was angry with him or not.

"Why?" she asked, barely holding in her rage. "Why did you tell her?"

"Because she had a right to know, dear. Why are you so angry with me? Why are you afraid of telling her about me?"

"Because she'll think I slept with you in order to get the position and I can't have that." Jason wrapped his arms around her and kissed the top of her head. Some things were just not worth stressing over. He could feel her body trying to pull away from him, but he held on.

"Jane, Jane, I am in your life now. Don't do this to me."

"Do what?"

"Shut me out. Close me off from your pain."

"But what you did-"

"Was necessary. How old are you, anyway?" Jane let her chin fall to her chest; deep down. She knew he was right. Thirty-three years old and still afraid of your parents was not a healthy attitude. Jason released her and walked into the kitchen, satisfied at what he had done. Jane, still standing in the middle of the living room floor, saw her imaginary friend who waved to her then disappeared.

"Jane, how about Indian delivery tonight?" Jason asked from the kitchen. "I'm in the mood for some Nan bread and chicken curry."

"Sure," she said without any emotion in her voice, but Jason pretended to overlook it. He knew he was right in what he did. She walked into the bedroom and closed the door behind her, wanting some privacy to change into her bedclothes. As she changed, she noticed a regular sized black leather journal lying on Jason's side table. She finished changing then stared at the book then at the door.

"Jane, I'm going out for some merlot. I'll be back soon. Do you need anything?"

"No." She did not want to face him right now. Her eyes glanced at the journal once more and she listened for Jason to leave. When she heard the door close and the locks turned, she ran over to his side of the bed and sat down, pulling the journal from its spot. She felt like Indiana Jones as she did this: were there booby traps connected to the journal? Would her taking it from its spot upset the gods? She shrugged; her imagination was way too active. She opened the journal and began to read.

10 April 2006: J. looked slightly tired today; wonder what's wrong with her? She has been looking tired lately. Maybe stress. She is still beautiful, though. She needs a vanilla latte. They seem to make her happy. I wonder does she know that she is a goddess. A being that must never be soiled by mortal thoughts and ways, but one who deserves only grapes and wine, followed by passionate lovemaking for hours then a perfumed bath. She must be worshipped and cared for because that is the least anyone can do for her. She is my goddess, if she will have me. She means more to me than my own life. J. is my life, my breath. I see others look at her and wish they would go away. I don't want them looking at her. I know I am jealous, but it is healthy to feel that way, right? God, I just want to talk to her. You know, she reminds me of me so much; perhaps that's why I feel so close to her and yet so far away.

Sadly enough, I miss London and my parents. There I go again, blubbering like some old fool- No, I should not say such things about myself. I no longer feel like an old man. J., just by being in the same room with me, makes me feel alive and wonderful. She is everything to me and I am forever grateful.

She thinks I can't see, but I can. She has no idea.

One day, if we ever become closer, I want to take her to London. Thank goodness I suggested her for the journal assistant position. She is perfect for the job. I wonder if she knows she is-

"Jane? I'm back!" She placed the journal back on his table then walked out as if nothing happened. Jason was in the kitchen, trying to open the bottle. Jane walked in and grabbed two glasses then held them out when he was ready to pour. His eyes were on her the entire time, but she refused to look at him. When both were filled, she handed one to him then took a sip from her own as both stood in the kitchen.

"I am sorry, Jane. I wanted to do the right thing. I am not ashamed of you and you should not be ashamed of being with me." She looked up at him, hearing the emotion in his voice, knowing that he was right. She was 33 years old; why hide what was purely normal?

"Jason, I'm sorry for how I acted," she replied. "You're right."

"Of course I am." She punched him in the arm while laughing.

Paul pulled her aside when he saw her walking up the stairs to their classroom. He spent the past couple of days thinking about what he was going to say to her and now that the time was here, had no clue whatsoever. She looked good; her skin glowed and there was a spring in her step. Dr. Phillips had not made it yet so he had to be fast.

"Jane, I need to talk to you." Jane stopped and smiled at her best friend then reached in her messenger bag for her cigarettes. As soon as she found one, she lit it up and took a deep puff, exhaling it to the autumn winds.

"Paul, why so glum, chum?"

"I saw you. . . and Dr. Phillips together."

"OK..."

"He kissed you." Jane dropped her cigarette; her hand was shaking too hard to hold it.

"Where did you see us?"

"At Wydham's. Roger and I were there for our anniversary."

"Funny, so were we." Paul looked at her as she tried to light another cigarette, her hands shaking. "Have you told anyone?"

"No, no one. In fact, I would not have known if I hadn't seen the two of you together." He placed a beefy hand on her shoulder. "I won't tell anyone, but I am dying to know!" The old queen was back, ceasing Jane's nervousness. She hugged her friend tightly then lit her cigarette with no qualms. "You know those things'll kill you."

'Yeah, well, so will standing in front of a microwave for too long." She blew out a perfect stream of smoke then said, "Ask."

"Well?! How did it happen? Did he. . . oh my god, did he make a move on you when he asked you to stay behind that one day?"

"No, but he did ask me to be his assistant for his project."

"Hmmm, well, good for you on that one, but when?!"

"OK, OK," she said while laughing as she took another drag from her cigarette. "He asked me to come over that night to help him with the preliminary stages of work. Then, well . . . that's when it happened. We had sex and I spent the night with him." She took another drag and blew out a perfect smoke ring. "In fact, I spent the entire weekend with him."

"Girl, did you really? So, what's he like outside of class?"

"Well-"

Just then, they noticed Dr. Phillips walking towards them. Jane extinguished her cigarette and smiled while Paul watched with sly eyes.

"Hello Jane, Paul." He smiled at both of them, showing off all of his teeth, but his eyes were on Jane, of which Paul took notice.

"Hello, Dr. Phillips," said Paul, drawing out the word doctor. "Seems like you're in a good mood today."

"I am actually, thanks! Don't tell anyone, but today's class will be cut short today. I have to work on my research project. Jane, will you be able to meet with me for this?"
"Of course Ja-Dr. Phillips." He smiled then walked inside the building. Paul waited several seconds then smiled slyly at her. Jane waved her hand in protest, but he asked anyway.
"So. . . . meeting up with him, huh? For research, I take it?" Paul then took her arm and led her inside for class, laughing all of the way.

He let them know immediately that class was going to be short; he smiled as the class erupted into laughter and beginnings of plans for longer lunches and the like. His eyes glanced over to Jane who was talking to Paul and he smiled.

He saw the professor smiling at her and wanted to scratch his eyes out. Bloody little pieces. Tiny, blunt little pieces.

Jane walked back home, her black messenger bag bumping against her thigh, her mind swirling around with the autumn breezes. Jason had left earlier and was waiting for her at home.

He wanted to scratch his eyes out. He knew where she was going, but was powerless to stop it. All he could do was watch. He wanted to know why he loved her.

"Mum, it's me, Jason."
"Darling, how are you? I can barely hear you. Must be this damn hearing aid."
"Doing great, Mum, look I have to tell you something important. Will you get Father on the line?"
"Wait, dear, I think he's in the garden puttering about. Hold on." Jason closed his eyes; could he tell them?
"Jason, is that you, my boy?"
"Yes, Dad, how are you?"
"Doing well! Have you met any movie stars yet, son?"

"No, Dad, not yet," chuckled Jason. "Look, I've got something to tell you both, something wonderful."

"Oh dear, you've been promoted to Dean?"

"No, not that. I'm . . .in love."

"Jason, my boy, how wonderful! Who is the lucky woman?"

"Jason, in love, eh? About time you moved on from that horrible slut of an ex-wife!"

"Theodore, shush!"

"Well, it's true. So, who is she?"

"Her name is Jane Amanda Collier. She's an exceptional woman. She's . . . also in one of my classes. She's the exceptional student I was telling you about some time ago."

"Dear, is that right? Should you be dating one of your students?"

He dug his nails into his palms so hard that blood trickled from the wounds. He did not notice.

"I love her. She loves me. We are perfect for each other."

"Well . . .if you're happy, son, then we're happy for you as well."

"She'll be coming with me to London; I want you to meet her."

"Of course, dear, of course!"

"As long as she doesn't sleep with your friends, then she is all right with me."

"Theodore, shush! Now, dear, have you heard from Lucien?"

The blood trickled faster down his hands.

"No."

"Dear, why won't you speak to him?"

"I hate him; why should I concern myself with his well being?"

"But, son-

"No, buts."

"Well, he has been asking about you. Wants to know how you're doing. You know he moved to the States recently?" Jason almost fainted from shock.

"Lucien . . . here?"

"Of course, dear, that's why we asked you if you've heard from him. He said he wanted to make amends with you. He wants to apologize, Jason."

"Damn it! Did you tell him where I was?"

There was silence, but Jason knew. "You told him," was all he said.

"Son-"

"Dear-"

"Mum, Dad. I need to go now. Goodbye."

He had to get ready. Lucien would find him soon enough.

Jane walked in the house, finding Jason sitting on the couch, smoking a cigarette. She knew he had not touched a cigarette in seven years so something must have spooked him enough. His eyes were red rimmed and he looked terrible. She dropped her bag to the floor and walked over to him, sliding her arms around him without a word. He put out his cigarette and kissed her lips, holding her face in his hands. Jane knew something was wrong; his normally soft and tender kisses were replaced with this new kiss, a kiss of urgency and anger.

"Make love to me," he said as he led her to the bedroom and closed the door.

He came inside of her, releasing stress and frustration, his mind wandering to Lucien.

"I spoke with my parents today. They told me a person from my past moved here recently."

"Was he a friend of yours?"

"He was; we grew up together. Lucien was always the better looking one-"

"Jason-"

"No, I'm serious. He was smart, cunning, daring; he was everything I wasn't."

"Jason, please, don't tear yourself down like this. I think you're wonderful. If I didn't, I wouldn't have moved in with you." Jason hugged her tightly, not wanting her to see his tears trying to fall from his eyes. "So, what happened? Why did the two of you stop talking?"

"He did something to me, something that I can never forgive him for."

"What?" Jason looked away, trying badly to hide his tears.

"He. . . .did something to me that I can not talk about right now. Maybe sometime later when the time is right. Trust me on this, please."

"Of course. So, when was the last time you heard from him?"

"I can't remember, actually. I still can't believe he moved here to seek me out. He probably wants to use forgiveness as a way to weasel back into my life."

"Whatever he did to you must have been horrible."

"Yes, Jane, it was."

When the man walked in the store, all eyes flew to him. He was an attractive man who carried himself well. His clothing and manner were impeccable, almost flawless, as if he awoke from his bed perfectly dressed. He caught the eye of one woman and winked, causing her to blush instantly. He chuckled and walked through the department store, knowing that their eyes watched him, knowing that they would be thinking of him in their dreams that night. Poor silly fools.

He did not care about them. He wanted only one person and she belonged to the professor. He chuckled as he walked; why did she want him? Of course, he thought; she hadn't met me yet. Of course. Images of her flew through his mind; what she would look like naked, the way her face lit up when she smiled. The sound of her skin being cut, tenderly, lovingly, quick and clean with no fuss . . . at least from him. He would know soon enough.

When he reached the customer service desk, he turned on the charm even more. The woman seated at her desk looked to be a homely sort, one who lived alone. She wore clothing that aged her, placing her in a category of standoffish librarian. She was probably still a virgin.

"Excuse me, miss?" The woman looked up and almost died. She blushed, not sure what to say to this man. He was stunning.

"Y-yes?"

"I need to open an account here. What do you need from me?" She stammered and began pulling out papers for him to sign, fumbling miserably. The man chuckled softly, enjoying her clumsiness. He could have her in bed with a snap of his fingers and yet, because it was too easy, he did not want to take the chance. Too, too easy. She handed the forms to him and a pen then sat back and watched him with hungry eyes as he found a seat and began to fill them out. When he finished minutes later, he handed them back to her and she completed the information in her computer.

"Congratulations," she said breathlessly, "you now have an account with us, Mr.- " she looked at the screen to get his name, "Lucien Gilchrist."

"Thank you, my dear. When should I receive my card?"

"Oh, in about two weeks." She hesitated for a moment then- "I know you get this a lot, but are you from England?"

"Yes I am. London born. I moved here several months ago."

"How nice."

"Yes, it is, isn't it?" He held her gaze a little too long for normal interaction, the smile still there on his face. "What's your name?"

"Lydia. Lydia Brentwood." He smiled even wider.

"Tell me, Lydia Brentwood, are you free around 6pm?"

"Why, yes I am!"

"Would you be interested in accompanying me to dinner tonight?"

"Yes, yes!" She sounded as though she was having an orgasm right there. Too, too easy, he thought, but what fun.

"I'll come by here and pick you up. How does that sound?"

"Wonderful!"

"See you at six, Lydia." He smiled once more then walked out, leaving her with sexual thoughts already playing in her mind. Too easy. He had three hours to kill and then what fun he would have.

Six came with Lydia waiting outside of the store, checking her watch to make sure it was not broken. Once Lucien left her desk, everyone who witnessed the transaction between them flew to her desk to get the details. When they found out she had a date with him, they couldn't believe her good luck. During her lunch break, she bought a new suit and new shoes; she wanted to make sure she looked her best for him.

At 6:01, he arrived in a black sports car, pulling right up to her. He got out of the car and walked over to the passenger side, opening the door for her.

"You look lovely, my dear," he said as he grazed his lips against her cheek. She wanted to faint; this beautiful man actually kissed her on the cheek! They got in and soon they were off. The interior was black leather with ergonomic seats. Mozart's Requiem was playing in the CD player, soft and haunting, while Lydia smoothed out imaginary wrinkles in her outfit for the millionth time.

"So, tell me, Lydia, what do you do for fun?"

"I read mainly, trying to keep my mind sharp."

"Reading is good for the mind; don't ever stop." Lydia giggled and smoothed out her outfit once more.

They had a wonderful dinner followed by coffee and pastries at one of the local coffee shops. Lydia, finally relaxed enough to talk, wanted him desperately. She noticed how his eyes kept glancing at her body; she had to make a move or else.

"Lucien?"

"Yes, Lydia?"

"I . . . was wondering if you'd like to drop me off at my place."

"What about your car? Didn't you leave it at the store?"

"No, I walk to work."

"Oh." Lucien knew he had her. "Sure, I would be delighted."

Thirty minutes later, the two were kissing in her living room. Lucien fumbled with her outfit, trying to remove it while not breaking the kiss. Lydia was in heaven; finally, after so many years of being alone, a man wanted to make love to her. She pulled at his shirt, feeling the lean muscles underneath and sighed. Soon, they were naked in her bed, with Lucien giving her body tender kisses. Lydia smiled in the dark and allowed this charming and attractive man take over. He slid inside her and she almost screamed; it had been too long for her as she let this man make love to her. Each thrust made her sigh; he made no sound. Let her be in heaven, he thought. A small part of him was actually enjoying it.

Suddenly, he stopped.

"What's wrong?" she asked as she tried to catch her breath.

"Nothing my dear, but I think it's time we had some fun, don't you think?" He reached down and pulled up what looked to be rope. Lydia giggled nervously; was he going to tie her up? She had never done that before, but one only lived once. . . He reached over to grab her wrists and tied them tightly together. The rope felt soft and did not burn her skin. He then rolled her over on her stomach and spread her legs apart. "Is the rope too tight, dear?", he asked.

"No, not at all."

"Good."

Five minutes later, Lydia Brentwood began to scream. It hurt, she kept yelling, but Lucien was no longer paying attention to her; the knife was now in control. Amazing how much blood came from one spot, he thought then decided to try another area. She was fading fast, the screams no longer audible, but he was far past caring. She was only walking meat as far as he was concerned. Meat that could be broken with a single thought, a glance, or in this case, a surgical knife that had been waiting to taste red again. This cow was nothing compared to Her. It was because of Her that he had to do this. Soon, very soon, he thought. Too easy.

Jane sat on the couch reading a book when Jason arrived home. He looked tired and worn, but he still had a smile on his face. He flopped on the couch and pulled her towards her, giving her a kiss on the lips. When he pulled away, his eyes seemed to sparkle as he looked at her. She smirked.
"OK, you have something in mind tonight. What is it?"
"I'm in a great mood, Jane. Let's go to Fincher's. My treat." Fincher's was the largest independent bookstore in the city; three floors of books, music, magazines, and anything else. Jane tried not to go to Fincher's too much because she always walked out completely broke.
When they arrived, she ran off towards the Dark Words section; Fincher's was the only bookstore in the world that had a fully stocked Goth section of books, music, and accessories separate from the rest of the store. She spent so much time there that the employees knew her by sight, even going so far as to offer her the position of manager of the section. There were tables and chairs with black lace for people to sit and read or converse with dark and haunting music playing in the background. Jane saw several friends and waved then began walking through the aisles, looking for something new.
Several minutes later, Jason found her reading the latest Goth Beauty magazine and surprised her with a hug.
"My little dark goddess," he said with a chuckle. "Did you see anything?"
"Oh, just five books and this magazine, plus the latest CD from one of my favourite Industrial groups." Jason took her

items and walked off to pay for them while she continued to walk around, still trying to find more items to buy.

The two soon left and walked down the street to a small restaurant for a cozy dinner. The night was beautiful and soft; people were out with their loved ones or by themselves, giving in to the warm night. Jason took her hand in his and held it as they walked along while she had their bag of purchases.

"Nice night," he said and whistled a tune. Jane wanted to say something, but remained silent, enjoying her time with him.

When they reached the restaurant, Jane plopped in her chair and placed their bags in the third chair while he took the seat opposite her. Every table had a lit candle, creating a warm and romantic tone. There were several other couples in the place, but each were lost within their own conversations.

Their orders were taken and soon the two were sharing a bottle of merlot. Jason poured for both of them and handed a glass to Jane.

"To us," he said, raising his glass.

"To us." They toasted then took a sip. Jane looked over at the kitchen door and noticed a group of waiters standing there, staring at the two of them and smiling. Feeling slightly goofy, she waved at them and to her surprise, they all walked over to her table. She turned her glance to Jason for an answer, but noticed that he got up and walked over to her then got down on one knee. The tears were already flowing down her cheeks as he started his speech. Even the other couples walked over to their table to see what was about to occur.

"Jane," he began in a slightly waving voice, "I love you, but you know that. I love you more than life itself. In fact, it was you who made me realize that there was a life to be lived out there. I know I am not a perfect person to live with and I know I can be slightly boring at times-", he said as his own tears began to fall, "but I am glad you are with me. Jane Amanda Collier, will you marry me?" Jane shook her head yes, smiling and crying at the same time, as he pulled out a ring box from his pants and opened it, revealing an engagement ring that no college professor could have bought on their salary. It was white gold with three medium sized diamonds in it. He slid it on her finger then took her hands in his own. "'I love you, soon to be Mrs. Jason Andrew Phillips." The crowd around them began to clap soundly as the happy couple hugged each other, their tears coming together in such a natural way.

He screamed; he saw what he did, heard what was said, saw her accept the ring then kiss him. He had to act.

Two weeks later, while Jason was off at the grocery store, Jane sat on their couch, reading the book <u>The Woman in White</u> by Wilkie Collins. Jason had introduced her to his work and she devoured each book within two days. The heater hummed through the entire home, giving off warmth and comfort. Jane yawned then snuggled deeper under her blankets, trying hard to keep her eyes open as she read. The living room was so comfortable, so warm. She closed her eyes.

The door flew open, causing her to fall on the floor. She removed herself from the tangle of her blanket, but was soon pushed to the floor by a very strong hand. She looked up and saw a figure crouched over her wearing a black ski mask that covered most of its face except for extremely blue eyes and thin lips. She wanted to scream, but kept herself calm. She closed her eyes and tried to slow down her breathing.

"Now, now dear, don't close your eyes," said the figure in a strong and deep British accent, causing her eyes to fly open. "I want to see your browns." She stared into those eyes, not wanting to look anywhere else, and continued to be calm. The figure lowered its face to hers, emitting a strong scent of peppermints from his mouth. He looked at her entire face, turning it left and right, then back to full front. "Do you know who I am?"

"No." She tried to keep her voice from wavering, but failed. The figure chuckled softly.

"I'm surprised Jason hasn't told you yet." Her eyes flew open wide in recognition.

"Lucien," she breathed as he chuckled again.

"Good, good. Now, don't try anything, understand?" She nodded her head yes. Lucien released her face then got up from the floor and sat on the couch. He motioned for her to get up and sit next to him which she did. When she did, he took her hands in his gloved ones and began to stroke them tenderly as if they were lovers. "So soft," he murmured, his eyes focused on her hands, "like silk. No wonder he is in love with you. Tell me, do you love him?"

"Of course I do."

"Of course. What a beautiful ring," he murmured. "Did he tell you I was looking for him?"

"Yes."

"I see. Did he tell you why?"

"No, only that you had done something horrible to him in his past and that he would not mention it." At this Lucien began to laugh.

"Well, well, Jas, it seems my reputation precedes me," he murmured then tightened his grip on her hands. "So he said nothing, absolutely nothing?"

"No."

"Hmmm. I wonder if I should be the bearer of bad news then," he said in an almost thoughtful tone, shaking his head as if disagreeing with an invisible person. Suddenly, he straightened his shoulders, looked at her square in the eyes and said, "You know he was once married."

"Yes, he's already told me this."

"He claimed that his friend Jeremy had carried on an illicit affair with her, yes?" She nodded in agreement. He chuckled again. "My dear, you have been fed a lie. Jeremy never touched her. In fact, Jeremy was and still is a fairy, or what you PC Americans call a homosexual." Jane felt her stomach lurch; was he telling her the truth? Lucien saw the doubt clouding her eyes and knew he had her. "Yes, my dear, Jeremy never touched her.

I did." The cold tone was not lost on her; Jane tried to pull her hands away from Lucien, but he held a firm grip, even with the gloves on. "In fact, I did more than just fuck her. Let's just say that my knife and I had a rather good time with her organs." Jane began shaking all over and soon felt something warm running down her legs. She glanced down to see that her bladder had lost control. She wanted to cry. Lucien looked down at the floor and sighed. "Jane," he said to like a parent scolding a child as he got up with her arm in his vice-like grip.

He led her to the bathroom and sat her down on the toilet seat while he took on the face towels and held it under warm water then lathered soap into it. Once he had it right, he pulled off her stained clothing and underwear then spread her legs wide open with no restraint. He took the soaped up towel and began to clean her legs and sex in a tender manner. Jane looked down at him in a numb way; she felt powerless. Was that really what happened, she thought? Did Lucien really murder Jason's wife? She blinked once. Lucien finished cleaning her up then washed the towel once more and wiped her down again.

"I hate to see you like this," he murmured in am almost caring tone as he finished up. Once done, he hoisted her up on her feet then led her to the master bedroom and sat her down on the bed. He stood over her, watching her stare off, and for a brief moment, felt sorry for her. He knelt between her legs and laid his covered head on her naked lap.

"Jane," he whispered, "I am going to lay you back on the bed. Don't fight me."

She did as she was told.

Finally, after so many times of wondering, now here he was, making love to the professor's woman. She felt delicious as he explored every crack, every fold, everything that was her as he made love to her. She had her eyes closed which made him angry for a brief moment, wanting to pull out his Bowie knife and "help" her to keep her eyes focused on him, but decided against it. He simply wanted to know. Jason, for once, was the lucky one; he had chosen a goddess.

She lay there, not wanting to see.

Her imaginary friend sat and cried because it was powerless to help her.

He turned once and saw it sitting there, then later pulled out the knife.

When he finished with a long sigh, Lucien rolled off her and got up to get dressed. Jane's eyes were still closed, but now she hugged herself carefully, holding back her tears. The cuts on her body still hurt, but thankfully, none of them were deep.
"You know," he said as he slipped on his pants, "I had rather hoped you would have put up more of a fight to make it spicy." He cocked his head, waiting for an answer, of which he knew he would not get one. He sighed. "Jane, if I wanted to kill you, I would have. I would have done to you what I did to his pretty little wife, but I did not. Oh how I dreamt of doing such nasty little things to you, things that would have given you nightmares for the rest of your life, but you see, I only left a couple of love bites on you. Consider yourself lucky that my knife was already satisfied. You are something special." Once he finished, he crept on the bed once more and lay next to her, caressing her cheek with an ungloved hand. "I. . . .love you." She opened her eyes in astonishment just as he removed his ski mask and pulled her towards him. His face, she thought as he kissed her. Even in the dark, she could still make out his face. His lips felt dry and thin like paper while hers were numb.

Jason arrived much later due to a fellow professor asking him out for drinks after closing up his office at the university then grocery shopping slightly drunk, which was actually kind of fun for him. He hiccupped slightly, grinned, and then let himself in the house, not noticing that the locks were loosely attached to the door. He missed Jane and couldn't wait to see her.

However, once he walked into the very brightly lit living room, he knew something was terribly wrong: Jane sat on the couch completely naked and covered in cuts and bruises, legs crossed in an almost impossible knot while she stared off into space. A large yellow puddle stained the carpet near her feet.

"Honey," he said carefully as he walked up to her, bags forgotten on the floor by the front door, "what happened?" For a moment, Jane continued to stare at the floor, feeling cold and rather untouchable. She wanted to be alone, giving her time to process what had happened to her, but she wanted to feel Jason's arms around her. Instantly, she began to cry, causing Jason to run over and tenderly place his arms around her. He could smell the old urine on the carpet.

"Jane," he repeated, "what happened?" Jane began to shake in his embrace as she said one word that caused him to shake in terror as well. He was now completely sober.

"Lucien."

He called for an ambulance.

"I was reading, waiting for you, when the door flew open and he stepped in, wearing a ski mask. He pushed me down on the floor and he-"

"Please don't cry. I'm here. Go on, I need to know everything."

"He. . . .told me things. About your wife. About Jeremy. Is it true?"

"Is what true?"

"Jeremy. . . is he a homosexual?" Jason wanted to pull away from her, but she held on tightly like he was a life saver. "Is it?"

"Jane-"

"No, I want to know. Is it true?"

Silence.

"It is, isn't it? Did you do that so that you would not have to tell anyone about what really happened? About Lucien and how he-"

"Jane. Don't."

"So . . . that's true as well. Is THAT why you refuse to see him? Because of what he did to you?" Jason got up and walked into the kitchen in silence, leaving Jane to her own thoughts and more questions than answers. When he returned with a large glass of water, she said immediately, "Did you ever press charges against him?"

"Yes. He spent some time in a mental ward for the criminally insane." He took a deep sip from his glass then said, "What else did he do, Jane?"

"I had an accident," she pointed at the dried urine, "So he took me into the bathroom to clean me off. He then led me to the bedroom and-"

Jason placed fingers over her mouth to silence her; he already knew what he had done to her. Jane did not cry when she told him, but she was concerned. About his face. About his mannerisms. Something was not right.

"Jas, about his face-"

"Yes?"

"He looked-"

Just then, someone knocked on the door. With some relief, Jason got up to answer it. Two young men in uniform came in and Jason led them to Jane. She had slipped on a robe for modesty, but did not bathe in case they needed to examine her thoroughly. They asked her general questions, checked her cuts and bruises, then loaded her in the ambulance and drove off to the nearest hospital with Jason behind them in his own car. He had his own thoughts to muddle through.

Lucien sits in a dark room, not wanting to move a muscle for fear he might lose her scent. Jane is a goddess, he thinks over and over again as he licks his lips. Sweet, sweet Jane, how my knife adored you. He does not want to forget.

Jason is trembling as he follows the ambulance with his fiancée inside. He wants to tell her that he loves her and that he will protect her no matter what, but now he is not so sure. He wants to talk to his parents and ask, for the millionth time why they told Lucien of his whereabouts. He wants to forget.

Jane is laid back on the stretcher, her mind whirling like mad. Did she really see what she thought she saw? Was it because of the dark room? No matter what Jason may try to tell me, she thinks clearly now, I know what I saw. She closes her eyes and does not want to forget.

The cuts were sanitized and bandaged and soon Jane slept in a middle-sized bed in the hospital thanks to a sleeping pill. Within five minutes of taking the pill, she closed her eyes and knew no more. Jason arrived just as the nurses were assisting her into the bed and set up his own sleeping arrangements in a corner with two chairs and some blankets provided by the nurses. Jason, after much fidgeting and turning, finally found a comfortable position and fell asleep as well. Neither dreamed.

Lucien opened his eyes to darkness. He blinked several times for good measure then slowly got up from his resting spot and walked around the small room. There was very little light to see, but he did not need it, for his thoughts were engrossed in Jane and how much he missed her scent. He had lost her essence while he slept which was horrible. He had to get it back, now that he knew why Jason loved her so much: it was because of her scent. He sniffed the air, trying to possibly feel for any trace of her, then sighed when he realized he had lost it all. He had to get it back. There was only one problem: her "friend". He hadn't counted on seeing it and did not even know she had one., but that was a minor concern.

Jason awoke to Jane coughing. He scurried from his corner and rushed to her bed, immediately grasping her hand and feeling her forehead with the other. Her eyes were open only a crack, but he knew she could see him. She tightened her own grip on his hand.

"Dear, how are you feeling?" he asked, not noticing that his voice sounded gravelly and worn. "Would you like a nurse to come in?"

"No nurse." Her eyes blinked several times then closed as she sunk back into her pill-laden sleep. Jason watched her for a moment then returned to his corner and fell asleep as well.

She dreamt. At first, all she could see was darkness, making her feel good and cozy, but soon images began to appear, images of him looming over her then next to her as he removed his ski mask. For a moment, she was unsure as to what she saw, but now deep in her sleep, she was certain. Lucien looked just like Jason, but his face was covered in darkness. . . . no, rather, the darkness swirled around his face. Was Lucien actually Jason's brother or was there more to the story than he was letting on? Soon, the images faded again and she resumed her dark sleep.

She opened her eyes to sunshine and Jason looming over her with a two day old scruff of a beard on his face that held tired, but still sparkling eyes. She smiled and reached for his hand.

"How are you feeling, dear?" he asked.

"Much, much better," she replied in a voice that was not completely happy. She had to know, for her own sanity and sake. "Jas, about Lucien-"

"Yes." His grip on her hand tightened for an instant.

"His face. . . Jas, he looked just like you." Jason released her hand and walked over one of the sun filled windows. She closed her eyes and sighed; this was not getting her anywhere.

"Jas, is he your brother?" He whirled around to face her, his face a mask of anger.

"Jane, how can you say such a thing? He is not related to me at all!"

"But he looked just like you. . . .but darker."

"Well, I can safely say that he is not related to me in any way, Jane." Feeling satisfied, he turned back to the window and the bright sun, leaving Jane to muddle in her own thoughts. *He never truly answered the question and I don't care what he says*, she thought as her imaginary friend suddenly appeared and laid its head against her chest. *I know what I saw.*

Two days later Jane was back in their home, cleaning up as best as possible. It still hurt to move too quickly, but she still wanted her body to be active. She still attended her classes and when one of her classmates asked about her condition, she claimed that she had intercepted a burglar trying to break into her home. Lucien violated her in the worst possible way; she felt she would see him again soon and she was not sure if that was a good thing or a bad thing.

Jason began preparing for their trip to London even though Jane thought it was a bad idea. Although they still worked on the project, Jane felt that the trip now was only a way to escape for Jason rather than a time of research and some fun. She could tell that he was trying his best to hold it all together, but it still slipped through his fingers like pancakes covered in syrup. At night, she heard him moaning in his sleep, always about keeping someone away from Lucien. Several times, Jane would sit up and watch her soon to be husband's face contort under the duress of the nightmares, sweat pouring from his face, as she wondered if she needed to wake him up or not. Then, after a few minutes of moaning, he would go back to sleep and the sweating would end, leaving Jane with still more questions than answers. She wanted to talk to him about it during the day, but he looked so haggard that asking him would probably be break him. So, she remained quiet . . . and fearful.

   Jason sat on the couch, trying to read the newspaper, but failing miserably.
   "Hello Jason."
   He turned around so fast that he almost lost his footing and fell. Jason blinked several times then stared into the face that was the source of his nightmares for years. Jason looked into Lucien's face and wanted to vomit. Lucien was, as always, dressed well and held a calm manner. How did he get in here, Jason wondered then noticed that Lucien was smiling at him while holding out his slender hand for Jason to take.
   "Come come now," he said when Jason refused his hand, "surely you can't still be angry with me from that incident-"
   "She was not an incident, Lucien. She was my wife."
   "That she was, Jason, that she was, but remember; she was more than just your wife." Jason wanted to cry; a door that had been closed all those years was trying to open, ready to reveal the old wounds and force the memories to surface. He never wanted to face those memories again, not while he had Jane in his life. He looked at the hand, saw the face of the man who still terrorized his dreams, and took his hand reluctantly. Jason began to tremble while Lucien embraced him like a lover.
   "Now," he said in a muffled voice, "doesn't this feel better? Can you ever forgive me for what I did to you, Jason? All those years ago and yet you still held onto the anger, the rage against me. I did what I had to do, Jason, for all of our sakes. She was going to put you away, Jason. She was going to take you away from us. We couldn't have that, now could we?" He sighed as he began running his hands through Jason's hair, causing Jason to moan softly. "When Jane showed up, however, I was jealous of you. She is so different than her; she loves you and I, foolishly enough, wanted to know why. I am sorry for what I did to her. Can you forgive me? My intent was never to hurt you or really her, but you know how I am. You of all people

know what lingers in my mind." Jason said a muffled yes, causing Lucien to slow down his strokes through his hair, giving off an erotic scent. "You remember, don't you?" he whispered in his ear. "You remember what it used to be like? You and me, Stephen, Daniel, Terrence, Agatha, and little Charlie, you remember little Charlie? He misses you giving him little sweets when you thought none of us were looking, but we all knew. That's why we love you and still do, Jason. Come back to us." Jason, worn out and weary, leaned his head against Lucien's shoulder and began to cry. Just then, he felt someone tugging on his sleeve. Jason looked down and saw little Charlie standing there, dressed in his schoolboy clothes while eating a big chocolate bar. He took a big bite of the bar, chewed it then smiled up at him like a son looks at his loving and adoring father. Jason smiled back and tousled with his black unkempt hair, causing him to laugh a full chocolate laugh, splattering chocolate all over his pants, but Jason did not care. He missed little Charlie.

"We've missed you too," said Lucien as he turned Jason's face towards his own. He smiled then pulled him closer for a kiss, a simple kiss, one that would make everything better-

"What the hell is going on?!" screamed Jane, shocking Lucien and Jason as they pulled away from each other in a guilty admission of their sin. Jane stood in the doorway, clutching her shoulder bag, her mind not believing what she had just seen. The man she loved and the man who violated her . . . in a lover's embrace? Jason walked over to her to offer help, but she waved him off and walked with shaky legs to the couch. She felt betrayed and worse. It felt as though her core self, once strong and loving, now was dry, brittle, and forever broken. Tears fell down her face, but she did not pay attention to them. She was numb. Lucien stood to the side with a slight smirk on his face; this had gone on too long and now it was time to get it straight again. He walked to the couch and sat down next to Jane who did not cringe. He sighed and ran a slender hand through his hair, trying to figure out the best way to explain it all.

"I wanted to know what he saw in you," he began, "and I understand. You truly are a treasure. However, he needs me just as much as I need him. That is for certain." Jane looked at his smiling face and wanted to scratch his eyes out. How could he say this to her?

"What do you mean, he needs you just as much as you need him? What, are you lovers or something?" She looked up at Jason's pleading face, waiting for some sort of explanation, but instead received silence . . . and a bit of fear.

"I mean-

Lucien then got up, walked over to Jason-

And stepped into Jason's body.

Jane stared with wide disbelieving eyes as the two men now became one. Jason's body trembled for a moment then he stood up straight and tall. It was Jason and Lucien at the same time, like a superimposed photograph. He looked down at Jane, who was still trying to hold it all in, and said in a voice that sounded both his and Lucien, "I told you, Jane; he needed me. He was never the same when he pushed me out, was the never the same after he killed his wife."

"B-but I thought-"

"Jane, he killed his own wife, but under my influence. She was the worst kind of wife one could imagine; she wanted to send him away to a mental institution. She needed to be taught a lesson and that is what I do, Jane. I provide lessons." He took a step closer to her. "You need not fear, my love. He loves you, and I feel the same way. In fact, we all do." He moved his arm in a sweeping motion to indicate that there were others, but Jane saw no one. Jason/Lucien chuckled then said, "I forgot, you can't see his other personalities."

"Other personalities?"

"My dear, our Jason has a touch of schizophrenia. In fact, his parents, his loving parents that he spoke to about you? They've been dead for twenty years., but don't worry, he didn't kill them. They died in a boating accident and he witnessed the entire event. Seems that did the old boy in finally, although he was born like this." Jane could not stop shaking as she reached in her messenger bag for her cigarettes. "You don't need those," they said in a kind tone. "We want to make sure our baby is healthy." Jane looked at them in disbelief, as if everything else had made sense, but this new piece of information was unbelievable; a baby? She dropped her unlit cigarette and placed her hands over her flat stomach. She began to cry.

"How long?"

"Two weeks."

"Two weeks," she replied to no one. Just then, she felt a flutter against her right arm. She looked over and saw her imaginary friend seated next to her. Jason/Lucien looked at the imaginary friend and acknowledged it with a nod.

"You can see my friend?" asked Jane with disbelief in her voice.

"Of course we can, Jane. We've seen your friend all of this time, but we, well, Jason, was not sure if he was going to tell you or not." Jason/Lucien closed their eyes then opened them and suddenly, he was completely Lucien. Jane stared at the man; although it was Jason's face, everything else had changed to a leaner version of himself. His face, however, held swirls of darkness, the same darkness that she witnessed the first time she met him. "I was so jealous of you and Jason," he said in a conversational tone, "and I wanted to know just why he was so attracted to you. I even killed a woman in biding my time for you. When I got you, however, I realized just how special you truly are." The imaginary friend moved closer to Jane in protection. Lucien noted the move and laughed. "My dear, dear imaginary friend," he cooed, "If I wanted to hurt her, I could have done so, but that is not my intent. If you have not figured it out by now, I am stronger than Jason and so I shall speak for him regarding this matter." The imaginary friend looked at its friend then floated to the side of the couch; Jane immediately felt vulnerable. Lucien took a seat next to her and she could smell scents of peppermints, rust, and dust coming from him. He was a walking enigma.

"So," he said while rubbing his hands together, "where shall I, or we, begin? How about I start with the fact that our boy Jason has a very troubled mind, so troubled that he was institutionalized for half of his life on this planet, hmmm? Or, how about the fact of Jason having about six separate personalities?"

"Are you one of those personalities?" asked Jane, now completely numb and strangely enough, accepting of the whole situation. She wanted answers and finally, she was going to get them no matter the "source".

"I am and yet not," said Lucien. "I am the darker side of Jason, the one that wants to hurt people with shiny knives and pain, the one who used to come out when Jason was in a foul and black mood."

"Did he kill his own wife?"

"Technically yes and no. True, it was his body, but it was all my action. In fact, it was that act that separated me from his body. Frankly, I was glad to be gone from his body; too many people in there for my taste. So, I left and enjoyed my freedom, leaving a hull of a man. That is why he blames me for his ex-wife's murder; he truly thinks I did it, which of course I did, but it was still his body."

"So . . . were you ever caught?"

"No." He said nothing further on the matter, his eyes focused on something inward. Jane looked at him with concern; she had to keep reminding herself that although this man looked like Jason, it was not. She reached out and touched his hand, almost recoiling when her warm fingers touched his cold and dead ones. Lucien looked down at her hand covering his then at her pleading face, no longer knowing what to say to her regarding this mess.

"Is Jason still inside of you?" she asked. "Can he hear me?"

"Of course he can, but right now he wants me to do all of the talking. Right now, I have the answers you want. Jason would only cry then scoop you up and carry you into the bedroom. As much as I would love to do that as well, right now is not a good time." Jane shook her head in agreement and was silent for a moment, allowing this new information to be processed in her own mind.

"Jane, I know this is hard, especially when all of this is coming from a man who attacked you, but in order for all of us to get through, I want you to listen to everything that I have told you," said Lucien.

"And I have," replied Jane, now visibly shaking, "but you must understand that this is something I never would have expected, Lucien. I was looking forward to spending the rest of my life with Jason as his wife." She stared at her feet, not wanting to look at anything else, but her feet; at least they did not have split personalities that could also be separate people. "I wanted to be his wife," she whispered.

"I still want you to be." Jane, hearing the change in voice, looked up and saw Jason with his sad blue eyes and warm skin. Lucien, for the moment, had taken a back seat, allowing the couple to be with each other for a while. He knew Jason wanted to be there for her during this moment. Tears fell from her eyes as she embraced the man she loved with all of her heart.

She still wonders who she talks to when she is around him, but none of that, strangely, matters anymore. He, or they, love her and that is enough. Sometimes, when Agatha comes out and invites her to tea and scones, she wants to burst out laughing because he will dress up in a dress with pearls and a little pillbox hat. She wants to laugh, but then decides not to because it would be impolite and she loves him. She wonders if she will ever accept it when Lucien steps out of him to be his own person from time to time, but then realizes that she still has her imaginary friend to talk to when things get too rough.

She does not ask questions when he returns home with blood on his clothes. Deep down, she knows what he did was wrong, but could never tell anyone about him. All she can do is watch the play continue to unfold, piece by piece, until all of the players and pieces are assembled and the final curtain falls with a muted hush. That is all she asks for now.

He refuses to seek additional treatment; he claims it would kill him and she believes him. He still speaks to his parents and she laughs when he tells her of his father's antics or his mother still trying to regain her youth and beauty. She knows, though. She knows that they are dead, rotting away in a cemetery, but she refuses to tell him that. She knows that somewhere amid all of the layers, he too realizes that his parents are truly dead. She loves him the way is he is although his actions leave her with more questions than answers. She meets all of them and they welcome her into their family. Even little Charlie hands her a piece of chocolate with a smile that will soon lead her to kiss his soft face over and over like a mother does to a child. She loves them all, even Lucien whom she has forgiven in her own way.

Soon, they are married.

Soon, she has his first child, a boy that they name Theodore, after his father. Lucien acts as uncle, for he is the strongest personality of them all. He cradles the child in his strong arms and nuzzles its soft downy hair. He is safe around Lucien.

Soon, they move to London: he teaches at Oxford while she completes her first novel about a grown woman who still talks to her imaginary friend.

Soon, they make love every other day; sometimes, Lucien joins them. At times, she can see two faces peering at her in the dark.

Soon, she is no longer afraid and it comforts them.

Goth Poetry

Kimberly Richardson

The Beginning of the End....

Come in, come in, my dearest guest
Please take the chair to relax and rest.
For I have been alone these 400 years
Enough time to survive my enemies' taunts and jeers.
And now, they're all dead, thanks to me
To see their dying faces filled me with glee.
But I digress, my dearest friend,
I see your heart is broken and needs to mend.
So sit back and listen to this black clad freak
While I read from my book...

Le Livre du Poesie Mauvais Gothique!

A Night With Edgar (Allan Poe)

One night, as rain poured from the sky
I sat with my friend Edgar, drinking tea and eating pie.
Our conversation was lengthy but our eyes were bleak
I did not fear him, my tongue was not meek.
I asked him of his poetry, his rhyme and reason
And why people loved him during Winter, the bleak season.
"It is because I am sad and lonely," he said with a sigh
I fail at smiling, no matter how hard I try.
My verses come out like a bunch of dead roses
And I write my characters like corpses in poses.
"Perhaps you can help me," he said with desire
To rid my soul of this deplorable mire."
I told him I would help, to reach success evermore
Perhaps I would ask my friend, a woman named Lenore.
Through the night, my knowledge of him raised me to a maven
And not once was I disturbed by his arrogant raven.
Soon, the night gave way to the day
And still we conversed with no servants in the way.
When the time read a quarter to three
He whispered in fatigue, "I must flee."
"For soon all you've told me will leave my mind
So I must write it down and leave nothing behind."
He thanked me and kissed my hand like a gentleman
And soon was out the door to formulate a plan.
Now I was alone in my large home
Wishing him success, to no longer be alone.
But soon I felt a sensation that seemed to attack,
With dread I turned around; that damned raven was back!
He stared at me with cold and baleful eyes
And right then and there I knew it was I whom he despised.

I raised my hand to my forehead in anguish and fell to the floor
With the last word I heard was. . .

Nevermore...

A Dying Wish

The moon is full, my love
And the stars are bright
Please stand still, my love
You're causing quite a sight.
My grip on the knife is loose
Due to the squirting of your blood
Now dear, please don't faint
Or fall to the ground with a THUD.
My love, do not fear me
For my love for you is strong
This knife was your gift to me
And not to use it would have been wrong.
So, my pale dear whom I still love
Let me hold you in my arms
And watch the blood flow from your gown
Your dying is a charm.
Now your eyes are closed in Death
And I am not in surprise
For in three days you shall return
As undead with violet eyes.
Our love goes beyond the grave
For we are more than this
You had to die to become undead
To live in nocturnal bliss.
And now I turn the knife to me
The shiny blade is long

And soon I will fall to the earth
To be with you ever long.

Kimberly Richardson

Confession of a Corporate Goth Woman

Absence makes the heart grow fonder
Or so I've been told
But I prefer the loneliness
To warm me in the cold.

I dress in black from head to toe
With a veil or top hat
To walk the town on a Saturday night
Or to a coffeehouse to chat.

I love the feeling of my velvet dress
Against my cold skin
And a glass of Absinthe
To make my head spin.

For I am in love with the night
And all things dark and bleak
The clubs give me refuge from the normal
While the scent of cloves makes me weak.

Now, I have been asked
By many people, short and tall,
"Why is a black girl into Goth
When it seems evil, after all?"

I tell them that I like being this way
To be my own self, 'tis true
To be a Corporate Goth standing on her own
Seems the right thing to do.

Soon, people walk away in disgust
Thinking that I am wrong

But they don't know such bliss
While listening to a Voltaire song!!

Kimberly Richardson

A Love Beyond

I danced at night
When the stars were bright
I could not help but smile.

For I was among the dead
in my velvet dress of red
as the shadows blended in with my dance.

The graveyard comforted me
As I dared not flee
for I was in a place of peace.

As the clock struck midnight
suddenly I saw a light
held by a figure walking towards me.

"Madam", said the figure
"You've given me quite a shiver,
Since I thought I was the only one here."

I stared into his eyes
barely concealing my surprise
as I recognized who stood before me.

It was my lover, Malachai
a young man who recently died
now come back to haunt me.

"Sir," I cooed like a dove
"Do you not remember your love?
It has been only a year!"

He looked at me up and down
while on his mouth there was a frown
as he tried with all of his might to remember.

Without warning, I took his hand
That felt rough like sand
and held it to my heart that beat wildly.

"Can you remember this", I cried
"Surely, you must try
For I was dancing here, thinking of you".

Soon, his eyes grew wide
As it all clicked inside
He fell to his knees, sobbing.

"My love", he said with tears
"I feel like I've been gone for years".
His black hair shook with every sob.

"I remember being dead
And all that was said
to me, one of the youth of the dead.

The King of the Dead came to me
In the Dead City
telling me that I was needed-

"I have heard of your time above
and the object of your love
So I will give you a choice.

You can either stay here forever
Or return to above but sever
your contact with the dead for a limited time".

Kimberly Richardson

"So, I was brought back to this place
To be again a member of the human race
And I knew I had to find you.

But, since I had been dead
I had forgotten your dress of red
And so I took you to be a stranger."

His dark eyes looked at me
I felt stuck to the earth like a tree
For what could I do now?

"How long will you be on earth
in the city of your birth
before you must go back to your place of rest?"

He suddenly took me in his arms
And I fell once more to his charms
His scent of myrrh engulfed me.

"My love", he said with such lust
I felt I would burst
if he did not make love to me right then and there.

His kisses felt like paper
and soon my sight began to waver
as I allowed my passion to consume me.

When we finished, we laid side by side
Watching the moon no longer hide
It was then he told me the rest of the story.

"My darling, I lied to you
Unfaithful, not true
for there is more to my story".

"The King gave me life, of course
to ride back on a black horse
but there was a job I had to do-

"Since you desire to find your love
You must take her from above
and bring her here for all Eternity.

Show her your passion and zeal
make her a nice deal
for she will not accept anything less."

"So, I am to take you now,"
He stood up to bow
then grabbed me to take me away.

"Malachai, this is madness," I cried
But something inside of me died
for I knew there was no escaping this.

We walked to the horse
that would help us on our course
And soon we were on, front and back.

He wrapped his arms around me
and suddenly I could see
The gates to the Underworld plain as day.

We galloped at a fast pace
As if we were in a race
for the sun was now about to rise.

Instead of trying to scream
I laid against him, as if in a dream
for I knew that there was no other way.

Kimberly Richardson

And now, I am dead.
Yes, (Laughing), I still have my head
I was assured that I would keep it.

Malachai and I are still together
no matter the weather
that haunts our fair dead city.

Do I mind being dead? No.
Where else would I want to go?
It was for him that I danced that night.

Now my tale is complete
I am glad we could meet
Now, if you don't mind, I think you should stay.

Tighter, My Darling

The pain is too hard to think or dwell
I feel like I have landed in Hell
(not a bad place to be!)
For this torture is done by myself
To create the image that I am a slender elf.
Thank the gods I do this once a week
Or else my future would truly be bleak!
But I am a slave to fashion, and Gothic at best
Perhaps I need to increase the tightness on my corset.

. . . .sigh. . . .
. . . .too. . . .hard. . . .to. . . .breathe. . . .

Kimberly Richardson

Black and Red

My pretties, black and red
Such a beauty to smoke in bed
For I take pleasure and delight
While holding a clove cigarette to a match light.
The smoke reminds me of a chilly October night
Dressed in black, giving the normals a fright!
The paper crackles and tastes of sweet candies
And men who smoke them turn into Wilde dandies.
Now with all this praise of them, you'd think they were good
And should be a replacement for food
But brothers and sisters of the night, that can not be
For it's not cool coughing blood at a quarter to three!
But, I do not mind about the spilled blood
That comes out of my mouth like a red flood.
For I am of shadows and everything bleak
. . . but I think I'll quit next week.

Demons and Tea

She comes to me like a dark beauty
But I feel I must do my duty
Or else I will be dead.

This woman who now stands before me
Holding her mug of tea
Asked me to join her for warmed blueberry scones.

We sit at her black table
And keep in mind I must sill be able
To do this dirty deed.

She asks me if I would like jam
And I tell her "No madam,
Because I am on a diet, please understand."

I look around her house
Now feeling timid like a church mouse
As I watch her pour a cup of tea for me.

Suddenly, I jump from my seat
And scream, "This time I must complete
The job I came here to do!"

She looks at me in surprise
And widening her violet coloured eyes
She asks me what she has done wrong.

I say to her, "You are pure evil
Since the period of Medieval
And I am here to slay you, you demon from Hell!"

Kimberly Richardson

She calmly sips her dark Oolong tea
Then she begins to laugh at me
And says, "You have the wrong place, my dear."

"Oh, yes, I am a demon, don't get me wrong
But the one you want is named Zyrfong
And he lives down the street at number 13."

Dear reader, I must confess to thee
That I felt slightly out of key
As I whisper the words, "Wrong demon?"

She bats her violet eyes while smiling with long fangs
While brushing out of her eyes her black bangs
And asks me, "Now dear, some more tea before you run?"

I must confess, dear reader, I did stay for a while-
I began to like her and her toothy smile
And where else could I get such lovely scones?

So, the demon named Zyrfong that I want to kill
Is right down the dark lighted hill
But for now, my present company is more important to me.

Vampire in Heat

I must confess, I am in love with you
And I do not know what to do
Because you are alive and I am undead.

My love, why do you hide from me?
Is it because I can not drink tea?
I wish I could, but I just can't.

Is it because I sleep during the day
So as not to get in the way
Of the eternal blazing sun?

Or is it because I have to quench my thirst
Is that the problem that is the worst
That lingers on your mind?

I'll do anything you want me to do:
Wear crosses or dye my hair blue
Or perhaps I should grow a beard.

My darling, I want to be with you
Can you not see that what I say is true
For I want to be with you always.

If you and I became lovers
There would be no others
And for my thirst, I would drink from packets cold.

I see that you are changing your mind
My dear, see how kind
I am to you because I love you.

Kimberly Richardson

Take my hand, dear, while I lead the way
As the night slowly changes to day
Let me take you, dear, to my place of rest.

Don't worry, there is enough room
I hope the scent of rotting earth will not make you swoon
For I have had this casket for 300 years.

Now we are alone, my darling Violet
No need to worry, I did not forget
My packets of blood, should the thirst take me.

Good night my dear, think of me when you sleep
And remember you have my heart to keep
Literally on your bosom, nice and red.

Ethereal Girl

My breath comes out like whispers
My glances are too fast to see
For I am lithe and frail-
A thimble full of water weighs more than me.

For I am an Ethereal girl
Obsessed with dark Victorian ways
Dressing in heavy black from head to toe
And dreaming of former days.

The tears I cry are not out of pain
Nor are they for a lost love
But rather I cry because I must-
My tears, not a blessing from above.

Rivet heads scare me
And perky Goths I do not understand
And yet all eyes turn towards me
Frailty is my strength, mine to command.

I spend my time in graveyards
Listening to the whispers of the dead
People think I am off kilter-
But oh, if they could only see inside my head!

For I am an Ethereal girl
Who believes in fairies with wings
And reads novels of madness without any cures
Along with other morbid things.

Please understand, if you can
That I am flesh and blood, truly here

Kimberly Richardson

But do not stare at me long enough
For I might just disappear...

The Renshaw House

See the house upon the hill
The one that stands tall among the trees?
There is a story behind that place
Come, sit and listen, if you please.

For this is a tale of madness and grief
And blood that covers the walls.
A damned and tortured soul lives there
Its wailing heard through the darkened halls.

Long ago lived a family named Renshaw
Who built the house you see now
Back then the house was full of laughter
with flowers fresh and sweet milk from their cow.

The family consisted of husband and wife
And two children, ages fifteen and sixteen
Wolfe and Violet, a boy and a girl
Both with dark hair long and full of sheen.

Their parents were proud of their children
As everyone in the town could see
They indulged in their every whim
Like musical instruments, books, and archery.

The town loved the family
Who exuded pure and simple bliss
But soon the atmosphere began to change-
Something soon was amiss.

The young master Wolfe began to brood
And lock himself in his room

Kimberly Richardson

He stopped going out on his daily walks
Catching the eye of every woman, causing them to swoon.

He cared for none of that foolishness
For he loved only his books
But soon, everyone began to realize
Something else had him hooked.

At night, he would lie awake
Dreaming of a woman fair
Whose deep eyes caused him to stumble
And catch him always unaware.

Finally, he could stand it no longer
He had to tell his father soon
For if he did not release his feelings
He would surely swell up like a balloon.

On a dark and rainy night
When his father was in the study reading
Wolfe walked into the room
With a look that was surely pleading.

"Father," he said, "I need your help
For I am in love
With a woman who is strong and fair
But whose heart is gentle like a dove."

"My son," said the older Renshaw
"That is wonderful news tonight
But tell me, son, why did you come in here
With your face full of fright?"

"My love can never be satisfied
To compensate for the tears I have wept.
Father dear I love my sister

My wonderful, wonderful Violet."

Father stared at his son in shock
As he ran his hands through his hair
His legs began to shake with anger
As he now sat in his leather chair.

"You will not speak of this to anyone
Not even your mother Ruth June
For this is an abominable confession
Now go, go to your room!"

Wolfe went upstairs to his room and sulked
For he was not ready for sleep
He closed his eyes and laid on his back
Preparing him for thoughts black and deep.

Soon he had a plan created in his mind
That would take away his grief
He got up and walked to his sister's room
Where he knew she would be fast asleep.

He opened the door carefully
To reveal Violet's slumbering pose
He tiptoed to her carefully
Noticing she had lips like a rose.

Suddenly, Violet opened her eyes
As she tried to make some sense
Why her brother was in her room
And why his face was tight and tense.

"Wolfe," she said in a sleepy tone
"why are you here?
Is there something wrong with Mother or Father
Please tell me, dear."

He walked up to her bed and sat down
His eyes a clear and deep blue
He looked into the eyes of his sister
And realized what he had to do.

His body began to tremble
As he leaned forward with lips soft and wet
Then soon his felt his sister's lips touch his
His own, his Violet.

For a moment, he closed his eyes in happiness
Knowing that this was right
But soon he felt his body pushed away
Followed by a scream of fright.

"Wolfe, why did you do that?" she yelled
As she gathered her sheets in a tight knot
"Are you in a trance or a deep dream
Or suffering from a fever hot?"

"Violet, I want you for my wife,"
Was all he could say on that night of fate
He held out his hand for her
To make her his eternal mate.

Violet pushed further away from him in disgust
Her eyes became dark as the night sky
"You are of my own flesh and blood
I feel I shall die!"

"For you are my brother and not my lover
And we are only in our youth
How could you think of me in that way
How could you be so uncouth?"

For a moment there was dead silence
From both brother and sister Renshaw
Suddenly Wolfe's blank face turned to anger
Holding out a hand with nails like claws.

"If I can not have you with your consent
On this romantic night
Then I shall do what I had planned to do!"
Said Wolfe with his eyes full of moonlight.

I shall not tell you of the details, fair listener
Of the act that was committed that night
It is too horrible to speak of
Nothing could have made it right.

Once over, Wolfe kissed his sister's face
That was covered in tears and sweat
He smiled in the darkness, his love was shown
With no moment of regret.

Suddenly, the doors were thrown wide open
Revealing their parents in their nightgowns
They saw who was in their daughter's bed
And soon on their faces appeared frowns.

"I told you not to act on your desire,"
Said their father as he walked up to the bed
"You may have satisfied your incestuous lust
But still, you can not be wed."

Their mother stood by the door in shame
In seeing her children like this
Soon, her mind reflected back to happier times
When their halls were full of bliss.

Kimberly Richardson

"Violet dear, come to us now,"
Said their mother with a trembling hand
"We know you are innocent in this affair
A confession we will not demand."

Violet tenderly got out of bed
And walked to her parents as if in a dream
Leaving poor deluded Wolfe alone
Suddenly, he began to scream.

"I want my sister for my wife
And no one else, for she is fair
She will soon have my child
A true legitimate heir!"

His eyes were full of madness
As he stared at everyone with hate
Their parents with Violet turned to leave the room
But of course, it was too late.

Soon, the halls were full of screaming
As blood now covered the walls-
A young man was now insane with anger
Answering the maddening call.

The others tried to flee him
With cuts on their bodies from his knife
But they were too slow for a of person of madness
As they tried to run for their life.

Violet stumbled and fell down hard
Much to her surprise
And soon her own brother was upon her
With those maddening and gleaming eyes.

He raised the knife above his head
Preparing to stop her life with one swipe
He wanted to give her his heart
But soon he would have hers, warm and ripe.

"I love you sister," he said with tears
That fell down his pale face
"But you turned away from my love
And that is something I can not erase."

The knife fell, Violet screamed
And soon there was blood on the floor
As father stood to watch this act
Allowing their mother to run for help to the front door.

Soon, his bare feet were covered in blood
As he stared in shock and dismay-
How did his son get to this point?
What did it? Was he always this way?

He watched the knife go in and out
Of his daughter now bright red chest
Then watched with horror as Wolfe took the knife to his own
And well . . . you know the rest.

Mother and father escaped from the house
Out into the night so cold
Then sat on the ground, weeping frozen tears
They suddenly felt so old.

Neighbours came from their houses
Wondering at the strange sight
They placed blankets around their now frail frames
Letting them know everything would be all right.

Kimberly Richardson

But as they looked back at the now dark house
And the two corpses that lay within
They knew they could never go back
To face the horrors within.

They left the town and their home of dreams
To escape from their pain and shame
Their memories of Violet and Wolfe, however
Were still kept alive, like a flame.

You think my story is now told
But I have something else to say
For one of the children that lay on the floor
Did not die on that cursed day.

My mother was a changed creature
A woman who gave in to fits of fear
For she dared not trust any man
Who tried to come too near.

Her brother, Wolfe, had destroyed her spirit
And damned her precious soul
Making her eyes turn into a pure black
Blacker than the darkest coal.

She spent her years in a hospital
Then to an asylum where I was born
I could never face my mother properly
Her spirit had been torn.

Before she completely lost her sanity
She told me of her getaway
From her home and her dead brother
And begin her life in a new way.

It seemed that her wounds were not deep
From his jealous knife
And so when she realized he was truly dead
She ran for her life.

She never found her parents
For they had traveled far away
That was the fact that drove my mother
To insanity on that bleak day.

I am the child of that cursed union
On that desolate night
Please do not look at me that way
Do not look at me in a heinous light.

My mother died recently
I was the only one to bury her properly
For although her mind was completely addled
I cared for her tenderly.

I am a good citizen, a woman of self respect
Who lives alone with my many books
I am invisible to all, however
People pass me by without second looks.

I am quite happy, you see
Because I know I am alive
I also know I am not mad
Allowing my father's curse to thrive.

So, that is the tale of that sad house
And the events that no one could defend
The day has turned to night, dear listener
For my story is now at an end.

Kimberly Richardson

Flower of Depression

I grow all sorts of flowers
To compensate for a single life
Bringing in sorts of flora
Without any mental strife.

I do not sell what I grow
For all of my plants I use
Each one is a wonder to behold
Each one is a Natural Muse.

However, there is one plant
That I cherish above all
Created with leaves of a deep purple hue
And it is not so tall.

I call it my midnight plant
The flower that represents the bleak
I feel it is a part of my own soul
Without a single sign of being weak.

For its daily nourishment I use
People's sorrows and their pain
Collected from stories I hear
From strangers now and again.

At night, when the moon is full
And the winds are silent here
Under a watchful gaze of your eyes
From the petals, several tears.

My poison ivy creeps along
And my Venus Fly Trap looks ready to attack

But I never thought in a million years
I would be buying my midnight plant Prozac!

Sometimes, I wish I could give my flower
Laughter and joy, happiness and glee
But all of that would have an opposite effect
Killing my flower, you see.

This flower is a reminder
That even sadness and depression are a part
Of the balance we call Life-
To give it respect is a start.

My flower of darkness and ennui
Is beginning to look slightly pale
Do you have any tales of woe
That are currently up for sale?

Kimberly Richardson

A Beat Tribute to Clive Barker

CLIVE!

B
A
R
K
E
Are you there, listening to me?

Deep, deep, in the dream sea

The dream C

Woven

Like the. . .
         . . . weaving of the world.

R! Are you there, sitting in Abarat, waiting for sweet, sweet Candy-

. . . man?

Jesus wept, you know.

CLIVE!

Adoration
Completion
Obsession

Transformation, all an Illusion. . .
. . .such sights to show you. . .

Kimberly Richardson

Opheliaholic

She is my Death Muse, this woman of fame
For she died a death that brought much shame.
Her madness drove her to kill herself one day
Because love and truth somehow got in the way.
Hamlet, that bastard, the one who was unsure
Giving way to her wondering if she was still pure.
But, truly, dear lady, I love thee with my heart
And I wish we could never be apart.
Even though you are of fiction and I am real
I want to still tell you how I feel.
I dream of you every night when I am alone
Deluded to think I could call you on the phone
We are centuries and countries apart
But that does not stop the beating of my heart.
I am an Opheliaholic, I do much confess
I would feed you sandwiches made of watercress.
Rose petals would bless your every move
I would kill anyone who hated you just to prove
That I will forever be here for you, my drowning beauty
Spending my time with you, an honorable duty.
I would stay away from rivers, oceans, and seas
To keep you from going insane again, for you to please.
Perhaps I will get my wish to love you someday
But unfortunately my own madness has gotten in the way.

Lines About Goths

Perkies are the ones who jump around and tease
Victorians, with just one look, will bring you to your knees.

Elders are the ones who began it all for the rest
Vampires think it's funny to walk around with a stake in the chest.

Deathrockers sport their mowhawks black and tall
Punks, alive not dead oi!, still wonder about the sense of it all.

Egyptians remind me of Akasha from Anne Rice
Fetish always keep me amused with their latest sex device.

Cybers are the newest ones; they look like Neo and Trinity
Corporates drive to Goth Night in their shiny black Inifinitis

Divas show off their body, no matter what their shape or size
Dark Fae look so cool with their violet coloured eyes.

So, there you have it, a small slice
Of the counterculture that I love and call home
No matter what your taste, leather or lace,
A Goth is never truly alone.

Now, I wanted to save this last part
To mention one other group
That sometimes gets lukewarm treatment
Or thrown completely out of the loop.

Kimberly Richardson

Rivet Heads, or lovers of Industrial music
Keep the beats going hard and long
As for me, well, I vent out my frustrations
Dancing to all of my Front Line Assembly songs!

Ode to the Topic that is Hot

When my dark soul needs a touch up in bleak
There is only one thing that I must seek
For the place to go is the Topic that is Hot
To find out what is in and what is not.
Black shirts picturing Jack and Sally
And graphic novels about a homicidal maniac named Johnny.
Lenore, the little dead girl, is the one I like best
To go rather well with my PVC vest.
Let's not forget the latest Gothic Beauty
To complete my Gothic reading duty.
Too many items to choose from, from Mod to Punk
I don't think I'll have enough room in my trunk!
Soon, I must go, although leaving is hard
But I'll have to go because I've max out my credit card!

Kimberly Richardson

Journal Entry on a Dark and Stormy Night

How nicely does the whip make a cracking sound
Across the skin so pale?
To make the marks of red welts
Some as large as a whale.

I do this to you because I love you
And because you are also mine
Now get on your knees, my wonderful pet
And lick my boots till they shine.

I am your master, never forget
And you are beneath me
And if you have trouble remembering that
I'll bind you tight until you see.

I love the way your skin turns red
When my hand or whip takes control over me
Now, now my pet, no tears please
And darling, try not to flee.

At last, the time is over
When our play time must come to an end
Now here, my pet, take some of this salve
To use for your skin to mend.

Perhaps when I am old
I shall write my experiences to date
To give the world a new view
Of what to do with your mate.

I know there is something in my actions
And in knowing I am no façade
I hope for my name to coincide with pain
I am. . . The Marquis de Sade!

Kimberly Richardson

Werewolves Anonymous

OK, OK, is everyone here?
Can you hear me, those in the rear?

I think we're all here, so let us begin now
And get answers to our questions: the why, the how.

I see we have some new faces tonight
That's good; be with us rather than out in the night.

Brothers and sisters, we come together rather than kill
Flesh and blood for our stomachs to fill

Now, for the new people, my name is Lucien Dawes
Who used to terrorize a small town with my sharpened claws

Women were my weakness when the moon was out
People would tremble to my howls and shout

"It's the Werewolf Lucien, coming for our women fair
To kill them outright and drag the bodies back to his lair!"

I would kill a woman once a month to keep them in fear
And give them plenty of reasons not to come near.

But suddenly, I was overcome with a strange thought
Wondering at first if it was a fiendish plot

Why did I want to kill women once a month to feed
To hear them scream and watch them bleed?

I wanted to live as a human, to no longer give in
To my beast ways, committing such a horrible sin.

So I left the town with a note on my door
Letting the townspeople know I would trouble them no more.

I traveled far away, enjoying the sun on my back
And when the moon came out, I would suppress any attack.

I arrived here, several years ago
Trying to keep up with the city's frantic flow
When the moon would come out, I held my ground
Seeking peace to change my life in a manner profound.

Now, I stand before you, a werewolf who controls the beast within
Never to hide in shame or live in sin

The moon still affects me but on a lesser degree
Overcoming it gives me a joyful glee.

There now, my tale is done, pass me a cup of tea?
And so, if everyone would repeat after me?

To the moon I do so plead
To maul no one, making them bleed
The beast and I are one in the same
To live I must overpower the urge, making it tame
We are werewolves, fur of black, white, red, and grey
To live peaceful lives and keep it that way.

Kimberly Richardson

A Darke Woman

See how she comes toward me
In this black night
She who is my Darke woman
By the moon her face alight.

She dresses in black clothing
Of period or modern fair
Her skin is as pale as milk
Ravens' wings the colour of her hair.

Her eyes are smoky and full of mystery
That drive me to insanity with every glance
Her movements seem to not be of this earth
Her being would surely kill me, given the chance.

I love my Darke woman, my gothic treasure
She who is of the night and of shadows bleak
She is not for the faint of heart,
Nor the solemn or the meek.

I hunger for her body
And treasure her intelligent mind
If she were to ask me to follow her
I would and leave everything of value behind.

She is my dark muse
The one who teases my sexual desire
And yet I have not had one kiss from her
Throwing me into an impossible mire.

I do not even know her name
Or where she lives during the day

But that is how our love must be
Must our relationship be this way?

She seems to sometimes not notice me
When I glance at her from behind a tree
Watching her pick violets and lilies
In her own way, she sets them free.

So, my time watching her is about to end
And I must go home back to my wife
Whose constant nagging and bothering of me
Gives me enough reason to end her life.

So, I must go home, dear reader
To do what must be done
To murder my wife, to take her life
And bury her in earth warmed by the sun.

Once the deed is done I will then shout with happiness
And prepare my home for my darke faerie
I'll feed her delicacies from around the world
And wine made with grape and blueberry.

So, do whatever you need to do to prepare
For your new life with me
Soon my home will be our home. . . .
And do not even THINK of trying to flee!

Kimberly Richardson

Our Daughter

When I was 30, I met a man named Lucien Aloysius Holmes
During a funeral of a dear friend
He took me in his arms and loved from then on
My formally broken heart he did mend.

We both realized that we were drawn
To the gothic side of life
We both wore black from head to toe
And not once did we live in strife.

We danced in gothic clubs, we drank red wine
We gazed at the moon during our graveyard walks
I loved the way he said my name
And how his skin was as white as chalk.

Soon, we were married
In a church lit with candles short and tall
Afterwards we left for our honeymoon
At his home in England, Abysmal Hall.

A year later, we had a child named Danae
Who looked just like her father dear
Our families, dark and creepy just like us,
Would often visit the baby, traveling from far and near.

We wanted our child to follow our footsteps
Of loving history and reading poetry
But I am sorry, dear reader, to tell you this
That was simply not to be!

When she was older, she began to clean out her room
Clearing it of all that we had bought for her

She no longer wanted anything to do with our way of life
Instead wanting a bed spread made of (sigh)….pink fur!

She dyed her raven black hair to blonde
And changed her cloaks and capes for pretty powder blue dresses
She wanted to spend more time with the popular girls at school
And claimed we were the source of her teenage messes.

"I can't bring any of my friends here," she would wail
"Because I am not like you
You enjoy reading macabre books and dancing in graveyards
I am sorry but that will not do!"

What could we do, Lord and Lady of Abysmal Hall
To make our daughter understand
That we loved her very much, no matter what
But we were the parents who had the upper hand?

We knew that many of her friends' parents
Knew of our "dark" lifestyle and found it to be quite tame
They still treated us with respect
And we did the same.

Danae's friends, strangely enough
Wanted to get to know us better
But Danae would not allow it, saying she was embarrassed
But we decided to have a party, causing her to fretter.

Her friends and their parents showed up
On Friday the 13th with the sky one black cloud
Lucien, my beloved, dressed in his black suit with velvet vest
And I in one of my Renaissance dresses with my spider black shroud.

Kimberly Richardson

People walked through our home
While servants offered them food and drink
Danae's friends were asking us all sorts of questions
Leaving her alone, giving her time to think.

Their parents enjoyed themselves on our hospitality
And no one complained of the décor
We were the perfect host and hostess
Not one item of food or drink was spilled on the floor.

When everyone left, smiles on all their faces
We closed the door behind them and laughed with glee
Danae suddenly came out of one of the side rooms
With tears on her face for us to see.

"I am sorry, Mother and Father, about how I treated you
About how I thought my friends would react.
It seems I was wrong and I do apologize
Please, please do not be angry for my previous attack."

We said nothing to her but took her in our arms
And loved her as our daughter fair
"We wanted to prove to you that we are human, just like you
With same worries and cares."

She understood that although we are different than most
People accepted us for who we are
That we would welcome anyone into our home
No matter where they lived, near or far.

We are still the gothic couple of our area
And our home is still open to all
We respect our daughter's wishes to how she wants to dress
Wearing bright orange platform shoes to make her look tall.

One afternoon, many years later, she called
With happiness evident in her voice
"Mum and Dad, I met a young man named Forrest
He reminds me of you, I had no choice."

"He swept me off my feet during a lunch
When I took a break from work
I wondered who the black clad freak was
Who stared at me, I thought he was a jerk."

"But, I found out he was a vice president
Of a company down the street from me
I told him that I was a lawyer and my last name-
You should have seen how his eyes lit up with glee!"

"So, now I am dating a Corporate Goth
A man who would do you proud
And yes I am in love with him, as he loves me as well
If I could, we would shout our love out loud!"

So, there you have it, our daughter is in love
With a man who is like us in our Gothic way.
A lesson learned, our daughter finally growing up-
They're coming over for tea and blackberry scones later this day!

Kimberly Richardson

Mayhem, A Wonderful Thing

See how the axe falls to chop
Off the lovely head of Annabeth Elizabeth Watt.
Watch the head fall quietly into the basket underneath
Soon, her body will be buried in an unmarked plot.

Another person, a victim, is found
To whet the axe's appetite for something thick and red
Perhaps the axe's owner will find the victim out on the streets
Or maybe while they are fast asleep in their bed.

Sometimes, when the owner is asleep
The axe gets restless, tired, and worn
Sometimes, only for a moment, it wishes other things
Like wishing it had never been created . . . or born.

But soon those thoughts leave the axe's mind
Once the owner wakes up, ready for more
Suddenly, it loves its master dearly
No thoughts about the owner being a bore.

So, off they go into the night
With no noises, screams, or wails giving them away
And I, the writer, dreaming of their future hellish plots and mayhem
Wondering if I'll meet them some day.

Mayhem, a wonderful thing
Better than insanity, although madness is quite fun
To instill fear into hearts of mortal men and women
Never to rest until the job is done.

Ah yes, mayhem, a wonderful, delightful thing

Tales from a Goth Librarian

To pass the time away when I have no books to read
Listening to the screams of the victims
As they try to reason, their voices ready to plead.

Jack the Ripper, now there was a fellow
Dash and dapper, melting into the London night
Following women in back alleyways and trash ridden streets
His face, I am sure, gave them quite a fright.

But, sadly I never met him
Wanting to shake his hand and not be a bother
I wanted to show him my work, to let him know I understood
You see . . . he was my father!

And so I sit, here in my padded cell
Waiting for the day when I am released and set free
Everyone thinks me to be a danger to myself
Everyone except my axe and me.

Those stories of murder, well, I committed those acts
Wanting to follow my father's way of life
To show the world just how brilliant he was
By using his wits and his trusty surgical knife.

So, now I lay my head down to sleep
Closing my eyes to the images that appear in my mind
My axe sleeps next to me like a friend
Dreaming of peeling people like an orange rind.

Kimberly Richardson

A Last Look

The sun is now high in the sky
And soon, dear listener, I must fly.
For my depressing poetry is at an end
With no more shadows of despair to defend.
I hope you have enjoyed my words of black
You must have, since you did not get up once for a snack.
But, on a serious tone, I must say
That not all Goths are evil and full of decay.
Some of us are dark and spooky
And give normals looks that are quite kooky.
However, most of us are good people who do give a damn
Rather than shut up tight like a clam.
I for one believe that ALL people are good
No matter your race, background, or your neighbourhood.
People need to get over the "black is Satan" crap
Too many people fall into that easy word trap.
So, that is my rant, hope you enjoyed it, so there!
And by the way, if you must know, I DO wear leather black underwear!

Thank you and good night. . .

Discover other fine Kerlak publications at:

http:www.kerlakpublishing.com

CPSIA information can be obtained at www.ICGtesting.com
Printed in the USA
LVOW081258030312

271323LV00001B/6/P